Pescadero

A NOVEL

HOLLIS BRADY

Palo Alto Publishing

Softcover: 979-8-9877277-2-0
Ebook: 979-8-9877277-3-7

This novel is a work of fiction. All events, characters, and names depicted in this novel are entirely fictitious or are used fictitiously. No representation that any statement made in this novel is true or that any incident depicted in this novel actually occurred is intended or should be inferred by the reader.

https://pescaderonovel.com

Cover Design: Swapan Das, Bigpoints
Interior Design: Lorie DeWorken, Mind the Margins
Cover photo: Cavan Images/stock.adobe.com
Back cover photo: Pixabay.com

For more information, contact:
Palo Alto Publishing
Palo Alto, California 94306
info@paloaltopublishing.com

For Wendy, who put this book into me,

and Annie, who pulled it out.

Part
I

Leave-Taking

1
Western Nebraska

The moment fourteen-year-old Hilde first realized her family was falling apart was at a Denny's on I-80 between North Platte and Ogallala. Later she would remember that moment as something akin to passing through an invisible curtain, a barrier that separated her life in Kenosha from everything that came after, in Pescadero, on the rural coast of California.

It wasn't one of her father's chilly silences, the kind that drove the family deep into their private recesses like fish in a frozen pond. And it wasn't one of her mother's fiery eruptions, though her white-knuckled grip on the steering wheel made it seem like she was exploding from home like shrapnel.

It was just a small thing, really, not much more than a gesture. It was Ethan, her older brother, her rock. It was Ethan who made her understand that the ground beneath her was liquefying.

They had stopped midafternoon for a *quick bite*, her mother's code for We will not be dawdling here. When Ethan opened the car door, the first thing Hilde noticed was the wind—hot and rife with the odors of west Nebraska feedlots. These were nothing like the sweet, fecund smells of Wisconsin dairy farms.

"Lock the car, Ethan," her mother said, throwing the keys in his direction. They clattered on the gravel at Ethan's feet. "You drive the next leg." She headed for the restaurant without looking back.

Hilde struggled over the boxes in the back seat, climbed out of the car, and stood up straight for the first time in four hours. She peered across the landscape, shielding her eyes against the hot sun. A low, concrete church sat across the highway between a tire store and a 7-Eleven. Power of the Blood Evangelical Church. Below it, in press-on letters: *Heaven has strict immigration laws. Hell has open borders.*

"Where *are* we, anyway?" Hilde said, hiking up the cutoffs around her skinny frame. Her straw-blond hair riffled in the wind.

Ethan scooped up the keys, put them in his pocket, and headed toward the restaurant without comment. Hilde watched him go, his tall lanky body hunched over the way it was when his wrestling coach sent him onto the mat. He was such a star back home.

She turned and took another look at the dry, flat land. "Cripes, it's hot!" she said to no one in particular. A gust of wind blew grit in her eye.

She followed her brother into the restaurant and slid into the booth opposite him. The table was sticky, and the ketchup bottle needed wiping. A couple of bills left by a previous customer lay in a small metal tray near the sugar. Her mother was nowhere to be seen.

"We gotta be halfway there by now, right?" she said, taking off her round, wire-rimmed glasses and rubbing her eye. She'd hated her old glasses, the powder-blue ones she'd worn since third grade. But these, they made her feel smart.

Ethan picked up the menu and studied it in silence.

The air-conditioning kicked on, and Hilde felt arctic air hit her sweaty neck. "Ethan," she said, tracing the edge of the table anxiously with her fingers. "You think things'll be better in California?"

"Dunno," he said sullenly. His wheat-colored hair stood up in spikes, a result of his habit of running his hand through it when he was irritated.

"Once we get there—and get the farm going? Better?"

"I know *squat* about goats," he said, almost to himself.

"That's not true. You know how to milk cows. You did it all last summer at Schroeder's farm." She needed a response from him—anything, really.

Ethan shrugged and looked away.

THIS WAS THE WAY it had been—Ethan surly, withdrawn—ever since the big announcement at supper on that hot, sticky evening a month ago.

"Guess what!" her mother had said in that singsong voice that never delivered good news. They were sitting around the supper table midway through a takeout bucket of chicken. "I have something special to tell you. Want to know?"

Hilde noticed her father rise abruptly and pick up his plate.

"Just tell 'em, Janine," he muttered and disappeared into the kitchen.

"*I* want to know," Hilde asked, sensing the need to support her mother.

Janine turned toward her daughter. "Next month this time," she said, widening her eyes for effect, "we'll all be in California!" Her smile seemed pasted on.

Ethan's steel-colored eyes jumped from his plate to his mother's face. "What?" he croaked.

"We're gonna clean out Uncle Karl's place. Get some goats. And start making cheese. You won't *believe* what those fancy restaurants in San Francisco will pay for goat cheese!"

She glanced at the kitchen. "Dad's coming later. After he sells the house."

"Sells the *house*?" Hilde said, incredulous. "We're *moving*?" She scanned the surroundings. Dad was nowhere to be seen.

"Wait a minute," Ethan said, placing his fork down carefully. "What about school?"

"What about it?" Janine replied innocently.

"What about school? What about four weeks from now when practice starts?"

"Hang on a minute, Ethan," Janine said, her hands held up against his words. "Hear me out. I've already talked to the school out there. They have a terrific sports program—wrestling, basketball, track. It's smaller than Tremper. But that'll be nice because it'll be easy for you to make your mark."

"Make my *mark*?" He looked like he'd just regurgitated bile.

"I know, hon. The wrestling thing. But California is *such* an opportunity, and you being a senior, it'll be a piece of cake to make the team out there. The walk-on who turns out to be a star! A great story!"

Hilde watched her brother's face turn to stone as her mother continued to pitch, laying out the charms of the move—the sunny climate, the ocean surf, the golden hills. Mom clearly thought a good dose of romance, entangled with a little logic, would bring him around.

He stood up, threw his crumpled napkin on the table, and stalked off.

Hilde sat motionless, waiting for her mother to react—maybe to ask her what *she* thought, how *she* felt—but Mom did not. She just started clearing the dishes.

Just before bed, Hilde crept downstairs to the rec room where Ethan holed up most of the time. He was stretched out on the sofa, arms cradling his neck, eyes closed, earbuds in ears. She sank down on the steps and waited for him to notice. She wanted to talk. She needed to talk. *The giants have gone crazy,* she wanted to say, *and we have lost control. Do you see it, too?* A terrible pressure between her temples made her feel like her head was about to explode. She needed to hear from him because his voice always calmed her. Anchored her. With him to talk to, she knew she would be able to make it through.

She waited for several long minutes, but he didn't open his eyes. He had gone dark.

THE STOPLIGHT IN FRONT of Denny's turned red, green, and red again without a single car passing beneath.

Ethan stared at it and then shoved the menu to the edge of the table. "Asinine," he muttered.

"What?" Was this an opening?

He turned and looked at her, and for a moment, she saw him soften. "Scout," he said, using the nickname he'd made up for her when she was nine and he was eleven, "if you were driving on a deserted road, and you came to a crossroads—like that one, with a stoplight—and there was no one else around, would you stop?"

She looked at her brother. She wanted to say whatever he wanted to hear, but she wasn't sure what he was looking for. "I guess so," she offered.

Her response clearly disgusted him. He turned back to the window.

She looked away. She had failed the test, though she didn't know how. Her eyes stung. She picked up the menu and held it close to her face.

DENNY'S WAS EMPTYING OUT, though they had yet to order. Hilde put down the menu and looked around for her mother. When she turned back, she noticed the dollar bills that had been sitting in the little tray near the sugar were gone. She looked up at Ethan, down at the tray, and up at Ethan again.

"Ethan?"

His earbuds were in, and he was tapping his finger on the counter to a beat only he could hear.

"Ethan," she said again, reaching across and stopping his finger with her palm.

He pulled out one earbud. "What?"

"You can't do that."

"Do what?"

"You can't take that money."

Ethan replaced the earbud.

"Really, Ethan," she said, grabbing his wrist to get his attention. "You can't." This was not like Ethan—trustworthy, dependable, the one who got the summer job because everyone in town knew he was so solid.

"Shut up, Hilde."

She drew her hand back as if she'd been burned. He so rarely used her real name.

Janine slid into the booth, holding up damp, limp hands. "Of course," she said, vexed. "No paper towels in the john." Forcing a smile, she picked up the menu. "Now, what's everybody gonna have?"

Hilde glowered at Ethan. She would never rat him out, but she wanted him to know that she knew what he had done. She needed him to be reliable. Especially now.

A waitress appeared with an order pad in one hand, a pencil in the other.

"Ethan?" her mother said, studying the menu.

"Not hungry," Ethan said.

There was a pause. The waitress, pencil perched on pad, looked over at two men eating burgers at the counter. One of them was pulling a wallet from his pocket.

"We're not stopping again till the motel, Ethan, so choose something."

"Not hungry," Ethan said again in exactly the same tone.

"He'll have a burger," Janine said to the waitress. "She'll have a grilled cheese. And I'll have a BLT."

BEFORE THE MOVE, THERE had been arguments between her parents, some worse than others, but then things would fade to a chilly normal, and Hilde never could quite tell whether her parents had forged a truce or were waiting for the next round. The not-knowing kept her perpetually on edge.

"Did you fix the truck yesterday?" she heard her mother say one Sunday morning at the breakfast table as she was coming down the stairs.

Her father grunted and kept reading the paper.

Her mother picked up a fork, reached across the table, and tapped his water glass lightly.

"Darrell?" she said, annoyed now. "The battery? Did you fix it? I've got work tomorrow."

Hilde stopped in the shadows at the foot of the stairs. Her mother's back was turned away, but she could see her father over her mother's shoulder.

"I'm aware, Janine," he replied coolly, turning the page and straightening the paper with the palm of his hand. "I didn't have time."

Her mother cocked her head. "You didn't have time?"

"No." After a long silence: "I'll see what I can do."

"Today?"

"Yes."

"Today," she said with disdain. "Really?"

"Yes, Janine. *Today*."

"Well, that's not a great plan, Darrell. Because if it needs a new battery *today*, you can't buy one. It's Sunday. Nothing's open. In case you've forgotten."

He stiffened, took off his glasses, and looked at her. "I'm sorry, Janine, but that's not in my control."

She sat back. "What's not in your control?"

"When the stores open."

"Oh," she said. "But if you'd worked on the truck *yesterday*, you would've been able to buy a new battery if you needed one. Right, Darrell?" She sounded like a professor teaching logic to a recalcitrant student.

"Look," he said, unaffected. "If the truck craps out, call Jeanette. She'll take you."

"If the truck craps out and I call Jeanette, I'll be late. And if I'm late, they'll hire somebody who isn't late. You get that, Darrell? They don't like it when you're late."

Hilde could feel the muscles in her neck tighten.

Her father gave her mother a long, cold stare. "You know, Janine, your little bookkeeping gig—it's not a career. It's just a job."

"Really?" She rocked back in her chair, her hands clutching the edge of the table.

"Yeah, really." He was revving up now, something he rarely did. "In fact, why don't you just quit. Stay home and clean up this place. Look at it! The kitchen's a mess. The laundry's piled high. And there's so much clutter in the hall, I'm surprised somebody hasn't broken a leg."

She jutted out her jaw and crossed her arms over her chest. "A fabulous idea, Darrell. I'll stay home and we'll all just live off your salary."

"Yeah. Good idea," he said acidly. "You should think about it."

"Let me give *you* something to think about, Darrell." She rose now and leaned over the table, her fingers braced wide against the Formica. "*I* pay the bills. And despite your precious position at that Podunk college, despite all those little twenty-somethings scurrying around—*yes Mr. Sabin, no Mr. Sabin'*— whenever you need a cup of coffee, *you* don't bring home enough money to cover the bills. *Surprised?*"

His shoulders went rigid. He folded the paper carefully, stood up, tucked it under his arm, grabbed his jacket, and headed toward the back door. Then he turned and growled, "You know, Janine, you can be a real ballbuster sometimes."

"Really?" she spat, her voice dripping with fury. "Well then, Darrell, why do you stay? Why don't you just get the hell out! Because I can't *stand* the sight of you!"

A wave of nausea overcame Hilde.

It was only when Ethan laid a hand on her shoulder that she found some mooring. "C'mon, Scout," he said gently, pushing her toward the rec room. "Let's go play some video games."

DENNY'S WAS NOW VIRTUALLY empty, and still no food. Hilde kept glancing at the door to the kitchen. She knew how testy her mother could become when she was made to wait.

Janine took a map from her bag, unfolded it clumsily, and stared at it.

"You know, Mom," Ethan said, breaking his silence for the first time that afternoon, "there's an app for that."

"I know," she said irritably.

Ethan rolled his eyes.

Hilde wished she were back in the hot car. "So how many goats are we getting?" she asked, hoping to distract her mother.

It worked, for once. Her mother turned toward her and breathed out slowly. She focused on something in the middle distance for a long moment.

"Fourteen," she said finally, managing a small smile, "at first. Next season, we'll have more. Ethan'll do the milking, and you and I'll make the cheese. We've gotta get the machines working again. Not sure how long they've been out of commission—probably since Karl died. But we'll figure it out." She blinked and looked around. "Where's our food, anyway?"

The waitress backed through the swinging door with a rolling cart of clean dishes. When the cook put three plates of food on the serving counter, she parked the cart, picked up the plates, and delivered them to the table.

"Finally," her mother said, loud enough to embarrass Hilde.

"Anything else?" the waitress asked, wiping her hands on her apron.

"Yes. The check, hon. We need the check."

HILDE TOOK A FINAL bite of sandwich and watched while her mother pulled out a bright pink jar of lip gloss and a hand mirror from her straw bag. She was making more of an effort these days. She'd let her hair grow, and just before they left, she'd streaked it—a first. She'd done it herself in the bathroom with a box from the drugstore. And she'd bought a few new things—hoop earrings, a halter top, even an ankle bracelet. But the lip gloss seemed—somehow—over the top. Like something the girls Ethan dated would wear.

"You know," Mom said thoughtfully, using her pinky finger to apply the gloss. "This is a new chapter in our lives. And a new chapter deserves a new beginning." She dropped the lip gloss back into her bag, pulled out a Kleenex, and dabbed the corners of her mouth. "I've been thinking about going by a different name. Jasmine. I like that name."

"What's wrong with your name?" Hilde asked, surprised at how unbalanced the suggestion made her feel.

"Oh, I don't know. Janine feels like the name somebody would give to a Wisconsin milkmaid."

"You are a Wisconsin milkmaid, Mom," Ethan said. "You grew up on a farm with thirty Holstein."

Janine stiffened but said nothing. Finally, her eyes landed on Hilde. "Sit up straight, honey. You look like a camel."

She snapped the mirror shut and slipped it back into her purse. "No more stopping till we get to the motel," she said, standing up and gathering her belongings, "so if you need to go, go now."

Hilde slid out of the booth and headed to the restroom. Janine rose, picked up the check, and turned toward the cashier. Ethan sat a minute longer, eyes down, cleaning up the fries on Hilde's plate.

As Hilde came out of the restroom, she spotted her mother through the plate glass window. She was standing in the sun beside the car, searching for her keys.

Ethan had gotten to his feet and was heading toward the door, wiping his hands on his jeans. As he passed the counter where the two men had sat, his hand darted out and scooped up the bills next to the empty plates. He slipped the bills into his pocket and strolled out into the sunshine.

2
Witness

There. The Pacific. See it?" Janine said from the front passenger seat as the car lurched over the hill. Ethan took his foot off the accelerator and let gravity take over. The highway wound down precipitously, disappearing into a grove of trees.

Over the treetops, Hilde could barely make out the ocean. A white mist hung over it, blurring the horizon.

It was not what she expected, this great mass of water—nothing like the blue Pacific she'd seen in pictures. It was cold and unfriendly, a gray-green roiling mass that looked as though some enormous beast was moving just beneath the surface.

At the bottom of the hill, they passed an abandoned fruit stand and a roadside shop selling rusted lawn sculptures. A Christmas tree farm sat between two large greenhouses. They dead-ended into a two-lane highway that edged the water.

"The Coast Road," her mother announced. "I thought we'd never get here. Go left."

The Pacific appeared on their right, much closer now, alive and restless.

You could hear it through the cracked window, and you could smell it in the air.

Hilde stared at the dark waters, wondering what was beneath the surface. Dolphins? Whales? Great whites?

As the highway dropped closer to the water, sand started blowing over the road. The wind buffeted the car, pushing it into oncoming traffic, causing Ethan to tighten his grip on the wheel. It was August, but this definitely did not qualify as a summer day.

After another stretch of road, her mother looked up from the map in her lap. "Slow down at the bottom of the hill. See that sign? That's where we turn."

The wind died as they turned inland. A large white bird with a graceful neck and yellow beak lifted its head and watched them as they passed by the cattails that lined the road. Weather-beaten cottages appeared, separated by low, well-tended fields. In one of the fields, farmworkers were still harvesting crops, even though daylight was fading.

They came to a crossroads in the center of town, a single stoplight hanging by wires above the intersection. On the far corner sat a beat-up tavern with a neon sign flashing *Liquor*. Several massive Harleys were parked in front. On the near corner was a nondescript gas station whose mini-mart had been turned into a hole-in-the-wall diner. *Taqueria de amigos,* the sign said. Everything was so different here.

"Turn left," her mother said. "And park there." Ethan pulled the car to the side of the road. "I'm gonna pick up the keys at that antique shop. Hilde, take my wallet and go see what you can find in that store over there. We need something to eat tonight. Ethan, stay with the stuff."

Hilde got out, crossed the deserted road, and ducked into the store. A soda fountain took up most of the front half of the place, with chalkboard menus posted high above the grill, and jars of pickles and cookies on the counter. A large man in a butcher's apron was standing behind the cash register, cradling a phone to his ear and scribbling on a pad.

There weren't many customers in the place—two men in biking shorts eating burgers and a young couple sharing a bowl of ice cream. An older woman with short-cropped hair, in a flannel shirt and jeans, was sitting alone at a table by the window, reading a paper and picking over a plate of onion rings.

Hilde headed for the groceries, which were stacked on small shelves in a corner behind a kiosk of maps and travel guides. Happy to see something she recognized, she gathered up a box of Pop-Tarts, a jar of instant coffee, milk, bread, mayo, and three cans of tuna. Comfort food.

As she turned back, she noticed a small, olive-skinned man in a dirty T-shirt and jeans standing at the door. He took off his straw hat, fingering it for a moment as he looked around. His black hair was matted and disheveled, his eyebrows were thick and bushy, and a scruffy mustache traveled down the sides of his mouth. The heels of his pointy-toed cowboy boots were worn to a nub. One of the workers from the field.

Tentatively, he picked up a bottle of water and a bag of corn chips and took them to the register, depositing them on the counter. Then he dug into his front pocket and pulled out a bill.

The woman eating the onion rings looked up.

The man in the butcher's apron hung up the phone, pursed his lips, and stared at the farmworker for a long moment. He seemed to be considering his options. Finally, he took a step toward the bill, scooped it up, stuffed it in his apron, and turned away. He pulled a pencil from behind his ear and began to inventory the pickles in the jar on the counter.

The farmworker looked around anxiously, as if trying to figure out what to do next. For several seconds, nothing happened. Then the woman with the onion rings rose from her chair and ambled over to the cashier, stopping just beside the farmworker. She rested her hand lightly on the counter.

The man in the apron turned. For a long moment, they stared at each other.

"Evening, Carmine," she said finally.

He shoved the pencil behind his ear, dug in his pocket, counted out some change, and smacked it down on the counter in front of the farmworker, scowling at the woman. The farmworker scooped up the change and scurried for the door.

The woman pulled several paper napkins from the chrome holder on the counter. Then she gave him a little smile and headed back to her onion rings.

"Hilde." Ethan was standing at the door. "We're done here. Let's go."

Hilde gathered the boxes and milk carton awkwardly to her chest. She took them to the counter, where the man in the apron took her money and made change without incident.

"Bag?"

"Yes, sir."

He eyed her. "It's extra."

"Oh," she said, slightly embarrassed. "Well, then—no, sir."

Hilde gathered the groceries in her arms and turned, hoping Ethan would help her, but he was already heading back to the car. She could feel the cold milk carton through her jacket as she clutched it to her belly. She crossed the street, fumbled with the car door, and slid in back. The groceries tumbled over the seat beside her.

"What, no bag?" her mother said from the front seat.

Ethan glanced at his sister in the rearview mirror. "I've a feeling we're not in Kansas anymore," he said, and he pulled the car away from the curb.

BY THE TIME THEY found the house, it was almost dark. Everything on the road had been washed in a flat, gray light. There were no streetlights, just a few yellow patches from the windows of nearby cottages.

The house was a dirty white clapboard, with a green roof that needed shingles, and a front porch with a broken plank. Two rusted metal chairs and an old rocker sat on the porch, and a plastic flamingo stood at an entirely unnatural angle in the center of the tiny yard. A beat-up pickup was parked on the gravel driveway.

"Nice house, Mom," Ethan said dryly.

Janine ignored him. She headed to the front door and fumbled with the key. "I hope they turned on the electricity," she said under her breath. She flicked the light switch. A dim bulb hanging from the ceiling illuminated a sparse living room furnished with an old couch, an upholstered armchair, and a wooden table surrounded by folding chairs. A small bookshelf sat against the wall, its bottom shelf holding a few old books. Toward the back was a galley kitchen, and to the right, four stairs led to a dark hallway.

"This'll do," she said, cheerily. "Three bedrooms and a bath upstairs. Turn on that space heater, Hilde." She peeked into the tiny kitchen. "Cute, don't you think?"

Hilde didn't think it was cute. She thought it was depressing. The worn furniture, the mismatched table and chairs, the ugly curtains. *Is this the house—the California dream house—we've all been talking about?* she thought. The difference between what she expected and what she saw as she stood in the tiny living room produced an ache in the back of her throat.

Ethan set the groceries on the kitchen counter and opened the refrigerator. A wan light came from within. "Ooh, nice," he said, pulling out a cottage cheese carton with no top. "How long d'ya think this has been here?" The smell bloomed as he set the carton on the counter.

"Ethan, help me with the bags, please," Janine said as she headed outside. "Hilde, get rid of that."

Hilde picked up the carton, unlocked the back door, and found a garbage can near the back steps. After dropping the carton in the can, she stepped away and took a deep breath of sweet night air. In the failing light, she could see three outbuildings—a loafing barn, a milking parlor, and a small house where she assumed the milk was stored. Between the buildings were several fenced pens. And beyond them was a field—mostly brown, with a few patches of green shrubs, certainly nothing like the lush fields of summer alfalfa that surrounded their Wisconsin home this time of year. Bisecting the field, she thought she spotted a streambed, but she neither heard nor saw water.

While her mom and Ethan lugged in bags from the car, she climbed to the upper floor and began to explore. The bedrooms were furnished simply, with bare lightbulbs in the ceiling that cast deep shadows, giving each room a melancholy gloom. When she found the bathroom, she flipped on the light. A half-used bar of soap sat near the faucets on the turquoise sink, a rust ring circled the toilet bowl, and a fine black mold edged the shower curtain.

She stood mute, and her face grew hot. *Will I ever feel at home here? In this house? In this bathroom?* She caught her own image in the mirror, and her face began to blur.

"Hey, Scout," Ethan called as he passed the open bathroom door, his arms loaded with battered suitcases. "Come let's flip for the back bedroom."

Hilde had already finished two Pop-Tarts when her mother padded into the kitchen, clutching her robe around her thin frame. Had she lost weight over the past year? Her hair was thin and dry, and without any makeup, she looked wrecked in the morning light.

"Ethan up?" Janine said as she opened the cabinet. A jar of instant coffee sat alone on the bottom shelf. She filled the small aluminum pot with water, set it on the stovetop, and turned on the burner.

"Not yet."

"We've got to clean this place up today. I need your help. Yours—and that self-absorbed brother of yours," she muttered.

It didn't make sense, how she treated Ethan. He had tons of friends and teachers who admired him. He'd been on the school yearbook committee. He was a member of the student ethics panel. He was captain of the wrestling team. But none of that seemed to matter.

As if on cue, Ethan staggered into the kitchen, bleary-eyed and bare-chested, his shoulders perpendicular to his spine, his deltoids rounded and sculpted. His hair stuck out at odd angles.

Janine pulled out a chair and sat down at the table.

"Ethan, I'm gonna need to you to clean out the barn today. I don't know what's in there, but we've got to get it ready for the goats. And take a look at the equipment in the shed, will you? See if we can use any of it."

"Mom," Ethan said, holding up a hand to block his mother's words. "Coffee first."

He took a mug from the cabinet and peered into it. Using his index finger, he dug something from the bottom of the cup, examined it closely, and flicked it into the sink. "No protein before coffee," he murmured.

His comment made Hilde smile, but her mother didn't seem amused.

He piled several spoonsful of instant coffee into the mug and poured water from the pot on the stove. Then he sat down and leaned back in his chair. "Aaaahh," he said after taking a sip, "that's some Joe."

Janine gave him only a moment. "And that pickup in the driveway. It comes with the house. I want you to figure out if it runs, and if it doesn't—"

"Whoa, Mom. Hold on a minute. What happened to learning to surf? When we were all back home sitting around the dinner table"—he waved his hand in the air—"you said *you'd* handle the farm. We'd just hang out and enjoy our new California life. That's what you said, as I recall."

"Ethan"—desperation seeped from her words—"please. Think of this as a new beginning, . . . a California *start-up*. There are plenty of restaurants over the hill that'll pay good money for goat cheese. We'll supply them with the best."

Ethan scratched his chin. "I see," he said. "Entrepreneurs. Come to California, and we're gonna be entrepreneurs."

Hilde could feel the air turn frigid.

"Let me make this crystal clear, Ethan," Janine said, her voice now clipped and menacing, "I *need* your help. I need it because your father"—her whole body tensed now— "he isn't here. He's back home selling the house. And he's selling the house because, as you well know, his hours were cut at the college. And when money is tight, everybody in the family pitches in. You're seventeen—eighteen in a few months. Right, Ethan? You're not unaware of the importance of money." She stared at him, her hands clasped so tight around her mug that Hilde thought it might break.

Ethan stood up, scraping his chair against the floor.

"You know, Mom," he said, glaring at her, "all this,"—he swept his arm around the room—"all this is a pipe dream. *Your pipe dream.*"

He grabbed his jacket. In two strides, he was out the front door.

3

The Town by Daylight

Patchy fog hung in the air and obscured the little buildings that lined the street as Hilde trudged back from town, her backpack heavy with groceries. She didn't mind doing chores. Chores got her out of the house, and she had always liked being on her own. She wasn't a loner—she liked people—but she felt most *herself* when she was out of the house and away from her mother's influence. That control was a force field she had grown up with, and she felt powerless around it.

She passed by the bar with the motorcycles parked in front, and the musty old antique dealer, and when the sidewalk gave way to a gravelly path, she tucked her head and leaned forward, hooking her thumbs under the straps of her backpack to ease the load.

When she reached the little white church, she looked up. Sitting on the steps was a woman with a ladle in her hand, a large cooking pot beside her. Dixie cups were stacked nearby, and an old yellow dog snoozed at her feet.

"Water?" the woman asked, holding up the ladle and a cup. She had a soft, round body and spiky hair. Her jeans were baggy, and her blue work shirt was embroidered with bright-colored cactus flowers.

"No, thank you." Hilde knew not to talk to strangers, especially when they were offering something. She ducked her head and started to hurry by, but something made her look up again. Did she know this woman?

"It's cold. And fresh," the woman said, giving her a wry smile. The dog raised one eyebrow and looked at Hilde.

This was the woman from the country store—the one Hilde had watched the first day they arrived.

"No . . . but thank you," she said, remembering her manners. "I've got to get home." She pulled her jacket closer around her chest.

"Suit yourself," the woman replied. She gazed at Hilde for a long moment. When Hilde didn't move, she said, "New here?"

"Yes, ma'am."

"Where from?"

"Wisconsin."

"Wisconsin, huh?" The woman's eyebrows rose a little. "That's a long way from Pescadero. You live around here now?"

"Just around the corner. The house with the flamingo."

The woman looked briefly over Hilde's shoulder. "Ah, the Flood house. That's got some land behind it."

"Yes, ma'am. And a shed and a barn. And a creek, I think."

The dog got up and made his way over to Hilde. She put her hand down for him to sniff, and then stroked his forehead. The last thing she remembered about her own dog, Jupe, was stroking his furry face as he lay under the porch, unable to get up.

"That's Toby there. He seems to like you."

"Yes, ma'am." Her thumb traced the indentation between the dog's eyes.

Ethan had known the exact moment Jupe died. It was the fleas, he said. They felt the drop in body temperature, crawled out from the fur onto Jupe's pink underbelly, and hopped away. He knew those kinds of things.

"Do you have a dog?" the woman asked.

"No," she replied. "Well, not now." A sudden wave of grief overcame her, making her eyes sting. "But I have goats," she added brightly, trying to mask the shame she felt for showing emotion to this stranger. "That is—we'll have some soon. My mom's setting us up to make cheese. And take it over the hill to sell to fancy restaurants and such."

"I'm guessing you'll do well at that," the woman said, bemused.

Hilde squatted down next to Toby, dropping her backpack in the dirt. "Hey, Toby," she murmured, caressing his muzzle. There was something odd about this woman. Her clear blue eyes seemed to invite Hilde into easy conversation with no particular agenda, and she had a peculiarly powerful way of making Hilde feel seen. *She is nothing like Mom,* Hilde thought.

"Do you live here?" Hilde asked, glancing over the woman's shoulder at the church.

"Kind of. I live just up the street. But it feels like I live here sometimes. Most Sundays, I'm pretty busy with the congregation."

This woman was a preacher! In all the years Hilde had gone to church with her parents and her brother, she had never met a preacher who'd park herself on the church steps on a Wednesday afternoon in jeans and a work shirt.

"You ever get to church?" the woman inquired gently.

"Yes, ma'am. Every Sunday, back in Wisconsin." Memories of youth group flooded her head—Bible study by the lake, field trips to the planetarium, tables at the Christmas bazaar. But then another memory pushed its way into her consciousness—a freezing evening last January when she stood in the church parking lot for close to an hour waiting for her father to pick her up. He never showed. Finally, the youth minister noticed her and gave her a ride home.

"What kind of a church do you go to?" the woman asked.

"Christian."

The woman smiled. "Well, we're all mostly Christian around here. Are you Baptist? Lutheran? Catholic?"

"Oh. Lutheran."

"This church here"—she gestured behind her—"is just a little community church. Pretty much everyone comes here, except the Catholics. They go to St. Anthony's, across from your house. And that's about it for this town."

The woman's gaze drifted over Hilde's head and up the road.

Hilde turned and saw two wiry farmworkers toting backpacks, making their way toward the church. They were both in dirty jeans and work boots. Their frayed straw hats shielded their faces.

"*Hola, hermanos,*" the woman called as they came near. "*¿Agua?*" She held up the ladle.

The men looked up and stopped. Hilde could see that they were considering. The taller man said something to the other and then stepped forward.

"*Sí, señora. Gracias.*"

"*Bueno.* That's what I like. People who know what they want." She dipped the ladle into the pot, filled a Dixie cup, and held it out.

The man took three long strides toward her outstretched hand as if to avoid making footprints on the grassy patch in front of the church steps.

Hilde couldn't help noticing the dirt under his nails as he took the cup. She backed away.

"You fellas new?" the woman asked. "*¿Recién llegados?*"

"*Sí, señora.*"

"Ah. Well, I'm Nan, and this is my friend . . ." She looked at Hilde.

"Hilde." Her voice sounded tiny.

"Hilde. Yes." Nan poured out another ladleful of water into a Dixie cup. Motioning to the smaller man standing in the street, she said, "Hilde, take this to my brother over there, please."

Hilde hesitated for a moment, then took the cup and walked it over.

"Here, for you." She tried to speak clearly so he'd understand her, but she made it sound as though she were talking to a dimwit. Embarrassed, she looked down.

The man nodded and took the cup. The skin on his hand was dark and leathery.

She was entirely unaware of the pickup truck that stopped across the street. And so when her mother called her name, she jumped.

"Hilde, come here, please."

Abashed, Hilde glanced at Nan, who returned her gaze diffidently.

"Hilde. Now, please," her mother called again, this time with an edge in her voice.

"Don't forget your backpack," Nan said gently.

Hilde picked up her backpack and, without saying a word, crossed the street and climbed into the pickup.

Her mother sat motionless as she settled into the seat and fumbled for the seatbelt. The look on her mother's face—especially that tight mouth—made her queasy. She knew Nan was watching, and she wished her mother would just put the truck in gear and drive. Instead, Janine reached over her to the glove box, rooted around inside it, pulled out a small plastic bottle, and offered it to Hilde.

"Purell?"

4

Estranged

Ethan couldn't get the truck running by the day school started, so they took the school bus, a big step down for both of them. The bus, which ran from the flagpole in the center of town to the sprawling high school out on Butano Cutoff Road, carried a full load of kids, none of whom looked like Hilde. The girls, with their coffee-colored skin, lustrous black hair, and heavy makeup, looked years older than Hilde—and they clearly knew how to flirt with the boys, something Hilde was still working out.

Ethan sat beside her on the bus, silent and preoccupied.

When they got to school, he turned to her. "You know where you're going, right, Scout?"

"Yeah, I think so. I've got that letter here somewhere." She fished into her backpack and brought out a slip of blue paper with a map of the campus.

"Okay, then. Later." And he was off in another direction.

The main school building was a low, sprawling place made mostly of cinder blocks painted a monotonous yellow. Classrooms were lined up like shoeboxes, all open to the outside and connected by breezeways with corrugated roofs. The restrooms were located along a chain-link fence behind the office. And there was no gym. Just a massive blacktop with hoops at either end and a grassy field beyond. This was nothing like Tremper, with its overheated halls, its massive auditorium, its endless rows of lockers.

She had always liked school. She liked the order and predictability of it all. She had done well in her freshman classes at Tremper—algebra first, then English, gym, science, history, and band practice in the afternoon. But this place was chaotic, with kids spinning off in all directions and teachers going through the motions with tired eyes. Finding the back row in each class, she couldn't help but notice the notes being passed, the cell phones pinging, the whispering, the sniggers.

Lunch—there was no lunchroom—came from the vending machines lined up in the breezeway or the taco truck in the parking lot. The kids sat in clusters at small metal tables, poking and jabbing at each other as they ate, while she sat alone on the curb, picking at a granola bar.

By the end of the day, Hilde had lost her map and gained several heavy textbooks, which looked like they'd been handed down for longer than she'd been alive. She boarded the bus and squeezed into a rear seat, exhausted and yearning for a glimpse of her brother. He would know how to calm her fears, how to ease her sense of displacement. But by the time he swung onto the bus, the aisle was jammed with kids. She tried to catch his eye. She wanted him to look for her. But he didn't. She spent the ride back to town hypnotically watching the crop rows zip by.

When the bus pulled up to the flagpole in the center of town, kids piled out and scattered in all directions. Hilde stepped off the bus last and scanned the street. Three small, sun-shriveled men were sitting outside the taquería next to the gas station. And across the street, a couple of heavily tattooed bikers in full leather gear were revving their Harleys, ready to head out to the Coast Road. Nobody familiar. Nobody normal.

By the time she spotted Ethan, he was across the street, striding away to who knew where. She watched him go, wishing he would wait. Then she heaved her backpack over one shoulder and headed home.

THAT NIGHT BEFORE BED, Hilde burrowed into the back of the closet and pulled out the suitcase she'd brought from home. From a side pocket, she retrieved the photo she'd pulled from her dresser drawer while she was packing. It had been squirreled away in that dark corner of her bedroom for too long—never good enough to frame but, in some unfathomable way, too revelatory to throw away.

Now she needed to see it again.

The photo was badly creased, and the color was faded, but the image was clear enough. Here were her father and mother standing together at a dinner table before an enormous turkey, he with carving knife and fork in hand, she in a party dress over which she had tied a tulle apron festooned with sequined reindeer. What was so odd about the photo, what made it so hard to throw away, was the way they gazed at each other, her mother's eyes bright and shining, her father's mouth open in a slight smile, as if they were sharing a delicate secret.

Hilde turned the photo over in her hand. Someone had written a date on the back. The photo was from Christmas six years ago. She had been eight at the time.

Fingering the deckled edges of the photo, she could feel her throat tighten.

I don't remember them ever being like that. They look as if they really like each other. What happened to that spark? Where did it go?

She placed the photo in the palm of one hand and covered it with the other, pressing her palms together hard. The room blurred as she rocked back and forth.

Maybe love isn't all it's cracked up to be. Maybe it doesn't last. Maybe it isn't even real. Maybe it's just something people convince themselves of so they don't have to face life alone.

5

Don de Dios

On Thursday as Hilde walked home from the bus stop, she came upon a small commotion of people buzzing around a vacant lot just beyond the antique store. Several food stalls had been clumsily constructed, and baskets of vegetables and fruits were laid out on wooden tables together with jars of honey and nuts. Flowers overflowed from plastic buckets on the ground. A farmer in a frayed T-shirt with hands like sausages was weighing artichokes for a woman toting an armload of sunflowers. And off to the side, amidst a tangle of old metal bicycles, Nan was squatting beside a battered blue bike, wrench in hand.

"Hold tight, Mateo," Nan said to the farmworker steadying the bike for her. "It's loosening." She drove the wrench downward. The nut suddenly let go, spilling her onto the dusty earth. She rolled around on the sparse scrub grass, chuckling as she tried to get her knees under her.

As Mateo helped her up, she glanced Hilde's way. "Hey, Hilde!" she said, breaking into a wide grin.

"Hi." Hilde said shyly.

"You remember Mateo. Mateo, this is Hilde."

She did remember him. He was one of the fieldhands who had stopped in front of the church, though she had not heard his name.

Mateo nodded in her direction and went back to wrestling the wheel off the frame of a bike.

Hilde glanced around. "Is Toby here?"

"He is," Nan said, and she motioned to a nearby picnic table, beneath which sat a large bowl of water.

Hilde saw a black snout sticking out from the shadows. "Can I pet him?"

"Sure. Go ahead." Nan wiped her hands on her jeans.

Hilde sat down on the grass beside the picnic table. Toby raised his head and looked at her, beating his thick tail against the leg of the table. She touched his ear, which felt like velvet—soft and floppy—and gently ran her fingernails between his wide-set eyes.

"We just got a load of bikes from over the hill," Nan said. "We're fixing them up before we give them out." She pulled a bike from the tangle next to the table, stood it up on its kickstand, and started running her hand over the tires.

Hilde turned and rested her back against the table. "Who are they for?"

"Farmworkers. They live mostly in the hills, in trailers, on the ranches. Some newcomers are under the bridge just beyond your house—temporarily, until we find them something better. Anyway, they need bikes to get to work."

Hilde looked beyond Nan to the dry, wheat-colored hills that surrounded the town. She couldn't imagine riding a bike up those hills at the end of a day. "Can't they drive?"

Nan shook her head. "Most of 'em don't have licenses—leastways, not licenses that work in the States." She stuck her fingers between the spokes and pulled several back into position. "And if they're pulled over without a license, well . . . that's no good."

"No good?"

"It can get them deported."

"For driving without a license?"

"Mm-hmm." Nan struggled for a wrench that was just out of reach. "It wasn't always like that. But things have changed."

She held out an old-fashioned label maker, an odd-shaped gun with tape where the barrel should be. "Ever used one of these?"

"I think so."

"I could use some help. We need to make a label for each bike," she said and motioned to the tangle of bikes behind her. "It needs to say *PCC*—for Pescadero Community Church—and *Don de Dios.*"

Hilde tried to work out the Spanish.

"Gift from God," Nan said, reading her face. "I promised the sheriff I'd mark all our bikes so he'd know they're from us. I gave two bikes to a guy last week, one for him and one for his buddy. He was walking home along the Coast Road when the sheriff stopped him. Confiscated the bikes and demanded his papers."

"Why?"

"Thought he'd stolen them."

"Did he get arrested?"

"No, thank God. Just a citation. He came straight to my house and told me what happened. I called the sheriff and explained *I'd* given him the bikes. That they were from the church. Anyway, the sheriff tore up the citation and gave him back the bikes, but not his papers. And without papers, he can't work. Now he's looking for fifty dollars to get another set of papers. It was all my fault, really. I should have labeled those bikes from the start." She held out the label gun to Hilde.

It was close to four o'clock when Hilde finished pressing the last label in place.

"Nice work," Nan said. "If you ever need a job, let me know. I could use some help on Thursdays. That's the day we set up *La Sala* for the workers."

"La Sala?"

"It means *living room*. We share a meal together once a week in fellowship hall just behind the church. We eat, play cards, dominoes—and sometimes somebody sings. Those guys are pretty lonely up there in the hills, so it's nice to come together."

Hilde hesitated. She watched as Nan collected the tools scattered across the dry ground. Nan was clearly *not* someone her mother would invite to dinner. That short haircut, those spiky shoots standing straight up in front, that moon face, plump and lined and untouched by makeup. Nonetheless, there was something about this odd preacher—a way of seeing things—that drew Hilde.

But no.

"Thanks, but I'm pretty busy with school."

"Well, change your mind, you know where we are." She picked up a bright-colored tote that sat near Toby's water dish and pulled out a small jar of honey. "Here, this is for you. A thank-you for all the work you did today. It's honey from a farm over the hill."

Hilde was surprised, but she took the jar, warm from the sun, and tucked it in her backpack.

"Thanks. I like honey," she said.

After touching Toby gently on the nose, she gave Nan a little wave and headed home.

6

New Beginnings

They're here!

Hilde could smell the goats as soon as she stepped onto the front porch. She dropped her backpack in the kitchen and scooted out the back door.

Huddled in the small corral were over a dozen goats, their tails flicking, their chestnut coats gleaming in the sun.

She crept to the pen and gently squatted down, peering through the chicken wire. They were so beautiful, these little creatures, with long, sleek legs and perfect cloven hooves. Each animal sported a black stripe running down its backbone, and long, frosted ears. Several of the older ones moved toward her, sniffing the air in anticipation of a bucket of feed. She poked her finger through the fence and touched the velvet snout of a young kid, who looked back at her with liquid eyes. He found her finger and started suckling. Hilde could feel new teeth erupting from the gums.

Her mother appeared around the corner of the shed, followed by a solid-built man carrying a large sack of feed across one shoulder. She was in a sundress.

"I know how heavy that must be, Mr. Booher," she said. "I'm most grateful for your help."

"Call me Ned," he said with a wink. Janine smiled. He slung the sack to the ground, took off his ballcap, and wiped his forehead with the sleeve of his shirt. His dark eyebrows, slightly pocked skin, and square jaw gave Hilde the impression that he might have had enough rugged good looks to be in Westerns—many, many years ago.

"That feed trough's got to be moved, and that one there needs water," Janine said. "Then we'll be set."

Hilde had never heard this voice from her mother—soft and lilty. She stood up.

"Hilde! I didn't see you there." Her mother looked slightly embarrassed. "Honey, this is our neighbor Mr. Booher. He's helping us set up."

Ned Booher nodded at Hilde and touched the arced brim of his cap with two fingers. "Little lady," he said. He turned back to Janine. "Let me help you with that trough, ma'am." He unlatched the gate and bullied his way into the pen. The goats clustered around him, several of them attempting to chew his pants. He encircled the trough and heaved it up into his arms. Little flakes of feed floated onto his oversized chest. "Nice herd you got here. Nubians give you some flavorful milk. Now, where do you want this? . . ."

Hilde watched them disappear behind the barn. She was mightily annoyed by Mr. Booher, though she couldn't say why. Maybe it was because he talked like he was in a cheesy Western.

A scrawny kid stuck its snout through the fence and sampled her shoelace. She knelt again.

"Well, hello, you," she whispered, running her finger down the length of the animal's long ear. Finding the shoelace entirely dry, the kid pulled away, turned toward its mother, and stuck its snout under her belly, jabbing roughly once or twice before finding the dark, heavy teat. The kid suckled hard while the nanny flicked her tail. After a few moments, a much larger kid muscled in, crowding out the little one who bleated fiercely.

"That's not fair, is it?" Hilde said to the kid, scratching its bony rump.

She pushed through the gate and picked up the scrawny body. Holding him in one arm, she crossed the corral and found a length of rope hanging from a peg on the barn wall. She brought it back and looped it around the nanny's neck, shooed the larger kid away, and led the nanny into a small pen made of chicken wire she'd noticed behind the shed. She placed the kid gently beside the nanny and filled a bucket with food pellets.

The nanny began to feed, her lower jaw moving methodically side to side. The kid sniffed the pellets, circled once, and attached himself to an engorged teat.

"Don't worry, little guy," Hilde said. "Tonight, you get a full meal."

That evening, when Ethan came home, Ned Booher was sitting on the front porch, legs sprawled out in front of him, a can of beer in his beefy hand. Hilde had positioned her chair slightly behind his so that she didn't have to keep up a conversation. And Janine was perched on the porch railing in front of him, leaning in, one sandaled foot dangling from beneath her skirt. She turned when she heard Ethan's boots on the steps.

"Ethan. Here you are! Come meet our neighbor Mr. Booher. He lives up the hill."

Booher leaned back in his chair and grinned. "So you're Ethan," he said. "Heard a lot about you, son. Your mother tells me you already got a job at the deli in town. That shows moxie. I like moxie."

Ethan stood there, looking at him.

Janine broke the silence. "Go get another chair, hon, and join us. We're having hors d'oeuvres out here tonight. It's such a nice night."

Ethan looked at the plate of cheddar surrounded by Ritz crackers balanced on the porch railing. He managed an eye roll in Hilde's direction before opening the screen door.

He emerged a few minutes later, cola in one hand, folding chair in the other. In one quick gesture, he snapped the chair open and sat down, mirroring Booher's sprawl with his own.

Booher didn't notice. He was absorbed in conversation with Janine.

"Mine's just a little spread, fifty acres or so. Starts behind the elementary school and goes on up the hill," he said, stretching out his arm and sweeping it from left to right. "Small, but enough for me and the cattle. You can make a heap of money raisin' cattle, if you know how," he said, watching Janine's face for a response. "'Course, a lot of people around here prefer crops. Brussels sprouts. Garlic. Strawberries. Easier work." He leaned forward. "But not as lucrative, you know?"

"Mm, it's a wonderful place," Janine said, a bit breathless. "Gorgeous coastline. Beautiful sunsets. I love seeing the fields of artichokes."

"You're right, of course." He leaned forward and touched her lightly on the knee. "Not to burst your bubble, but let me tell you about the downsides. There *are* downsides, you know, and you may as well find out now."

"Of course," she said.

"For one thing, taxes. Sky-high. Not like what you got in Wisconsin. That's in part because this state is full of do-gooders who want to take everything you got and spread it around." He wiggled his fingers as if he were sprinkling glitter on the porch boards. "When I was growing up, this state was solid. Full of quality people. They took care of themselves, and they didn't rely on the government to give them a handout. Anybody could make good money here."

He took a swig of beer and burped gently.

Janine circled her ankle slowly as she listened.

"But now"—he flung his hand this way and that—"now we've got the socialists in San Francisco and the snowflakes in Hollywood. They just want to make everything free." He snorted. "They want to take the money we make from the sweat off our own backs—and give it away."

"Really?" Janine asked. She seemed to be doing nothing more than making space for his talk.

"Yes, they do, darlin.'"

Ethan leaned back in his chair, put his hands behind his head, and stared hard at Booher's profile. Then he asked in a flat tone, "And how do they do that exactly?"

Booher turned toward Ethan, happy to have another member in his audience. "Food stamps. Rent control. Unemployment payouts. Free health care." He ticked them off on his fingers. "And here's the real kicker. Most of those bennies—around here, anyway—they don't even go to *US citizens*. Nope. Most of 'em go to them migrants coming up over the border. Don't get me wrong. I'm fine with 'em coming up to work. We need that, in the fields. But next thing you know, they're bringing up the whole family—aunts, uncles, cousins, kids. And the wife? She's *always* pregnant."

He twisted in his chair and grabbed two Ritz crackers from the plate. "Slice me off a piece of that cheese, will you, darlin'?" he said to Hilde.

Ethan caught her eye as she leaned forward to offer the square of cheese she'd positioned on a cracker in the middle of a paper napkin.

"And all those kids," Booher continued, popping the cracker into his mouth, "they need to go to school, of course. And what does that mean?"

The conversation paused as he savored the cracker and cheese.

"Take our elementary school just down the road," he began again. "We had to hire three more teachers—*three more*—just to handle the load. And who pays for that?" He brushed crumbs from his chest. They landed on Ethan's boot. "And when the kids get sick, and they *do* get sick, they don't go to their doctor, no sir. Because they haven't *got* a doctor. Nope. They go straight to the emergency room, the most expensive place to go, and we treat them *for free*. All paid for by hardworkin' folk like you and me. We're bein' sucked dry. I see it every day. Sucked dry."

Ethan's boots scraped across the boards of the porch as he pulled his legs in. He bent forward and flicked the crumbs off his boots.

"Oh, pardon me. I seem to be on my soapbox," said Booher, offering Janine a toothy smile. "Now tell me all about yourself, Miss Jasmine. You do have a fine family here. Did you drive all the way from Wisconsin? That's a long way to be driving, for a woman on her own."

Ethan looked at Hilde. *Jasmine?* he mouthed.

Hilde gave her brother a little shrug.

AFTER GLANCING AT HIS wristwatch—a fancy thing with a large face and several tiny dials—Booher rose and picked up his hat. "It's been a mighty pleasure, but I still have work to do tonight," he said.

"Ethan," Janine said, "move the truck so Mr. Booher can get out of the driveway, please."

Ethan crushed his empty Coke can in one hand, placed it carefully on the porch railing, and headed down the steps. The pickup's puny grinding sound caught and failed twice before he could get it to move.

As Janine and Hilde watched, Booher hefted himself into his Chevy Silverado, revved the engine, and spun out of the driveway, waving his cap from the window of the truck as he disappeared up the hill.

Janine waved back.

They came back to the porch single file, silent.

"*Jasmine,* Mom?" Ethan said.

Hilde looked away. She could feel her shoulders inch toward her ears.

"Maybe," Janine said as she scraped the cracker crumbs from the table and dumped them over the porch railing, wiping her hands on her skirt. After a few seconds of dead silence, she turned and faced her son. Her tone was harsh now. "You know, Ethan. There's no reason why I can't call myself whatever I want. What's it to you?"

For a long moment, Ethan stared at her, as if he were trying to suss out what was happening. Then he said in a low voice, "I wonder what Dad is doing tonight."

Janine turned away. "Hilde, help me clean up."

7

Cloven

The next morning, Hilde was up at dawn. She did not want the goats to have to wait for their food. She dressed quickly and stole to the kitchen, where she grabbed some lettuce leaves from the refrigerator. Stuffing them in her pocket, she slipped out the back door and breathed in the cool salt air.

When she slid aside the barn door, the goats began to move toward her as if they were one body. She pulled the top off the bin that sat under the window and scooped pellets into buckets. The pungent, fecund odor reminded her of the tents at the Kenosha County Fair. As she filled the troughs, the goats began to bleat. One of the nannies smelled the lettuce she'd squirreled away in her pocket and nosed after it.

"Not for you," she said, nudging the animal away.

She left the barn by the side door and headed for the pen where she had corralled the nanny and kid. She hoped the kid had gotten his fill of milk last night, and she wanted the nanny to have the lettuce.

The pen was shrouded in shadow when she rounded the corner—but almost immediately she knew something was wrong. Several of the posts lay askew, and the chicken wire was twisted and matted down. She paused, then crept closer and peered into the shadows.

At the far end of the corral, she saw what looked like a large piece of burlap covering a pile of sticks, dark tar spread beneath. She stared, waiting for her eyes to adjust. No, it wasn't that . . . it was something else. She pushed opened the rickety gate and inched forward. As she moved, her foot caught on a stick in the dirt. She looked down. Lying over her foot was a disembodied leg, capped by a delicate cloven hoof.

"Nooo!" she howled. "No, no, no!"

Janine came racing around the corner of the shed, clutching her thin robe. Her eyes skimmed over Hilde and then fixed on the carcasses in the pen. "Oh, Hilde," she said, taking a step toward her daughter and putting her arms around her.

Hilde buried her face in her mother's robe. They stood together like two statues in the cold morning air.

The screen door banged, and Ethan appeared, pulling a T-shirt over his head. He surveyed the pen, his sister, his mother. "What the hell happened here?" he said, incredulously.

Hilde looked at him, her eyes shining. "I—I put them here because of the kid." She could barely speak. "He was so skinny. He couldn't get enough milk. He wasn't—he couldn't get in to feed—so I decided—I—"

"Jesus, Hilde! You put them *out here*? What were you thinking?" he said, fury in his voice. He knew from tending livestock in Wisconsin that coyotes love finding vulnerable prey away from the herd.

His comment cut her to the quick. She pulled away from her mother and faced her brother, her fists in tight balls, but she was shaking so much, she could not find her voice.

"Shut up, Ethan!" Janine said icily, glaring at him. "Had you been here—had you done what you needed to do—"

His face went cold. For a moment, the three of them stood there in stony silence, a monument to family discord.

"Llama," said a voice in a thick Hispanic accent. It came from the path that ran just outside the paddock fence. They all turned. "This field needs a llama. To keep the coyotes away."

A fieldhand in dirty jeans and work boots stood just outside the fence. He looked only a few years older than Ethan. His skin was ruddy at the cheeks and forehead, and his nose was long and pointed like an arrow. Strong forearms poked from the sleeves of his worn denim shirt, suggesting he was no stranger to hard work. He was holding a beat-up beach bike with a wire basket.

"What?" Janine said.

"*¡Disculpe!* I couldn't help but see."

Janine's eyes narrowed. "What's your name?" she said.

"Gabriel. My name is Gabriel, *señora.*" He removed his ballcap and clutched it to his chest.

"Gabriel. Yes. And how do you know all this, Gabriel. About llamas and such?"

A shy grin flitted across his face. "It's what people do around here. And also where I come from.

Ethan began to fidget.

"And where's that—where you come from?"

"Veracruz. Mexico. I grew up on a farm."

Her eyes narrowed. She was clearly taking his measure. "And Gabriel, do you know where to get a llama around here?"

Gabriel shrugged. "It wouldn't be hard."

Ethan snorted and looked away.

Turning and looking straight at Ethan, she said, "Good. Gabriel, I'll pay you ten dollars an hour to help me with this farm. Cash. Two hours in the morning, two in the evening. You don't have to quit your day job. Can you do that?"

Gabriel looked surprised, but did not hesitate. "*Sí, señora.* I can do that."

"Good. You can start this evening. And find me a llama."

8

Casting a Line

Gabriel pedaled hard into town, stopping outside the taquería where reception was strongest. He prayed his phone would work. It was always an iffy proposition since the battery barely held a charge. He punched in the number. A familiar voice picked up.

"*¿Miguel?* It's me, Gabriel. I need to speak to Joaquín."

"*¿Gabriel?* Long time, my friend! *Un minuto.* I'll send for him."

For several minutes, there was nothing but static on the line. Someone at the bar would have to run down the road and find Gabe's brother, so he was prepared to wait. Finally, he heard a breathless voice.

"*Gabriel! ¡Aquí estoy!*" I'm here!

"I have good news, *hermano*." Gabriel said. "I got the money."

"What? You have it *now*?"

"I'll have it when you need it. Just come.

"What about Fernando?"

"Fernando?" Gabe sighed. He knew his brother had developed a tight friendship with Fernando, but he wasn't sure why. "Is he ready to come?"

"Are you kidding? He's like a pit bull. I keep telling him we don't have the money, but he doesn't care. He's ready."

"Fine. Bring him. But tell him he needs to pay his own way. He's not your brother. Remember that."

Joaquín said something, but static jammed the line.

"Joaquín, *escucha* . . . can you hear me?" He began to talk slower, louder. "Listen. Don't try to cross at Tijuana. Go to Nogales. Or Agua Prieta. It's safer there. Call when you arrive. I'll wire the money. And get yourself a phone."

9

Outskirts of Mexico City

J oaquín, *compa*, pay up! You owe me for that call," Miguel barked from across the bar.

"Bill me!" Joaquín raised his hand in a high gesture that was part excitement, part goodbye. With that, he burst out the door and into the street.

Finally! It's happening!

It was something he had dreamed of for three long years.

In America with Gabe, we can do anything. We can start our own business—a truck farm, maybe, or an autobody shop. And we'll make money. Good money. Build ourselves a house out of cinder blocks, not tin or plastic—a sturdy one, capable of holding back the rain. With running water. And electricity. We'll keep a dozen chickens behind it, and we'll eat eggs every morning. And when we have enough money, we'll build another house. And maybe we'll each find a wife. And start a family. And the two families would live close. And the cousins would run in a pack. Little kids, big kids, kids everywhere . . .

That was as far as he could imagine, but it was enough. It was enough to propel his body home. He tried to keep his body under control, walking briskly down the dirt road, but soon he broke into a jog and then a run. He had to find Fernando. To tell him. They were heading north!

By the time he reached his makeshift home in the middle of Neza, he was breathless and his legs burned, but his mind vibrated with the news. He pulled back the tarp and ducked into the dim, humid space looking for Fernando, but the room was empty. It had rained that morning, so there would be fresh water today. Probably Fernando was out refilling the jugs. He picked up Fernando's bedroll—wet from a leak in the roof—and shook out the droplets, laying it over one of the two chairs that flanked the small wooden table in the center of the room.

From under his own bed—a piece of plywood perched on cinder blocks—he retrieved a beat-up cigar box. He placed the box gently on the table and pulled out a dog-eared map, just as he'd done so many times over the past year, ever since he'd found it while scavenging for lumber at a nearby construction site. It was a map of the northern half of Mexico and the southern half of America, and he had colored the routes north, all of them, imagining exactly how he would get to each of the various border crossings. He spread out the map with his hands and studied it again.

After several minutes, he rose and positioned one of the chairs at the head of his bed. Stepping up onto its seat, he reached through the corrugated metal sheeting that served as a roof and into the plastic sheeting that covered it. He groped for several moments, finally retrieving the small cloth pouch he'd been searching for. It felt satisfyingly heavy in his hand. He brought it to the table and shook out the contents. His mother's ring tumbled out, a large and showy silver disk bigger than a peso set with coral and turquoise stones. When he touched it, he said a little prayer, thanking God for his mother's foresight. He had never seen her wear it. In fact, he'd had no idea it existed until she got up off her sickbed one day and dug it out. She was not a sentimental woman.

When she showed it to him, she had looked him hard in the eyes and said, "Sell it, *mijo*. It is just a thing. It has no importance. Your dream. Your dream has importance. Sell it and turn it into your dream."

Her illness, her death had happened so quickly. She had said nothing. *Nada*. He had noticed the distended abdomen, the bloat, only a few weeks before she died, and he had hoped then that she was finally gaining weight. God knows she needed some meat on her bones. In Veracruz, in better times, she had been robust and strong. She had worked alongside her boys—Gabriel and Joaquín—in the fields, harvesting the maize to sell and beans to eat. They were not rich, but they were not poor in Veracruz. They ate from the land and survived on what they sold, and with the help of neighbors, they got by.

But then things changed. Governments made deals. And the markets were flooded with maize—maize from America, sold in Mexico. The prices were so low that they were forced to drop their own prices to compete. They did, and the next season they had to do it again, and the next. There was less and less money to put into seed, and less to pay for the gasoline to take the maize to market. After three years of scraping by, it became clear that the land could no longer sustain them. And so they moved to the capital looking for work. They ended up in Neza, at the eastern edge of Mexico City, on a piece of land that nobody wanted, with other displaced families, where they fashioned a home out of tin and cardboard and plastic, learning from their new neighbors where to collect rainwater and how to jury-rig the overhead wires so they could have electricity for a few hours each day.

Gabriel, seventeen at the time, found a part-time job at an auto-body shop, which kept food on the table for a few months. He liked the work, and he learned a good deal from the owner, a widower with a wealth of knowledge, no sons, and a shed full of tools. But one day Gabe arrived at work to find the place burned to the ground. It did not take long for the buzz around Neza to deliver him the story. The owner had failed to pay the *protección* he owed—whether he *would* not or *could* not, no one knew. Some kind of interaction had taken place with those thugs, and he had vanished into the night, leaving several cars still on the racks. The thugs swooped in, retrieved the cars, sold them to a chop shop in Mexico City, and—perhaps as a message to others in the community—burned the garage to the ground with the owner's two guard dogs inside.

Joaquín, who was fourteen, had heard the story straight from Gabe, who told it like a parable, a morality tale in which the hero finds himself faced with life-changing decisions. Stay or go. Fight or flee. Kill or be killed. He'd cautioned Joaquín about the gangs. He told him how they would soon come for him, luring him in ways that made life sound sweet and wild, and how they would make it difficult, even dangerous, *not* to join. They would spread money around, a siren call to the boys of Neza, and before long, he and those other boys would do anything—*anything*—for a few pesos and a sense of family.

"Be thankful," Gabe said. "You're skinny, short. They don't want you. Yet."

Joaquín was unnerved, both for himself and for his older brother. He was young, but he was not stupid. And so he fixed his eyes on contributing to the family's coffers. He began to help his mother, who had taken to fashioning large, colorful flowers out of paper to sell to tourists. He threw himself into the work, gathering up her handiwork and riding his battered bike past the open-air market and deep into the hotel district of Mexico City where the flowers would fetch quadruple the price. He made the trip every day except Sundays, bringing home enough money for the family to eat while Gabe looked for another job.

One day as he was headed into town with a stash of his mother's handiwork, an old woman stopped him on the road not far from his home and asked if she could borrow his bike. He could not say no to such a woman. It was not done. So he lent it, hoping against hope that she would bring it back. He found out three days later that she had sold it for food.

Joaquín told Gabe what had happened, so ashamed of his gullibility that he was unable to look this brother in the eye.

"*No llores.* No tears, brother," Gabe said, after Joaquín had finished. "You, *mamá*, and me—we have each other. We'll find a way."

That was the day Gabe decided to head north.

10

Goat Grave

Hilde opened her eyes to the gray light of dawn coming through the tiny window of her bedroom. For a fleeting moment, she could not remember what had happened the day before. But she felt the foreboding, that *something* had happened, *something terrible had happened.*

Then the obscene images bloomed in her brain. The tar. The burlap. The fragile bones—so white—sticking up from the mud. The black cloven hoof, *here* next to her foot. The tangle of bodies, *there* across the pen.

She turned onto her stomach, wrapped her arms around her head, and buried her face in the musty mattress. The pressure built around her heart, moved up her windpipe and seeped out her tear ducts.

I killed them. I put them out there, alone in that pen, facing the field. I set them out like bait.

She had conjured a horrific image in her mind's eye: the nanny, sensing a shadow moving across the field, standing up, sniffing the air, scurrying from one side of the pen to the other, looking for cover.

And the kid, raising itself onto its wobbly legs, darting after her like a Mexican jumping bean, not knowing why but becoming frantic as the menace skulked toward the pen. Together they would leap wildly at the fence, trying to scale it, getting legs caught in the wire mesh, crashing to the ground. And at some moment, there would be no cover, and no place to run.

Something between a gasp and a sob escaped her throat. She was *so* stupid! And that ignorance—*her* ignorance—had caused their deaths.

I should never have tried to help. I don't understand this place. I want to go home!

She curled in on herself and stayed motionless until her heartbeat steadied in her chest. Finally, she sat up and rubbed her eyes hard with the heels of her hands.

She saw through the window Gabriel in the morning light. He was already out in the big pen, tending the goats. Watching him move, touching the snouts of the nannies, greeting them, calmed her somehow. It was as if by his demeanor, he was accepting it all. Not blaming, but acknowledging and accepting. *Yes, two are lost, but life goes on, and the others need tending.*

She dressed quickly and stole out the back door. The air was cold and blurred by fog.

"Hey," she said, standing in the dirt just outside the gate, her hands deep in her jacket pockets. Was her face tear-stained? She wiped her cheek with the back of her sleeve.

Gabriel looked up. "Morning," he said, showing a hint of surprise.

"Can I help?"

"Sí, claro."

He handed her a bucket. She filled it with pellets from the bin in the barn and dumped it into the trough. Dust floated up and into the fog.

"They need fresh water. The hose is there," he said in his accented English.

She dragged the hose to the trough and turned on the water. The goats chewed the pellets, their eyes fixed blankly on the far side of the pasture, their ears and tails twitching.

Gabriel moved to the milking machines and checked the rubber hosing.

He didn't look much older than Ethan, but he acted older. He had an air about him that Ethan lacked. He carried weight on his shoulders. What kind of life had he had that made him like that?

"Where do you live?" she asked.

"Bobcat Creek Ranch. Off Bean Hollow Road."

"By yourself?"

"With others."

"You have family?" she asked.

"I have family, *sí*. But not here." He was wiping down the equipment now with a wet rag. After a minute, he added, "I have a brother. In Mexico."

"What about your parents?"

He hesitated. "My mother . . . she passed a while back. My father, a long time ago."

Clearly, she'd overstepped a boundary. Her cheeks burned. She changed the subject. "What's your brother's name?"

A tiny smile rippled across his face. "Joaquín."

"Is he younger or older?"

"Younger. He's"—he paused to calculate—"seventeen now. It's three years since I saw him."

"Oh, wow. That's a long time."

He nodded.

"And you haven't been home to visit?"

He shrugged. "It's not easy to go home."

She sensed a deep loss in his voice, and it resonated in her body. They had both lost family, but in different ways. She could understand his circumstances. There was no reckoning with death. But she couldn't understand why she was losing her family, why her parents would let it happen.

She worked with Gabe as the early morning sun burned off the fog. She helped him wrangle the goats past the loafing barn and up the ramp, crowding in on one another, to the milking machines. He attached the cups to the teats and showed her how to keep the tubing free of kinks until the goats were spent and ready to be shooed back to the pasture. She found she liked working beside Gabe. He was quiet and deliberate, and he seemed to have a silent pact with the goats that made them trust him. *He's a natural with animals,* she thought.

SHE TRAILED HIM THAT afternoon, too, watching as he set up a nursing bucket for the older kids—the ones who should have been weaned but who drove the younger ones from the teats. He punched a bucket with holes, fitted a hard rubber nipple into each hole, filled the bucket with milk, and set it in the middle of the pen. The kids muscled their way to the nipples and began to suckle, their jaws working and their small bellies growing round and hard.

She had been wrestling all day with how to ask the question. Finally, she screwed up her courage. "What did you do with the nanny and the kid?"

He stopped and looked at her quizzically.

"Their bodies, I mean."

His brow furrowed. "I buried them," he said simply. His black eyes watched her carefully.

"Oh," she said, looking away. "I'm glad." She'd been terrified that the carcasses had been dumped in the garbage somewhere where the buzzards could find them.

After a moment, he said, "Do you want to see?"

She looked up. "Okay."

He wiped his hands on his jeans and headed for the gate. She followed.

They crossed the grassy pasture in the late afternoon sun and hopped the dry streambed. A narrow path along the other bank led to a weather-beaten arbor overgrown with vines.

"Here," he said, pointing to the base of a red-barked madrone.

Hilde could see the newly turned earth. She squatted down and touched it. It was cold.

Gabriel picked up two branches from the ground. He broke off the twigs until he had two straight sticks. From the arbor, he pulled down a large vine, quickly stripping it of its leaves, and handed it to her.

"You can make a cross with these."

She looked at him. "How?"

He knelt and set the sticks on the ground, crossed one over the other, and wound the vine around the juncture. "Now pick a flower."

Hilde picked a yellow flower from a clump near a boulder. He tucked the stem beneath the vine at the center of the cross and pushed the cross into the soft earth.

For several moments, they stood side by side, surveying the grave and saying nothing. Then as dusk drained color from the land, they made their way back to the barn.

"Thanks. For showing me," she said, as he gathered up his backpack. "I hope you get to see your brother. Soon, I mean."

"I hope," he said. He gave her a little smile, mounted his rickety bike, and headed up the road.

11

The Border

The springs of the bus seat dug into Joaquín's bony backside as they pulled into Agua Prieta. Still, he was lucky to have gotten a seat at all, given the number of people crammed onto the wheezing vehicle. Nausea and heat had caused several travelers to get off in Janos, which had given him an opportunity to sit. But the smell of vomit lingered in the air, wafting up from the floor mats.

Fernando was asleep, his head thrown back. A fly buzzed near his gaping mouth.

Joaquín nudged him. "We're here."

The bus bounced hard. Fernando opened his eyes. "Yeah?" He looked dazed.

"Yeah. This is it."

The midday sun pounded the squat buildings crowding the road. *This is nothing like home,* Joaquín thought. The earth was barren, dry. And there were too many pawnshops, and ugly storefronts set out with tourist shirts and hats. And boots—so many boots—lined up for sale on concrete benches. In the distance, behind chain-link topped with razor wire, Joaquín could see the long, low factories—the *maquiladoras*—where Nike and Del Monte paid handsomely if you could get a job. But there were no jobs for men. The women took them all. They would always work for less.

At a crossroad, the bus pulled over. Joaquín stuffed his water bottle into his backpack. Fernando unrolled the shirt he had been using as a pillow and tied it around his waist. They waited until the others cleared the aisles, then picked up their stuff and hopped off the bus into the dry street.

And there it was. US Port of Entry, Douglas, Arizona—a clean, white stucco building stamped with an enormous government seal. Next to it, four lanes of traffic inched toward the inspection area. Men in uniform emerged from small booths, leaned over, and peered into car windows. They took papers and strolled around vehicles. Sometimes a driver would get out and open a trunk. Cameras and klieg lights were perched on tall poles, aiming inward.

"Impressive," Fernando said wryly, "how much they trust us, huh?" He hooked a hand in Joaquín's arm and pulled him away from the scene. "Come on. I wanna see the wall."

They found a narrow alley leading north. Joaquín's chest tightened as he followed Fernando up the alley. For all his bluster and impulsiveness, Fernando was a good traveling partner. He kept Joaquín moving forward. Somehow Joaquín had never expected to make it here by himself.

They stepped from the dark alley into the blazing sun and looked up. The massive wall was before them. It was made up of metal slats the color of dried blood and soared to three times the height of a man. At the top, flat panels welded to the slats extended the wall three feet higher. Joaquín had heard about these panels. They'd been added to make the wall just high enough to break the leg of a jumper.

Joaquín stepped up close, gripped the hot slats, and peered through to the other side. The sandy soil looked the same, the shrubs looked the same, and the sun beat down on the earth with the same ferocity on both sides. But that, that was America. *That* was the prize.

On the other side, a dirt road ran the length of the wall. In the distance, a white SUV with a green stripe sat motionless. Border Patrol.

Fernando shaded his eyes as he assessed the wall. "Okay. It's not so high. We can do this. Right, *hermano*?"

Back in the plaza, they settled under a scrub tree.

"Call the guy. You still have the number, right?" Joaquín said.

"Yep." Fernando took off his shoe and fished inside. One finger poked its way out a hole in the toe. He wiggled it at Joaquín.

"Find me the number, *tonto*," Joaquín said, trying not to sound annoyed.

Fernando pulled the insole from his shoe and fished out the small scrap of paper he'd squirreled away beneath it. He set it on his knee and flattened it with the palm of his hand.

Joaquín leaned over it. "This is it?" he said.

"Yeah. See?" Fernando pointed at the blurred ink on the paper.

"I *see it*. But I can't *read it*."

Fernando smoothed out the paper. He put one eye close and held his breath for several seconds, examining it closely. Then he made a face. "I sweat too much," he said, shrugging almost imperceptibly.

"For God's sake, Fernando!" Joaquín said, grimly. "We paid the bus driver three hundred pesos for that contact. Why the hell did you put it in your shoe?"

"Uh . . ." Fernando looked down at the ground, "I thought it would be safest there."

"Jesús ayúdame." Joaquín sighed. He lay down in the scrub grass to think, his lumpy backpack pillowing his head, and rested his arm across his eyes. It had been such a long, arduous trip—the jostling bodies, the potholes, the smells, the heat. He didn't know where he would get the energy to figure out what was next. His head pounded.

IT WAS LATE AFTERNOON when he woke. His back was stiff, and his tongue stuck to the roof of his mouth. He sat up and reached for his water bottle.

Fernando was no longer at his side. Where was he?

Fernando. Unpredictable. Unreliable. A guy who seemed to float along the surface of life like a water bug, unaware of the dangers lurking just below. He never took anything too seriously. He sidestepped trouble if he could, preferring to run rather than fight. And somehow, all of those traits served him well. He had a catlike ability to survive. Joaquín had learned this the first night they'd met.

Joaquín had been sitting at a small table in a cantina on the eastern edge of Mexico City nursing a beer when he spied Fernando at the bar. It was clear that Fernando was not Mexican. He had a moon-shaped face, ruddy skin, black eyes, and his feet rested on a large backpack—clearly in from somewhere south. Migrants were easy to spot—and there were a lot of them in those days.

Joaquín was feeling a bit buzzed and paying no attention to his surroundings when *un poli* entered. One could never trust *el policía* in this part of town. The man, who had legs like tree stumps and a pudgy, pock-marked face, surveyed the bar carefully.

He sidled up to Fernando and leaned in, one elbow on the bar.

"You. *Chapín.* You got papers?" the *poli* said, so the entire bar could hear.

Fernando looked up. Joaquín saw fear flash in his eyes.

"*¿Papeles, cerote?*" the man barked, his mouth close to Fernando's ear.

Fernando sank down into his shoulders. His thumb traced the neck of the bottle in front of him.

Joaquín had seen *policías* do this before. Need a little money? Look for the nearest migrant. Hell, it didn't even need to be a migrant. His own mother had been shaken down by these guys. They could always muster some reason. But the migrants traveled with most of their savings in their pockets. And they were the juiciest marks.

"No papers? Oh, not good for you," the man said. He moved in closer. "You listening, *chapín*?"

Fernando leaned away. For a long moment, he did nothing. Then he pulled a wad of bills wrapped in a rubber band from his front pocket. Without removing the rubber band, he placed the wad on the bar.

El poli raised his eyebrows. "All you got?" he asked.

Fernando nodded.

Satisfied, the man scooped up the wad and stuffed it in his back pocket.

When he noticed Joaquín frowning at him, he turned, ignoring Fernando now, and ambled over to Joaquín. "Problem, *pendejo*?"

Joaquín dropped his eyes.

"I'm talking to *you*," the man spat. "You know that guy over there?"

Joaquín glanced up at Fernando who was watching him intently. "No."

"He's nobody, right?"

"Right."

"Best he move on, right?"

"Right."

"Because we don't need no *chapines* here, right?" The man was standing over him now, his face inches from Joaquín's ear. He could smell the man's breath.

"Right."

"Good. Glad we got that settled." He smacked Joaquín on the shoulder. "Now you can buy me a beer."

As the man turned, the bottle hit his head with such force that he pitched forward. His body splayed across the table. Shards of glass skittered everywhere. Joaquín jumped up and threw his weight on the man's back, pinning him. As he did, Fernando jammed his hand into the man's back pocket and pull out the wad of bills. Then they locked eyes and bolted for the door. They ran through the dark streets, their feet clapping the dust, listening for footsteps behind them. After several minutes, they dodged into an alley and dove behind a dumpster, listening for their pursuer. But the street was eerily silent, save for a couple of cats growling at one another.

Fernando turned to Joaquín, his breath slowing, and grinned. "Buy ya a beer?"

They'd become friends that night, Joaquín letting Fernando sleep on the patch of dirt behind his mother's house. And Fernando had quickly made himself useful, tending the tiny garden Joaquín's mother had planted and feeding the two chickens she kept for eggs. Joaquín's mother didn't like *migrantes* who showed up in the neighborhood, but she had a soft heart, and Fernando's dark eyes, wide smile, and usefulness played on her. Soon she was cooking for three, and he was telling stories after supper, entertaining both Joaquín and his mother.

Fernando told them about home in Guatemala, on the sloped hills above Quetzaltenango, learning to work the land from the uncle who'd raised him. From his stories, Joaquín surmised that he grew up poor, but his good humor and resourcefulness had always seemed to produce food enough for the family's table. He was clearly proud of his ability to do what was needed to survive.

When Joaquín's mother asked how he'd crossed into Mexico, he hesitated only a moment before launching into his story. He'd found his coyote in a single day—a middle-aged woman who worked for a trucking company in the town over from his. She had three teenaged daughters and was looking for some quick cash for a *quinceañera* dress. He borrowed money from an uncle to pay her, and she added him to a haul she was arranging. Early the next morning before the sun became blazingly hot, he'd slipped into the back of a semi and settled himself behind a wall of crates in that dark, airless hold. He thought he'd be traveling solo, but she was apparently as resourceful as he was, and soon several other stowaways hoisted themselves into the trailer, each claiming a spot behind the crates. They seemed not to know one another and said nothing as they settled in, and so Fernando spent the next several hours listening to road noise as the truck lumbered west. The woman had told him she would text the truck's plates to her contact at the border when the time came, and the guard would arrange some kind of distraction—a thorough search of another vehicle, maybe— while her truck was waved through the gate without anything more than a brief slowdown. And that's exactly what happened.

The driver let them out near the freight yard in Tapachula where the trains were being loaded for trips through the Mexican heartland. For the rest of the day, Fernando hid in the undergrowth some fifty meters from the freight yard. Dozens of others—single men, women and children, too—waited with him, backpacks and black garbage bags nearby, ready to jump at any movement of the enormous freight cars sitting immobile on the tracks. A man with a clubbed foot gave Fernando a hand-drawn map of the rail lines, a faded paper that showed where each line was headed. But at that moment, he didn't care, so long as he was heading north.

In the waning light of the day, one of the big iron beasts in the yard woke. It clattered and strained, pulling its load taut as it began to roll. Fernando quickly gathered his belongings and loped toward it, looking for a ladder to grab. He was jostled by others fighting for the same handhold, their plastic bags bouncing against his legs. When he realized he was jockeying for position with a woman carrying an infant, he faded back and let her board. Finally, he found an open rung and, with a mighty effort, heaved himself aboard. By that time, the train was rolling so fast that the effort almost pulled his shoulders from their sockets.

Telling Joaquín's mother about the dangers of that trip made him feel *strong*, and her anxiety at what he described made him feel *wanted*, a powerful combination. He told her about climbing to the top of the boxcar and finding few places to sit, with so many traveling north. He described how the wind buffeted them as there was nothing to hold onto, and how they sat back-to-back to steady one another. And how everyone would flatten against the roof of the car as they approached a tunnel, sticking fingers in their ears to protect from the sounds of the beast as it passed through the tunnel at sixty kilometers an hour.

But he didn't tell her everything. He didn't tell her about the gangs who routinely boarded the trains whenever they stopped, swaggering across the cars, kicking the soles of travelers' shoes and demanding money. He didn't describe the *compañero* who, when he claimed he'd had no money, had been jerked up by the scruff of his neck and flung off the car headfirst into the railyard. And, of course, he didn't tell her about the boy whose legs passed too close to the wheels of the beast as he leaped toward its ladder. He had disappeared in one horrific moment. Fernando would tell Joaquín these things months later, after a night of drinking, but not in front of his mother.

What he told her was that by the time he reached Mexico City, he had no money. And so he'd decided to stay in the city to find some work and rebuild his stash of cash. That's when he'd met Joaquín.

Joaquín looked across the plaza. A figure was bounding toward him, a bag in each hand. Fernando had been *shopping*.

"Where have you been?" Joaquín said, annoyed.

"I got us a way," Fernando replied as he slid down beside Joaquín.

"A way?"

"A way, *hombre*. We're going over *tonight*. And I got us some supplies too." He dumped the contents of the bags on the ground. "Water, chips, and . . ." he popped open a Styrofoam container. Two fragrant tacos sat nestled inside.

Joaquín softened when the aroma hit him, but he was still angry at Fernando for losing the phone number they'd paid for. "Tell me about this *way* you have," he said, ignoring the tacos for the moment.

"Found us a coyote in the plaza. He's taking us up by ladder, down by rope. Tonight," Fernando replied, seeming to have picked up on none of Joaquín's skepticism.

"And where do we get the money? For the coyote."

"Haven't. Yet."

Joaquín looked at him.

"Well, I was thinking . . ." Fernando began. "You know your ma's ring? There's a pawnshop a block over. It's doing a booming business. You should've *seen* the rings in that shop." He opened the bag of chips and offered some to Joaquín.

Joaquín had sewn the ring in the lining of his jacket the night before they left. But he had made the mistake of doing it in front of Fernando.

He looked down and noticed Fernando was wearing a new pair of boots. Timberlands.

"Where'd you get those?"

"You know, I gotta to look good for the girls," Fernando said. "I can't show up in America with holes in my shoes."

Joaquín frowned. "Are you joking? You spent money on those? And now you want me to pawn my mother's ring?"

"Don't worry. I got 'em real cheap." He stuffed everything back in the bags, chips last. "C'mon. Pawnshop's only open till six."

By sunset, the plaza was full of men, all dressed in jeans and dark shirts, all toting backpacks. Waiting. When dusk overcame the square, they started to move. Singly and in small groups, they hoisted their backpacks and headed away from the plaza, some going east, some going west. All heading eventually for the wall.

"C'mon, buddy," Fernando said, hoisting his backpack on his shoulder. "I know the way."

By ten o'clock, they were three kilometers out of town, crouched behind an autobody shop. Others had joined them—mostly men with dirt under their nails, scruffy from the trip north, lean from the work of getting there. A lone woman, middle-aged and heavyset, pawed through her plastic bag, taking inventory of the things inside. A couple of teen-aged boys with flat noses and dark skin sat apart from the rest. *Brothers from Honduras, maybe,* Joaquín thought.

The younger of the boys rubbed his eye with his hand.

"It's okay," the other one whispered.

Joaquín looked at the boy.

The woman did, too. "How old is he?" she asked in a low voice.

Both boys froze. "Eighteen," the older boy said quietly.

"Yeah, right," Fernando snorted. "He's eighteen and I'm Chinese."

Everyone looked away.

The woman turned toward Fernando. "Where you going?"

"San Francisco." Fernando grinned, nodding at the lights on the other side of the fence.

The woman peered at him in the dark. "That's not San Francisco. That's Douglas."

Fernando kept grinning. "How do you know?"

"I live in the States. I know."

"If you live in the States, why are you here?"

"None of your business," she snapped. Then, "My sister's sick. I just needed to be here for a while."

Then suddenly, they heard an urgent, staccato hiss.

A burly man with a wooden ladder in one hand and a heavy coil of rope wrapped around his shoulder emerged from the dark. He motioned, and they circled around him.

"Listen carefully. You," he pointed to a wiry man who looked like he'd spent years heaving bales of hay around. "You first. Take this rope. Tie it at the top and use it to get down. Make sure you do it right. When you get over, head for that white house across the field—the one with the lights out. The back door is open. Don't go anywhere else. You got that?"

No one said a word.

"Stay there," he continued. "When it's safe, someone will come for you. The rest of you follow." Looking around the group, he spotted the woman. "You go last," he said to her.

She opened her mouth to say something but then closed it.

"Pay me now," he said.

People dug deep, fishing rolled-up bills out of cuffs and shoes and hats.

Joaquín noticed the Honduran boys standing motionless. "You got money?" he whispered to the older one. The boys just looked at him.

"They're covered," the coyote growled. He continued to collect money, counting it as it was passed to him. Then he flattened the bills, wound them around his ankle, and pulled his sock up over the wad. "This way."

At the wall, the coyote raised the ladder and set it in place. It clanked against the rusty pylons, which made everyone freeze for a moment.

"You. Up now." The coyote jerked his thumb toward the ladder as he passed the coiled rope to the hay baler who scrambled up the ladder with the rope over his shoulder. Joaquín could hear him grunting as he tied the rope in place. Then he rappelled down the other side, his boots thudding against the metal slats. When he reached the ground, he started running.

Every fiber of Joaquín's body was vibrating now. It was thrilling. They were *going*.

"Go, go, go—now!" the coyote hissed. Several more men clambered up the ladder, followed by the two Honduran boys weighed down by their heavy backpacks. Fernando danced in anticipation at the foot of the ladder. Through the wall, they could see feet hitting the dirt.

Finally, it was their turn. Fernando climbed quickly and surely, swinging his leg over the top as he reached it. Joaquín, who was holding the ladder now, noticed the woman looking up with trepidation. When he felt Fernando's weight lift off the ladder, he stepped back. "You first," he said.

She stared at him, panic in her face.

"I'll be behind you."

"Just give me a minute," she breathed.

Joaquín heard Fernando scramble down the other side of the wall and grunt as he hit the ground.

He turned back to the woman. "It's okay. You can do this," he said.

She stood frozen in place, fidgeting with her plastic bag.

Giving the woman one more look, he turned, grabbed a rung, and scrambled up the ladder. At the top, he threw one leg over. "Look. I'm here. I'll help you," he called down in a loud whisper.

"Hurry up. I need that ladder," the coyote hissed.

The woman gathered her plastic bag close to her body, hooked it over one wrist, and began to climb slowly.

The ladder swayed as the woman climbed. Joaquín grabbed the top rung and steadied it. She looked up at him, eyes wide.

Fernando hissed from the ground below. "C'mon, man. Let's go."

"Just keep coming," Joaquín said. When she got to the top, she was breathing heavily. She heaved herself onto the pylons and held on tight, her knuckles white in the moonlight. The ladder disappeared into the darkness below.

"I can't do it," she whispered.

"Yes, you can. Put your foot here and swing your other leg over. Hold on here. I'm gonna go down first, so watch me. Then when I'm down, turn around and do the same thing. Okay?"

She looked at him, terrified.

"Don't look down. Just keep your eyes on the rope."

Fernando's voice rose from beneath them. "Joaquín . . . *¡ándale! ¡Ahora!*"

THE PATROL CAR—A STANDARD-ISSUE white SUV with the green stripe—had sat all evening in the shadows at the end of the deserted road that ran the length of the wall. As the moon moved from behind the clouds, it revealed two bodies teetering unsteadily at the top the wall, some nine meters from the ground.

The engine revved, the headlights flicked on, and the van moved forward out of the shadows.

12

Spit

Hilde heard the truck lumbering into the pasture from her bedroom window. It was barely dawn, and the sky was a uniform gray. She jumped out of bed, pulled on her jeans and a flannel shirt, and sprinted out the back door.

In the pale, cool air, she saw the trailer rock and shudder as Gabriel unlatched its door.

"Easy, easy," he crooned to the animal as he extended the ramp from the trailer to the dusty ground.

Hilde peeked in the trailer. A great hump of fur was moving upward as the beast found its footing and raised itself onto its knees.

Gabriel slipped a halter deftly around its small head. He guided it backward down the ramp.

"Oh, he's so beautiful. What's his name?"

Gabe hid a smile. "He's a she. She doesn't have a name."

Hilde looked her over. She was tall and shaggy, with a heavy chestnut body and sturdy legs, a long neck, and a head she carried with great dignity. Her large, liquid eyes were bright, her ears perched high on her head, and beneath her velvet snout, Hilde could see two gapped teeth. She looked as though she were grinning.

"Oh! I love her!" Hilde said, her hand moving forward to touch the snout.

In an instant, the animal's ears flattened, and she spat. A fine cone of mist coated Hilde's face and chest.

"Ack!" Hilde backed up in surprise. She flicked her hands over her jacket, but she only spread the smelly film.

Gabe chuckled. "She needs to get used to you. Give her time."

The llama blinked her long lashes in mock innocence.

Hilde spit out the flecks in her mouth. "Pah," she said, working her tongue around her teeth. She eyeballed the furry face with amused disgust.

Gabe led the animal to the barn, with Hilde tagging behind. He laid down some bedding, filled a bucket with water and poured some pellets into a pan, spreading them to the edges. The llama sniffed the air, her ears and tail twitching, and began to feed.

13

A Plan and a Lie

As Hilde entered, the cowbell on the knob of the deli door clanged, causing Ethan to look up.

"Hey," she said, tentatively.

"Hi," he replied. He continued to wipe down the milkshake machine.

She sidled up to the counter and watched him for a moment. Then she sat down on one of the red leather stools. It was midafternoon, and the deli was empty except for a table in the corner where a couple was finishing a late lunch. The man wore a black windbreaker with racing stripes on the sleeve, and the woman, a peach-colored track suit. Mirrored sunglasses held back her blond hair. Tourists, obviously.

There was a long pause as Ethan poured coffee grounds into a filter and fitted it into the coffeemaker.

"Sorry. About the goats, I mean," he said flatly, not looking at her.

Hilde nodded. "Yeah." She ran her finger along the edge of the counter. The dead carcasses flashed in her brain. Her vision blurred.

He turned, came over, and wiped down the counter in front of her. "Want a donut?" he said gently. "We've got apple fritters."

Apple fritters were a treat back in Kenosha. So many Saturdays they'd ridden their bikes to the Seven Eleven, him always behind her, watching out for her on the gravelly shoulder. He'd buy her the biggest, lumpiest fritter in the case, and they'd sit on the curb, her eating the doughy little toes one by one. The memory made her happy. She looked up and nodded.

He set a plate in front of her. "Fritters are the most popular thing around here, aside from the artichoke bread," he said.

She broke off a toe of the fritter, the glaze crackling like mica beneath her fingers. "Gabriel found us a llama," she said, nibbling on a toe.

"That was quick." He turned away.

"He says when the next coyote comes, she'll go out there and face off with it—and all the goats will line up behind her." She watched Ethan, expecting he would feel the same comfort she did, imagining the large, shaggy llama standing her ground against a predator in the pasture, but he seemed unmoved. "She's really big. But Gabe can handle her."

"Gabe can handle anything," Ethan said dryly, scraping dried ketchup off a bottle on the counter.

She couldn't read him. She needed to feel she could lean on him, but she also needed to be straight with him. She needed him to understand.

"Mom doesn't know llamas. And when Gabe's not around, she . . ." Hilde paused, "well, she gets anxious. And she doesn't like it when you won't help."

Ethan straightened up. He pulled an order pad from beneath the counter, wrote on it, carefully removed the top page, and walked it over to the couple in the corner. When the man pulled out a credit card, Ethan turned his back to Hilde. "Sorry, sir," she heard him say, "the reader's broken. We can only take cash."

As the couple scrambled for their wallets, Ethan returned to the counter and started wiping down the soda machine.

She tried again. "Mom's going over the hill tomorrow to find restaurants to sell cheese to. She says the first batch'll be ready soon. She wants you back. She wants your help."

He looked at her in disbelief. "You're dreaming, Scout."

What was it that had changed in Ethan? When had he become so unreachable? Had it been like that back in Wisconsin? When Dad's hours got cut at the college, she remembered, things became tense at home. Dad was always unhappy about how Mom ran the house, and now he had the time to do something about it. He started by making sure everyone was up by seven even though it was summer. He posted a spreadsheet with chores for each family member on the fridge without getting anyone's buy-in. He had his ways, and he expected everyone to fall in line. But Ethan chafed at the rules. He already had a full complement of summer plans, and he was not going to be deterred. And for that, he became a particular target of Dad's wrath. They went at it on a regular basis, Dad demanding Ethan "step up," Ethan furious at being given no leeway, no say in his own life.

Finally, Ethan withdrew from the fight by withdrawing from the family.

Hilde remembered those last few weeks of summer before the move. It was as if her bright and brilliant brother had been body-snatched and replaced by this brooding figure who appeared at home only after dark, scavenged in the refrigerator, and disappeared behind closed doors for the night. That may have been the start.

And then there was Denny's. That was *so* not like him.

Across the deli's hardwood floor, the couple gathered up their things, leaving a pile of bills on the table. The cowbell clanged as they pushed open the door. Hilde tried again.

"I wish Dad were here," she said.

He turned to face her, putting both hands on the counter. "Scout," he said, "I need to tell you something."

She wasn't sure she wanted to hear. "What?" she said tentatively.

"Once he gets here, I'm heading out."

"Out?"

"Yeah."

"Out . . . where?"

"Dunno. Texas, maybe. There're good jobs in Texas. Jobs that pay real money."

"You're gonna get a job in Texas?" she said, astounded.

"Yeah. Maybe working on an oil rig."

"But why?"

"Why, what?"

She couldn't think straight. This was not part of the plan. Not at all. "But . . . what about college?"

"What about it?"

"Aren't you gonna go?"

Ethan squared his shoulders and looked her in the eye. "Look, Scout, in one month, I'll be eighteen. I don't need any more schooling. What I need is to get out of here."

What I need is to get out of here. The words felt like acid thrown in her face. She felt unmoored. Abandoned. "You'd—you'd just up and leave like that?"

"Soon as I have enough money." He seemed unaware of her emotions, which were making her stomach roil.

Just then, the large man with the apron whom Hilde had seen that first night lumbered through the rear door, weighed down by a heavy carton of canned tomatoes. "Sabin. This is your job, not mine," he growled.

"Yes sir, Mr. Cardullo." Ethan scrambled to his feet and disappeared into the back room.

She sat on the stool for several minutes, staring at the half-eaten fritter in front of her. Her mind was scrambling for ways to make her brother see things the way she saw them. She needed him. Here. He needed *to stay.*

When he didn't reappear, she rose and let herself out the door.

Across the street, four brawny bikers banged open the tavern door, beer cans in hand, and swaggered to their Harleys. They looked like a menacing police force, with their tattooed forearms and insignia-laden leathers.

She watched as they started their engines and roared out of town. When she turned back to the deli, she saw her brother through the plate glass window. He didn't seem to have noticed she was gone. He just went about his business, busing the plates and cups on the table at the window. As she watched, he picked up the bills that had been left on the table, glanced over his shoulder at the empty counter, folded the money once, and stuffed it in his pocket.

WHAT ETHAN HAD SAID, and then what she saw him do, sucked her into her head as she walked home. She passed by the seedy antique shop and the real estate office with unseeing eyes. It was only when she came to the little white church that she fully awoke to her surroundings. She stood there for a long moment, staring at the church and thinking about Nan's offer of a job. And as she did, she felt something shift inside her.

She'd spent so much energy over the last several months trying to make things better—pretending not to notice the icy silences between her parents, doing everything she could to avoid disappointing her mother, jollying up her brother. When was it going to stop, this ever-present need to figure out what people wanted, and to give it to them? She just wanted everyone to get along. But that wasn't going to happen. She was powerless, a bystander, buffeted by the emotions of everyone else in the family. And she was unable to control any of it.

From some untapped well beneath her heart, she could feel a dark and unfamiliar bile seep into her consciousness. It worked its way up to her brain and mixed with the gnawing angst that had been a constant companion since forever. She stood there expectantly, deliberately giving it space and allowing it to work its way through her. It wasn't anger, exactly, though it had the power of anger to motivate her.

It was fierce. It was a desire to claim her own.

14

Arizona Medical Foundation

The patrol car pulled into the ambulance bay. From the backseat, Joaquín could see the clinic's intake desk just inside the glass doors. Two male nurses in green scrubs emerged from the doors and helped the woman out of the SUV and into a wheelchair. Her knee was swollen to the size of a tree trunk, and her hands, which she held open as if she were praying, were raw from rope burns. As they wheeled her into the clinic, one of the orderlies gave her a tissue, which she used awkwardly to wipe her eyes. She'd hit the ground hard, that was for sure.

Once she disappeared into the clinic, the SUV started up again and headed west, with Joaquín and Fernando locked inside.

Still, Joaquín thought, *this is America. This is worth it.*

15

La Sala – the Living Room

The next Thursday after school, Hilde knocked on the back door of the church. She stood off to the side of the rickety stairs, wondering what she'd say if a stranger opened the door.

Nan opened it.

"Hilde. It's you!" Her face broke sunny and wide. "Come on in."

The room was warm and well lit, with several tables in the center. Overstuffed sofas and chairs that looked like they'd fallen from the back of a Goodwill truck were scattered about. An industrial kitchen took up most of one wall. Cooking smells filled the air.

"Welcome to *La Sala*," Nan said. "We're just setting up. Did you come about the job?"

Hilde was glad Nan hadn't forgotten. She made things so easy. "I did," she said.

"Terrific. We meet every Thursday for dinner, and we could use some help setting up. If you can come from—say—four to six, we'll pay you eight dollars an hour. We're pretty flexible. If you need to leave, that's okay, too."

Hilde was thrilled.

Nan introduced her around. A cook stirred a large pot of beans at an industrial stove. A skinny woman in jeans and work boots set the tables with paper placemats and plastic cups. And a man with the thickest eyebrows Hilde had ever seen seemed to be putting games around the room—dominos, checkers, cards, and puzzles of the US and Mexico. They all nodded amiably.

"We try to make it comfy here," Nan said, "so the men have somewhere to come after work. Otherwise, they just disappear into the hills. People get crazy when there's no family around."

Hilde nodded.

"You know any Spanish?"

"A little," Hilde said. She'd taken Spanish for a year back home.

"Good. Here's what you'll do. When the men come in, I want you to greet each one, in Spanish if you can, and ask them to sign in here. On this sheet. We like to keep tabs on them, make sure they're okay and all, and it gives them practice signing their names."

"Practice?"

"Some of them have a hard time with it. But they all want to learn. They have to sign when they send money home, and it can be embarrassing if they can't do it."

The first two workers arrived less than an hour later. They shuffled in, baseball caps in hand, battered boots scuffing the floor. Hilde offered an awkward *hola* and pointed at the sheet. *"Su nombre va aquí."*

Over the next hour, the room filled with men from the fields. They helped themselves to fragrant plates of rice and beans, set up game boards, and chatted amiably in Spanish.

One weathered worker with bowed legs and an enormous moustache arrived with an armload of flowers, which he presented to Nan. "They were throwing these out," he said. "I couldn't let them go."

"They're too beautiful," Nan replied, burying her nose in them.

After the plates had been cleared, the men settled down to cards and dominoes. A young farmworker picked up an old guitar that sat in the corner and started strumming quietly.

Nan came over to Hilde. "So what do you think?"

"I like it." It felt good to help.

As she gathered up the sign-up sheets, she noticed a photo of Nan in hiking gear, standing in a grove of redwoods with several other people. Her arm was draped casually around the shoulder of one of them.

"Is that your husband?" Hilde asked, pointing.

Nan looked amused. "That one? No. That's my wife. Pima."

Hilde looked at the photo again. Pima, dressed in jeans and a plaid flannel shirt, holding a small ukulele, could have been either gender. A flush of embarrassment crept into Hilde's cheeks.

"If you come next week, you'll meet her," Nan said. She held Hilde's gaze for a moment longer than necessary, as if she were trying to read her.

Hilde took a deep breath and looked around. A pink light had seeped into the room from the west-facing window. The slow strumming of the guitar, the buzz of men talking, the aroma of the food, the blush of the field flowers on the table—it all surrounded her like a warm embrace.

"I'll be here," she said.

16

La Hielera – The Icebox

Joaquín watched the colorless, arid earth rush by, interrupted by prickly gray-green scrub, as they traveled west in the back of the border patrol's SUV. The land looked just like the desert floor near Agua Prieta. And yet, *this* was America. This was the desert floor of America, and they were driving through it over a smooth, paved highway in a late-model van whose suspension rocked them gently, lulling them into believing things would be fine now, even though they were in the hands of *la migra*. Things would be fine.

They reached the cinder block building just as the sky was lightening. When the van doors opened, they scuffled out and were hustled into the building. Fluorescent lights played off the painted walls, and a wave of cold air hit them as they entered.

The man behind the steel counter wore a starched khaki uniform, together with a pair of incongruous blue latex gloves.

"Name," he said, looking over his glasses at Fernando.

When Fernando said nothing, he tried again, annoyed this time, "*¿Nombre?*"

Fernando gave his name.

We've only been in America for a few hours, Joaquín thought, *and they've already managed to capture our names in their computers.*

"Fingerprint him," the man behind the counter said.

A guard with similar latex gloves jostled Fernando to a side table. "Finger here. And here," he said, pointing first to an inkpad and then to a white card.

After processing, they were led through a set of doors to a holding tank in the center of the building. The room was entirely enclosed in glass, with wooden benches lining the walls. Twenty, perhaps thirty, bedraggled travelers were in the room—some propped up on the benches, many stretched out on the cement floor, asleep. A young mother slept in a fetal position on the floor, her arms wound tightly around her small daughter. A wizened old man knelt on the floor, hunched over a bench, his head in his hands, praying.

As they entered the holding tank, a guard handed Fernando two small packets without explanation.

"*Jesucristo,* it's cold in here," Joaquín said, looking around.

Fernando slid down the wall of the holding tank and opened a packet. He drew out a lightweight foil blanket.

"Gimme that other packet," Joaquín said. He pulled out another foil blanket and wrapped it around his body.

"You look like a burrito," Fernando quipped with a lopsided smile.

They sat silently side by side for several minutes, Joaquín turning over in his mind all they'd gone through—the clandestine meetup, the climb, the sound of feet hitting the ground, the safe house so near but so far.

"Those two kids—the ones who crossed just before us," he mused aloud, "I wonder if they made it."

Fernando pursed his lips. "If they didn't, they're in bigger trouble than we are. Two brown boys packing white powder—*la migra* don't take kindly to that shit."

Joaquín turned and stared at him.

Fernando stared back.

"Those kids," Fernando said, "they were running dope. That's how they pay. You didn't know that?"

Joaquín woke to a smack on the forehead. A plastic container of orange juice lay at his feet. He touched the point of impact with his middle fingers.

"You want that?" Fernando asked, eyeing the juice.

Joaquín picked up the container and handed it over. Fernando pulled off the top and downed it in one continuous slug. A young girl sitting on the floor nearby watched him do it.

"Ahhhh," Fernando sighed, wiping his mouth with the cuff of his shirt. He looked around. "Where's my backpack? I still got tortillas in there."

"Gone," said the man squatting across from them. His jeans were dust-caked, and he wore several days of dark stubble.

"Gone?"

"Yeah. They say they give you back your stuff. But they don't."

Fernando turned to the guard to confirm what he'd heard, but the guard was preoccupied tossing juice bottles. Fernando watched as he took aim at a sleeping woman across the room, arcing a bottle at her as if he were on a basketball court. It hit her just below the ribs. She sat bolt upright and looked around, dazed.

"Fuck him," Fernando said under his breath.

"This your first time?" said the man with the stubble.

Joaquín nodded. He pulled his blanket tight around his shoulders. "Why is it so cold in here?"

"Hmph. They tell you it's to keep the germs down. Nah. It's to let you know who's boss. You come in here hot and sweaty from the desert and spend a day in the freezer, you remember it. You get so cold your fingers turn blue. Your head starts pounding like there's somebody inside it with a jackhammer. You see sunshine out the window, but you can't get to it. It's their way."

Joaquín shivered. His gaze moved to the window. The morning sun had risen in a cloudless sky and was beginning to bake the dry earth just outside the windowpane.

LATE THAT AFTERNOON, A white bus pulled up. As if on cue, the people in the icy room began to gather at the glass door.

The man with the stubble struggled to his feet, stepping gingerly over the empty juice bottles. Joaquín and Fernando followed him out the glass doors. As they stepped into the sun, Joaquín closed his eyes and said a little prayer, welcoming the warmth into his body.

The bus passed through several small towns on the way to the border. The road was lined with liquor stores, fast-food joints, autobody shops, and payday loan stops. As they approached, the traffic thickened. Cars, buses, and trucks jockeyed for position beneath the signs that hung above the lanes. *Commercial vehicles left lane. Commuters center lane. Speed bumps ahead. Weapons illegal in Mexico. Pedestrian walkway.* And then *Welcome to Mexico.*

Joaquín sat in a window seat over the rear wheel, his knees thrust uncomfortably upward. A heavyset man who needed a shower sat next to him, overflowing into his space. Fernando sat in the seat behind.

As the bus moved forward, Fernando tapped Joaquín on the shoulder. "Check out those guys," he said, pointing to a pair of soldiers on the road ahead, peering into the windows of the vehicles that inched toward Mexico. Each carried a menacing, coal-black assault rifle. "Those are Border Patrol, right?"

"Yeah, I think so." Joaquín shrugged.

"Why are they checking people going *south*?"

"Dunno."

The man sitting next to Joaquín leaned over and looked out the window. "Them? They're lookin' for narcos."

"Going south? But haven't they already dropped their load somewhere in Tucson?" Joaquín asked.

Fernando hunched forward in his seat so he could hear better.

"Yeah, but they never go home empty-handed. They stock up on what they can't get at home."

"Like what?"

"AR-15s. Glizzies. Whatever they need."

Joaquín had heard that guns were legal in the States. "Where do they get 'em?"

The man snickered. "They buy 'em. At Walmart."

"They buy those kinds of guns *at Walmart*?"

"Hell yeah, man. Cash on the barrel."

Joaquín looked out the window. The Walmart they'd passed on the way to the border had a huge parking lot—and it was filled to capacity.

"So how do they get 'em past those guys up there?" he asked.

"They take 'em apart. Hide the pieces inside the wheel wells, behind the dash, stitched into the seat cushion. Some of 'em hire truckers from the States to drive the parts across—inside crates of toys, microwaves, food, that kind of thing—and then they reassemble them at home. It's good business—for everybody."

The bus pulled over just short of the border, and the doors opened.

"Out," the driver barked.

Border patrol agents lined the street. The bus disgorged its passengers, and one by one, they walked across the bridge back into Mexico.

JOAQUÍN COULDN'T HELP NOTICING the difference a quarter mile made. The sun-bleached pastel buildings of Aqua Prieta, with their broken stucco and peeling paint, seemed almost welcoming. Signs hung from iron hooks. *Farmacia. Casa de cambio. Dentista. Correos.* Anglos with fanny packs strolled through the open-air market with its jumbled display of sunglasses, pottery, blankets, lawn sculptures, and T-shirts. A mongrel sniffed for scraps in the trash along the street. Home.

"Now what?" Fernando said, standing in the middle of the dirt road.

Joaquín looked around, shielding his eyes from the sun. *Yes, now what? That is the question.*

The burly man, who had followed them through the pedestrian pathway, clapped Fernando on the back. "There's a place down there where you boys can get some free food. It's about two blocks. Good luck." He turned and disappeared down an alley.

The place was not much more than a hole in the wall. A small, pale pink building with no door, just a low doorframe with a curtain pulled over it, and a crooked sign—*Centro de Ayuda al Migrante*. As they stepped inside, a birdlike woman looked up from a desk.

"Hola, viajeros," she said, standing slowly. Her mousy hair was cut short, and a heavy metal cross hung around her neck. She was Anglo, but she didn't act it. She came around the desk and held out both hands to Joaquín. "You look tired, my friend," she said in perfect Spanish, her eyes searching his. "Come. Let's get you something to eat."

Feeling enormously grateful, Joaquín sank down onto a metal lawn chair in the tiny room. Fernando sat opposite, on a padded bench that looked like it had been scavenged from a pickup truck, complete with seat belt.

"I'm glad you found us," the woman said after she'd brought them each a fragrant plate of beans and rice which she'd heated in the microwave in the corner of the room. She watched them eat with a tiny smile on her face. When they finished, she collected their plates and said, "Wait a minute. I have someone who wants to talk with you." She disappeared into a back room.

Carlos, clean-shaven and in his late twenties, appeared from the back room. He was dressed in a Nike shirt and flip-flops. From his look,

Joaquín could tell he had a decent place to sleep. He had dark eyes—decent, but no-nonsense.

He shook both their hands and sat down beside them. "So," he said. "Sister tells me you're just back from the border, right?"

Joaquín nodded.

"Didn't quite make it," Fernando piped in, grinning.

"What do you plan to do next?"

Fernando looked at Joaquín.

After an awkward moment, Carlos tried again. "Some people at this point head home. Others, they try again. Which are you?"

"Not going home. No way," Fernando said quickly. He held his palms out against the idea. He turned to Joaquín. "Right? We don't have any money to go home. Right?"

Joaquín had not thought that far ahead, but it was true.

Carlos fixed his eyes on Fernando. "No? You know, if you guys want to go home, we can help. We can float you a bus ticket."

"We're not going home," Fernando said firmly. "Not."

"Guess not," Joaquín said.

Carlos leaned back in his chair. "Okay, then. I can't say I'm surprised. Most don't." He put his hands on his knees. "So let's talk about what you're going to do next."

They talked for half an hour, Fernando spinning out ideas, Carlos sorting through them, pointing out the pitfalls.

"Tunnel?" Fernando suggested at one point.

"The border's riddled with them," Carlos said, "but the narcos own them. And the cost—it's very high, man."

"River?"

"Possibly. Depends on where you try. You can find some decent guys out there with rafts, but you gotta watch the current, especially if you go at night. And some of those crossings, the water's so toxic you don't want to be in it."

"What about the wall? Again." Joaquín said, after listening quietly.

"They've been beefing up patrols—lacing the ground with motion detectors, setting up klieg lights. You probably saw. People living on both sides of the border are up in arms about those klieg lights—how they shine into bedrooms at night."

"Okay. The desert then," Fernando said, frustrated now. "We'll hitchhike out of town. Get to that part where the wall turns into a cattle fence—"

"You could," Carlos replied, "but that desert is deadly. You'll be out there four, maybe five days. And it's easy to get lost. Don't go alone."

"Okay," Fernando said.

Carlos paused and looked at them both, as if sizing up their stamina. "You sure?"

"We're sure," Fernando replied. He turned to Joaquín. "We're sure, right?"

Joaquín nodded almost imperceptibly.

"Okay. But understand. Those *polleros* try to fool you. They'll say they can get you across in a few hours, but it's not true. They'll lead you through irrigation canals, over rough terrain, into washes, wherever, and if you can't make it, if you slow up the group, they'll leave you out there. So don't let them out of your sight. They're the only ones who know the terrain."

Fernando's face became sober.

"This time of year," Carlos continued, "it's blazing hot in the day, and cold—*really* cold—at night. You gotta be ready for both. You have warm clothes with you?"

"We don't even have backpacks," Fernando said. "They took 'em."

"We can get you clothes," Carlos said. "You'll also need canned food. And as much water as you can carry. Find some gallon jugs and paint them black."

"Black?" Joaquín said.

"Otherwise, it's easy for *la migra* to spot you. Start with one in each hand, more in your backpack. You won't have enough, so watch for the water drums in the desert. They're big and blue. And sometimes have flags attached to them, so look up when you walk. You can get more water there. And do not—*do not*—drink the water in the cattle troughs. It'll give you the runs. And that'll kill you. Your biggest problem is gonna be dehydration. You got that?"

Fernando looked at the floor.

"And one more thing. Take matches. If you get lost, find some dried scrub weed and light it. They'll see your smoke and pick you up. It's better they deport you than scrape your bones up off the desert floor." Carlos paused. "You know how many bodies they deliver to us each year from out there?"

Both Fernando and Joaquín were silent.

"Four hundred last year. More, maybe. I don't want to be calling your mamas about you. You got that?"

Fernando picked at his fingernails.

"Wait here. Let me get you some clothes." Carlos disappeared into a back room.

Fernando got up and walked across the room to the wall. He seemed shaken. A poster hung above a small table. He stared at it for a long time.

Joaquín came up behind him.

"Read this to me."

Joaquín was surprised. "You can't read it?"

Fernando continued to stare straight ahead. "I didn't do so well in school." He glanced at Joaquín. "Well, truth is I didn't *do* school."

Joaquín looked at the poster—a photo of a man scaling a wall, probably the same wall they'd scaled days before. He was halfway up, straining to reach the top.

Joaquín read the words quietly. *To those who pass through this place: Having ventured out in search of a better life, knowing little of the dangers that await, you have been defeated by powers beyond your control. But remember this: You are the lucky ones. You are still alive. Your family waits at home, not for your money, but for your warm embrace.*

Fernando eyes glistened. "Not me," he whispered. "No one waits for me."

17

Day of the Dead

On the first day of November, Hilde stepped off the school bus beneath the flagpole, slung her backpack over one shoulder, and headed through town. Though the sun sat low on the horizon, the air still felt warm and soft—nothing like November in Kenosha. Back home, it was freezing by now, blustery, with a sky full of low, mean clouds that threatened rain, or sleet. This time of year, you could not break the hard, gray ground even with a heavy shovel.

She remembered all this because yesterday was Halloween, and Halloween mattered. It had always been the best holiday in Kenosha—better than Christmas. On Halloween, she ran in a pack with kids who'd known each other since first grade. Bundled against the frigid air by insistent parents, they would meet up at somebody's house, ditch their jackets and hats and scarves, and show off their costumes to one another. Then they'd set off through the streets, black ice crunching under boots, in search of loot. There were no eggs, no spray paint, no practical jokes. They had been raised by parents who took them to church and expected them to act right. It was the thrill of the hunt that propelled them through the cold night, oblivious to numb fingers and furious red ears, to the big houses near the park where they knew they could score full-size Heath bars. And it was an early adolescent taste for rebellion that allowed them to ignore the churlish comments of adults who reminded them they were really too old for such things.

But here in Pescadero, October thirty-first had passed by unmarked. Nobody roamed the streets in costume. Nobody rang the doorbell. None of the stores set out baskets of candy. There were plenty of pumpkins in the fields, but nobody carved them for their porch steps. Here, things were different.

Earlier in the day, just before she left for school, Hilde poked her head into the milk house looking for her mother. She had promised she would help sell their first batch of cheese at the farmers market that popped up every Thursday in the empty lot next to the deli.

"Mom, when do you need me there?"

Her mother was hunched over a tray of small molds, each lined with plastic wrap. She was tearing apart marigolds and bachelor buttons and arranging the petals laboriously in the molds.

"Gorgeous, don't you think?" her mom said, distracted. "Can't you just picture these cheeses on a fancy buffet? In a penthouse on a hill, maybe overlooking the Golden Gate?" She wiped her hands on her apron and reached for the cheesecloth bag that hung from a shiny metal hook attached to the ceiling, its milky whey weeping into a bucket.

"What time?" Hilde asked again.

"Right after school. There's lots to set up. Mr. Booher says there'll be plenty of people showing up today, so we want to be ready."

WHEN HILDE ARRIVED AT the lot beside the deli, it was buzzing with people. Tables were piled high with tomatoes and eggplant. Plastic baskets of radishes and strawberries were laid out in rows, and jars of preserves and honey were arranged on jury-rigged shelves. Hand-lettered signs pointed to bright green padrón peppers, three dollars a basket, and plump Early Girl tomatoes, two dollars a pound. But what drew Hilde's eye as she entered the market—beyond the booths, beyond the activity—was an elaborate tiered display that stood in the center of the lot. It was as tall as she was, and at least six feet square—a riotous display of candles, dried fruit, playing cards, rustic breads, soda bottles, and sepia photographs in silver filigree frames—all strewn with fresh marigolds. And there were skulls, too, dozens of them, lined up in neat rows.

"Hey, stranger. What do you think?"

Hilde turned to see Nan standing behind her. "I—it's very cool. What is it?"

"*Día de los Muertos.* Day of the Dead. It's an altar to honor the dead."

Hilde knelt and examined the snow-white skulls. Each was different, decorated with tiny sequins, buttons, and candies. "Are these—made of sugar?"

"Mm-hmm. And hard icing."

"Wow. Is this how they celebrate Halloween?"

"Not exactly. But both days are about remembering those who came before us."

"Look at all this food—"

"They say that on this day, the gates of heaven open and the ancestors' spirits come down for a visit. They come so far that people set out their favorite foods for them."

"For the people in the pictures?" Hilde was entranced.

"Yep. There'll be a party tonight to welcome them. And tomorrow, families will go out to the graveyard, have a picnic, and tell stories about the ancestors they've lost. It's a lovely way to remember where you came from, *who* you came from."

All those Bible stories Hilde had absorbed—that loaves and fishes miracle, raising the dead, casting out demons—had always seemed so far-fetched. They defied every known principle of the physical world.

But then again, she *did* believe in spirit. She believed because she had seen, *actually seen*, a spirit leaves its body. She'd seen it in the death of Jupe, how the light went out in his eyes as he lay in her lap. She had been stroking the fur between his eyes and talking to him gently. One moment his spirit was there, in his eyes, and the next moment, it was gone.

"*¿Pan de Muerto?*" A small, round woman stood beside Nan, holding out a pink bakery box filled with sugared buns topped with doughy crossbones. Her face was fabulously painted—all white with glittery spirals and curlicues around the eyes, and sequins above the brows. She looked like an elaborate sugar skull.

"Oh, absolutely," Nan said, reaching for a bun.

Hilde smelled the fragrant buns.

"Take one," Nan said. "They're special—and free today."

They sat together on a picnic bench at the edge of the lot, Hilde pulling apart the bun and nibbling the sweet bread.

"Can I ask you a question?" Hilde said tentatively.

"Sure."

"Do the farmworkers come to your church on Sunday?"

"Not usually."

"They come to eat on Thursdays," Hilde observed.

Nan shrugged. "Most of them go to St. Anthony's across from your house. They come from Catholic countries, and that's the only Catholic church in town."

"You don't mind?"

Nan let out a little laugh. "Not a bit."

"But . . .why?"

"Why what?"

"If they don't come to your church, why do you take care of them?"

Nan raised her eyebrows as she considered the question. "Well, 'I am my brother's keeper.' You've heard that."

"Yeah."

"Doesn't matter if they come to my church or not. Or any church, for that matter."

Hilde glanced up at Nan, who was looking out thoughtfully over the little open-air market.

"But it's a good question," Nan continued quietly. "I guess I also do it because I know how painful it is to be shut out."

"You do?"

"Mm. For sure."

Hilde wondered whether she dared probe deeper. She didn't know Nan well, but she wanted to. And Nan was one of those rare adults who seemed to welcome questions, answering them straight and clear, with no bull. So Hilde took a chance. "You mean—because you have a wife?"

Nan's lips curled in a tiny smile. "I knew pretty early I was different. I tried to hide it. But the older you get, the harder it is not to be yourself." She rested her hands on her knees and spread her fingers wide. "When my parents found out—you won't believe this—they sent me to a camp. To fix me." She eyed Hilde's face for a reaction. "But that didn't work. And so I came home. And that's when things got really rough. My mother coped as best she could. But my father . . ." she shook her head. "He called in the pastor, and I had a heap of counseling. But in the end, I was still me. And my parents—they're gone now—they were never quite able to get beyond the teachings of their little church."

"No?" Hilde said.

"So, yes, I've been shut out. It's a very dark place." She shifted her body and looked directly at Hilde. "But I was lucky. I made my way out here. I found a different kind of church. And I found Pima. And that made all the difference."

Hilde fell silent, considering what she'd heard. How was it that someone who'd been through all that could develop such—what was it?—strength at her core?

"Our first night in Pescadero," Hilde said, "I saw you at the deli."

"You did?"

"Yeah. We stopped for some food. And while I was there, a farm-worker came in. He wanted to buy something."

"Ah, yes. I remember."

"And Mr. Cardullo, he took his money, but he didn't give him change."

"Uh-huh."

"And you got up and stood by the cash register. And then he gave him the change."

"Yeah. Witnessing."

"Witnessing?"

"You stand up. And you witness what's happening. Often, that's enough."

Hilde gazed across the lot as she considered this thought. Suddenly, her mother came into focus, struggling with the legs of a folding table at the opposite edge of the lot. "Oh, jeez, I gotta go," she said, jumping up.

"Go, then," Nan said, shooing her away.

She sped across the lot and took hold of one of the table legs. "I got it," she said.

"Yeah, well, it would have been nice if you'd been here earlier. I can do this. Go get the molds from the truck."

By the time Hilde came back, her mother had set out crates of varying sizes, overlaying them with burlap. On the makeshift shelves, she'd placed several small metal trays.

"Okay, so we want to set out each little wheel separately. Let me show you," her mother said. She picked up a mold filled with cheese encased in plastic wrap. "Hold it like this. And turn it over gently. Shake it a little,"—she shook it—"and *voilà*. A perfect little cheese wheel, bachelor button on top. See?"

She laid the little wheel on the metal tray.

As Hilde watched, the cheese began to expand and flatten, and whey seeped from the seam of the plastic wrap.

"What the hell?" Her mother flipped the wheel over and pulled the plastic wrap apart. The creamy white substance started to move, spreading onto the tray. "Oh, dammit," she muttered.

"Uh-oh," a deep voice called from behind them. "Looks like you've got yourselves a little problem there, missy."

For a split second, Hilde couldn't identify the voice, but she knew she did not like the person it belonged to.

Her mother's demeanor changed instantly. "Oh, Ned, look," she said, holding out the tray. "What went wrong?"

"Well, now,"—he was clearly ready with advice—"it could be your temperature. I don't mean *your temperature*, honey," he said, moving in a little closer. "I mean the temperature you took the cheese to when you heated it." He poked his finger at one of the cheese wheels. "Then again, it could be the rennet. Old rennet'll do that."

"Oh, I can't believe this. It's such a mess!"

"Don't you worry. I'll come over tomorrow and check things out. We'll figure it out together. How 'bout that?" He put his arm around Janine's shoulders and gave her a squeeze.

Hilde stood there, feeling invisible.

As the sun set and the little bulbs strung along the edge of the lot switched on, someone set up a boombox and started to play salsa music. People left their picnic tables, stepped over the beer bottles in the grass, and began to dance. Hilde, who had dumped the runny cheeses in the trash behind the deli and packed the molds into her mother's car, wandered aimlessly among the produce booths before ending up at the deli with a bowl of bean soup, courtesy of her brother who was working alone that night. On her way out, she gave him a little wave, but he didn't catch it. He was chatting up a couple of Hispanic girls she recognized from school who had come in for ice cream. Both had glossy black hair and were strikingly beautiful.

She passed through the shadows at the edge of the lot, stopped just before the road, and looked back at the partygoers in the square. She wanted to go home. *I'm not a party girl. I don't know why. I'd rather sit with the goats.* As she stood there, her eyes taking in the colors and lights, she saw her mother dancing with Mr. Booher at the opposite end of the lot. They were moving to an insistent, sassy beat from the boombox, and his hands were gripping her hips. Her arms were raised above her head, and she was looking down and laughing.

HILDE ARRIVED HOME TO a house that was dark and empty. She moved through it quickly, out the back door to the barn. When she settled herself on the grass, her back against the rough timbers of the barn, the goats rustled, acknowledging her presence. She liked to sit still in the night air and look at the sky. She knew if she were back in Kenosha, sitting on the porch steps looking up, she'd be seeing the same sky, same stars, same constellations. The idea comforted her.

After a half hour, the kitchen light switched on and the back door swung open.

"You out here?" her mother called.

"Yeah, I'm here."

Her mother stepped onto the back stoop, looking up at the moon. She pulled her sweater tight around her thin frame and gave herself a hug. For a moment, she looked satisfied—happy, even. Was it because of the dance? She turned toward Hilde. "You check the water troughs? Everything battened down out here?"

Hilde heard her, but didn't take in the question. It was such a beautiful night. She wanted to remember the moment.

There was a pause. "Did you?"

The sudden change of tone made Hilde sit up straight. Before she could get to her feet, her mother descended from the porch and strode past her into the barn.

"Uh—" Hilde knew she was in trouble.

When her mother reappeared, she had the hose in her hand. "No. You didn't," she said curtly. She dragged the hose roughly from the barn.

"I'll do it, Mom," Hilde said, jumping to her feet. She reached for the nozzle, but her mother jerked it back.

"No, you won't. You kids think this is all a joke. You never lift a finger to help. I'm doing it all myself." She struggled with the gate that led to the pasture, pushing it with her hip, her knee, and then shoving it with her foot. The wood splintered with an ominous crack and the hinges gave way. "God dammit!"

Hilde could think of nothing to say, nothing that would placate her mother. She sank down again and waited to be told what to do.

"Go get me a flashlight. And some duct tape. Shit! And bring me a paper towel. I cut myself."

As Hilde held the flashlight, her mother crouched down and began to bind up the gate with duct tape, which did not want to stick to the splintered wood.

It was then that Ethan came around the corner of the barn.

Hilde saw him first. He was strutting between the two Hispanic girls from the deli, his arms draped casually around their shoulders, a beer bottle dangling from one hand. He looked like he had just won a varsity letter. And they were all three laughing.

Later, Hilde would remember how white those girls' teeth looked in the moonlight.

He stopped when he saw his mother.

For a long moment, Janine just stared at him. "Really, Ethan?" she said. Her tone was dark and ugly. Then, "Get those girls out of here!" She spat out the word *girls* as if it were dirt in her mouth.

"What?" Ethan looked stunned.

"Get them the hell out!"

"Mom, we're just . . . they're just . . ."

The two girls looked mortified. They unhooked themselves from Ethan's grasp and began to back up, as though they'd come upon a rabid dog. Ethan stood stock still in the moonlight, his face contorted in a mixture of fury and humiliation.

His mother flung the duct tape at him. "And come fix this gate."

She turned on her heels and stormed into the house, holding her bleeding hand.

"ETHAN, WAKE UP." HILDE was perched on the edge of his bed, on the small patch of real estate not covered by his sprawling figure. "Wake up."

He groaned and turned his head away.

"Wake up." She shook his shoulder gently.

Ethan put a hand to his forehead and ran his fingers through his hair. His eyelashes were crusted over, barely open. "What time is it?"

"Morning. Seven, I think. I'm sorry. We gotta talk. Please."

He sighed and sat up. "Ow," he said, rubbing his temples. Then he leaned his back against the wall, pulled his knees up to his chest, and rested his head on them. "Jeez, Hilde. What?"

He smelled of sweat. And beer.

"Ethan, I think we should go home. This place is not good for us. I think we should talk to Mom. We should go home."

Ethan let out a sigh. "And why's that?"

"Because . . . I don't know. Because. Maybe you could talk to her."

Ethan snorted. "Me? Not bloody likely."

"Well then, maybe you could talk to Dad. Call him. Tell him to come. He said he'd come, right? I think he should come now. What's stopping him?"

Ethan let out a sigh. "The house. He's gotta sell the house. You know that."

"Yeah, but he needs to know how we are."

"Are you kidding? How many times has he checked in since we've been here?" He held up his hand, his fingers making a big zero in her face. "We don't *need* him. And I'm sure as hell not gonna call him. Let him call us if he wants to know how we are."

She paused. "Ethan . . . last night . . ."

Ethan looked at her then, and she could see him replaying everything from the previous evening in his head.

"Last night—at the dance. I don't like Mr. Booher. And he's coming over today to figure out the cheese—why it didn't set up and all. You know it didn't set up, right? But I don't think—I think Dad should be here. To help. With the cheese, you know?"

He scratched his head, which made his hair stand up wildly. "You mean, you don't like the way Mom acts around Booher?"

Hilde's eyes widened. "Yeah."

"Yeah, I saw it," he said quietly.

Hilde was relieved. She was so used to being told that everything was in her head that this affirmation from her brother washed over her like a warm wave. She drew courage from it. "We should do something about it, maybe?"

His face changed, and his eyes flashed. "Like what?" he snapped. "Look, Hilde. I can't help here. It's not my problem."

"Not your problem?" She stared at him, incredulous.

"No. *Not my problem*." He threw the covers back, grabbed his jeans, jammed his legs into them, and disappeared down the hall.

18

Call Home

Ethan burst out the front door in long strides and headed toward town. Walking allowed him to clear his head. The rhythm of his boots pounding the gravel gave him some respite from the thrumming that had taken up space inside his brain. He didn't know when it had started, but this thrumming had become a constant companion—an acidic prickling in his shoulders, a tightness in his chest, an ache in his jaw. It all made him want to jump out of his skin.

But of course, he could not rid himself *of himself.* The only answer was to rid himself of his family, and to find a place where he could figure things out. On his own. Those jobs in Texas, jobs on the oil rigs, they paid two thou a week. And you didn't even have to find a place to live because you lived on the rig. He could do that. He knew he could. He could use his brawn, burn off some energy, make some money. And then, go to town and spend it however he liked. On girls. On booze. That'd be a good life. For a while.

Last night's scene near the barn played out in his memory. What the hell was wrong with his mother—yelling like that? Was she angry because the girls were Mexican? Her tirade had enraged him. Those girls were both *fine*. If his mother didn't want him hanging around with them, why did she bring him here?

And what the hell was *she* doing—with that smarmy rancher?

He let the rhythm of his steps take over, not thinking, just sensing—and the pulse of his own heartbeat, the cool air in his lungs, the ocean smells, the gravel beneath his feet began to calm him.

And when at last he felt balanced inside, he thought about Hilde. She was so upset this morning. And how had he reacted? Why did he find it so hard to dig down and find something reassuring to say to her? What made him bring down the curtain so quickly? Had he become too used to blocking out everyone? How ironic that he actually fed Mom's lines to her about selling the house, as if that were the explanation for Dad's absence. She had asked him for reassurance. And he had parroted back the official words, as if they made perfect sense. What was he becoming?

When he got to town, he found an empty bench in front of the antique shop and pulled out his cell phone. After holding it in his hand for several minutes, feeling the cool metal in his palm, he dialed.

His father answered.

"Hey," Ethan said. There was an annoying pause on the other end of the line. His father still insisted on a landline at home, so he never knew who was calling. But the silence kicked up the same irritation in Ethan he'd lived with for so long. *Remember me? Your son?*

"Ethan!" his father said finally, drawing out his name. "I didn't expect you to call."

"No? Well, here I am."

"So . . . how are things out there? Did you find the farm?"

It was clear that his father had not talked to his mother since their arrival two months ago.

"Yeah, we found it."

"And how is it?"

Such an asinine question. "Not great."

"Oh? That's too bad."

The best statement of empathy Dad can muster. "Yeah. The house has one bathroom. The outbuildings leak. The fences need repair, and the pickup only runs on Thursday and every other Sunday."

Silence.

Is he on the computer? "Are you listening, Dad?"

"I am." Defensively. "Just finishing up some paperwork. And how's Hilde?"

"Okay."

A pause. "And Mom?"

"As ever, Dad."

"That's good. Glad to hear it." He seemed to have run out of things to say.

"So, Dad. When are you planning to come out?"

"Don't know yet. Lots to do around here."

"You should come now."

His father chuckled, distracted. "You know I can't just drop everything, son. The roof needs repair, the kitchen needs—"

"Sell the house, Dad. Just sell it."

"Excuse me?" his father was finally alert, captured by Ethan's tone.

"Sell it. As is. Let somebody else figure out what color to paint the kitchen."

"Ethan, if I sold the house now—*as is*—we'd take a bath on it. And we can't afford that. You know that, surely."

"There're more important things than money, Dad."

"Really?" Annoyed now. "Clearly, there are things you don't understand here."

"No, Dad. There are things *you* don't understand." His voice was so tight he could hardly breathe.

"Enough, Ethan!" his father barked, icy now. "I sent you out there to help your mother. That's your job. And you need to step up. You can't just"—he paused— "you can't just wait for me to swoop in and save the day. 'Cause I can't, Ethan! I'm workin' my tail off here. So grow up. Put on your big boy pants. And start doing your job."

Ethan's backbone stiffened. He pulled the phone from his ear, stared at it for a second, and squeezed the disconnect button with his thumb, holding it down hard until his father's words stopped echoing in his ear. Then he closed his eyes and held it against his temple to cool down.

19

Safe House

It wasn't difficult to find black paint. Fernando found several spray cans in a dumpster while scrounging for plastic jugs. The jugs themselves were much harder to come by. In the end, they had to pay cash for them at the Super Blancos.

They were squatting in an alley behind a gas station, spraying the jugs in the late afternoon sun, when they were approached. Joaquín noticed the man first. He was standing in the shadows, leaning against a beat-up Nova with its hood in the air, its blackened body scavenged and burned. He had a hard face, with heavy brows and a nose that looked like it had been flattened in a bar fight. A scruffy beard traveled down his neck.

"Going soon?" the man said. He grinned and pulled a toothpick out of his mouth. Perhaps he had smelled the paint. Perhaps he had smelled the desperation.

Fernando looked up. "Yeah. Soonest," he said, shaking the paint can hard.

"Been before?"

"Just back," Fernando said, with a faint whiff of pride.

The man made a *tsking* sound with his tongue. "Gotta be more careful, *hermanos.* You get caught this time, they lock you up and throw the key in the nearest river." He picked his teeth, letting the idea settle in. "You're *felones* then," he said. "And they throw *felones* in prison."

"Yeah, we heard," Fernando said.

Joaquín eyed the tattoos on the man's knuckles.

"But . . ." the man said, sounding now like an unctuous used car salesman, "I can get you across safe and quick. Take care of everything. Guaranteed."

Fernando stopped spraying. He cocked his head. "Guaranteed?"

"*Sí,*" the man said, his eyes glittering. "We take you to the best crossing. Our men know the way because they've done it. Hundreds of times. Van on the other side meets you and takes you to Tucson—*all the way.* No extra charge. It's safer there. And from the bus station, you can get a bus to wherever you need to go."

Fernando glanced at Joaquín. "How much?" he said.

"For the two of you?" The man switched the toothpick quickly to the other side of his mouth. "Three thousand."

"Pesos?"

"Dollars," the man said. "Each. Half up front. Half on arrival."

Joaquín let out a long breath.

"We'll think about it," Fernando said.

Joaquín's head jerked toward his friend.

"You do that. And when you make up your mind, you find me here." He stepped out of the shadows and handed Fernando a slip of paper with an address handwritten in pencil.

They squatted in the dirt for some time after he had gone.

"What the hell, man?" Joaquín said, in a low, urgent whisper. "Where we gonna get that kind of money?"

Fernando turned his head and gazed in the direction of the wall.

Over the top of the squat garage, the metal pylons were fast becoming dark silhouettes in the fading light. He was quiet for a long time. Then his jaw tightened. "I'm afraid of that desert, of goin' it alone."

Joaquín looked down at the black jug before him.

"I have a cousin in Houston," Fernando said. "I can get mine from him. And you, you have your brother."

"THREE THOUSAND," JOAQUÍN SAID. "But I only need fifteen hundred now." He felt shame creeping up the back of his neck.

"What happened to the other money?" Gabe's voice sounded far away in the tinny phone Joaquín had bought.

"Most of it went to the guy with the ladder. It would have worked, but ..."

"But?"

"Some people *did* make it. It was just that we were the last, and this woman freaked out at the top and"—he paused—"and she kind of half-jumped, half-fell. She got hurt. Couldn't run. I tried to help her." He hoped Gabe would understand. "And that's when they picked us up."

Gabe was silent for a long moment. Then he said. "Yeah, okay. I have some saved. I'll borrow the rest."

"You can get it?" A wave of relief poured over Joaquín. He knew he could rely on his brother. He yearned to see him.

"I'll figure it out. Text me when the wire goes through."

TWO DAYS LATER, THEY picked up cash at the Western Union. They bought a few cans of beans, some tortillas, and topped off their water bottles at the spigot in the plaza.

Joaquín felt the fat wad of cash in his pocket so many times that it became sweaty and soft to the touch. He could not risk losing it.

At dusk, Fernando fished out the slip of paper from the man with the flattened nose. The first shopkeeper they showed it to gave them a hard stare and turned away. But people knew. And soon enough, they found themselves standing on a back street strewn with trash, in front of a small stucco building with boarded-up windows.

Fernando approached and knocked.

The first thing he saw through the crack in the door was a pistol, the barrel pointed at his left eye. He jumped back. "¡Mierda!" What the hell, man!

The door opened slowly—and a man with tattoos running up his neck eyed them suspiciously.

"Let 'em in," said a disembodied voice.

The door opened wide, and the tattooed man stood aside.

For a moment after they'd stepped inside, Joaquín could see nothing. The air was close and fetid. But as his eyes adjusted, he discovered that the room was packed with people—fifteen or twenty of them—all seated quietly on the floor, backpacks and water jugs in hand.

"*Hombres.* You made it." The man with the flattened nose was standing in the center of the room, toothpick still sticking from his mouth. "Come into the kitchen. Please," he said, removing the toothpick and flicking it away. "We'll settle up. And then you can make yourselves comfortable."

By midnight, most of the bodies in the room were draped over their backpacks, dozing. But Joaquín, as tired as he was, could not sleep. He sat upright, spine against the wall, thinking. The man with the pistol was not the only guard. There was another at the window, carrying a heavy assault rifle. This was much different from the group they had joined a few nights before. Joaquín studied both guards, his eyes flicking from one to the other as they stood watch.

After a half hour, Fernando stirred and sat up. He ran his fingers through his hair, looked at Joaquín. "*Ya vamos,*" he whispered anxiously. He pawed through his backpack, pulling out a Chicago Cubs jacket and ballcap he'd been given at the migrant aid center, and finally, the stub of a pencil and a paper napkin. "Here." He tore the napkin in half and gave a piece to Joaquín.

"What's this?"

"Write your name. And your brother's number," Fernando said, handing him the pencil.

"Why?"

"Just do it. I heard about this from a guy back home."

Puzzled, Joaquín took the pencil. He wrote his name and Gabe's number on the tissue-thin paper. Then he passed the pencil back to Fernando, who did the same.

"Now roll it up. Like this."

"Isn't this how we lost the coyote's number?"

Fernando ignored him. He took the little roll of paper and with his fingernail gently pulled apart the brim of his ballcap. He slid the paper inside.

"What are we doing this for?" Joaquín asked, waiting for the punchline.

"So they can identify the body," Fernando said quietly.

Part II

Dry Bones

20

Into the Desert

Up! Now." The men with guns moved around the room, kicking the feet of the sleepers.

One by one, people stood up, shifting backpacks and stretching stiff legs. Joaquín stumbled to his feet.

The man with the pistol threw a cardboard carton full of rags into the middle of the room. "One each. Tie it around your eyes," he said. "From now on, I see eyes, I shoot eyes." He raised his pistol to the eye of a youth who had just straightened up. The youth focused on the barrel less than a finger's width from his eye and froze. The man with the pistol chortled.

Once blindfolded, each person was instructed to hang on to the shoulder of another, and together they moved into the chill night air. Joaquín heard the growl of idling motors and smelled the diesel.

Fernando, whose hand rested on Joaquín's shoulder, gave a squeeze. "We're doing it, man," he said with quiet excitement.

"Stay in line. You six, two steps up, find a seat. The rest of you, to your left."

There were no seats left by the time Joaquín and Fernando boarded their van. As it lurched forward, they crouched on the floorboards, hoping not to get stepped on, and held onto the metal seat frames.

They traveled for close to an hour over bumpy dirt roads. Finally, the van stopped.

"Out," a voice barked from the front of the van.

The door opened, and the group spilled out into the dark. No one dared remove a blindfold. They stood a few feet from the van, facing every which way, waiting for instructions. None came. They could hear their backpacks and water jugs being thrown from the van, thudding on the earth beside them. Then suddenly, the van doors slammed, the engine revved, and the tires spun.

For a moment, no one said anything. Then one by one, they pulled off their blindfolds and looked around. The moon was a bright half-crescent, and the air was frigid. An army of saguaro cactuses stood nearby, silhouetted against the sky.

In front of them, atop an embankment, was the wall—but it was nothing like the wall in Agua Prieta. This wall was made from great metal X's connected by crossbeams and laced sparingly with barbed wire. It would stop a truck or a van but not a person.

Joaquín looked around at the small group of stranded travelers: three young *compañeros* straight from the farm, a skinny *indigéna* with a round face and reddish skin, a Salvadoran in a poncho, and two older men—one stocky, the other wrung out from overwork. And a slip of a woman traveling with a girl no older than ten. The girl held the straps of a Disney Princess backpack.

Joaquín found himself staring at the mother and child. He could not fathom that they would take this trek alone. He'd heard stories about women crossing. They would prepare themselves by seeking out contraceptives—one-month injectables—making sure they were protected before they started out. They knew the price for crossing, and they were willing to pay it. That's what Joaquín had heard.

Joaquín watched as the young woman scanned the dark desert, a mixture of fear and hope in her eyes. As she did, her daughter pressed in next to her. She helped the girl remove the blindfold from her eyes. Then she dropped to her knees, held the girl's hands in her own, and began to pray.

"Sssssst."

The noise surprised them, and they crouched instinctively. From a small thicket of manzanita, a figure emerged dressed in worn desert fatigues. He was compact, with thick shoulders, a barrel chest, and a shaved head that made him look as though he enjoyed flaying desert rattlers for supper. A tat—two teardrops on the cheekbone—drew attention to ferret-like eyes.

"Get your stuff. And stay low. We go after *la migra*'s next pass."

Fernando glanced at Joaquín, his eyes wide with anticipation.

The group scattered, gathering up backpacks and water jugs. They watched as the figure in fatigues dropped to his knees and crawled up the embankment, his backpack hardly visible as he moved. One by one, the others followed.

When Joaquín got to the crest, he peeked over, but all he could see was flat ground. He lay there with the others for a very long time. Finally, he heard the crunch of gravel under tires. A SUV appeared, moving along the road that ran parallel to the barrier, headlights illuminating the ground. Joaquín tucked his face in his arms as it passed, raising his head again in time to see a heavy tarp trailing behind, sweeping the dirt smooth. The vehicle moved at a steady pace, neither slowing down nor speeding up as it passed.

When they could hear the engine no more, the coyote rose up and moved to the crossbeams. "Now!" he said, parting the barbed wire. They scrambled from their hiding places and dove for the empty space.

Joaquín cursed as he passed between the wires, a barb scraping the tender flesh of his neck.

Then they were through, moving swiftly across the desert floor between the cholla and acacia. Joaquín eyed with alarm the prints left in the dusty earth by the three *compañeros* who preceded him. How long would it take for *la migra* to notice those prints? How far until they reached ground that didn't give them away? He could hear Fernando behind him, panting under the weight of the water jugs—one in each hand and one in his backpack.

They moved quickly through the desert, the coyote in front.

"*¡Apúrense!*" Hurry! the coyote called over his shoulder.

Joaquín kept his eye on the coyote's back. The man's gait was uneven, as though one leg had been broken and not set properly, though it didn't stop him from keeping a brisk pace.

After a half hour, the dusty earth began to throw up rocks—small ones, then ones big enough to turn an ankle—and the pace slackened. Feeling fully exposed on the barren land, Joaquín continued to cast his eyes toward the horizon, hoping not to see lights. Finally, the coyote led them into a dry wash whose banks surrounded and hid them, but the earthen bottom was littered with debris deposited there during the wet season. They picked their way gingerly between the boulders, rocks, and vegetation until the sky lightened.

Even then, they did not stop. As the sun rose, the temperature of the earth rose with it, and soon Joaquín could feel his scalp begin to sweat. For another hour, and another, they moved north across the barren land, speechless, each looking up only to take a bead on the person in front of him. Joaquín tried to look around to see whether the mother and daughter were keeping up, but every time he did, he felt dizzy, and a headache soon bloomed between his temples.

Finally, the coyote found a patch of shadow large enough to accommodate the group.

"Here," he said. "We rest for a while. Drink. Eat." His voice was distinct, raspy, as though he ate gravel.

A palpable sigh of relief escaped from the group. It was hot now, and the sun baked the earth around them.

They hunkered down, slinging their backpacks from their shoulders into the dust. Fernando twisted off the cap of one of the jugs he'd set beside him and took a long swallow. Then he lifted the jug, closed his eyes, and poured the contents over his head.

Whomp! The jug went flying, hitting one of the *compañeros* on the foot and landing on its side. Clear, clean water flowed from the neck of the jug into the parched ground. Fernando scrambled for it and then turned in fury.

The coyote was standing over him. *"¡Pendejo!"* Moron! The man hissed. "You do that, you die." Fernando looked up at him, wide-eyed, clutching the jug to his chest. No one said a thing. The coyote stood over him for a long moment, then kicked dust in his face and walked away.

Every pair of eyes focused on Fernando.

The stocky man picked up the cap that lay in the dirt and held it out to Fernando. "He don't want to lose you, *hermano*," he murmured. "He gets paid by the head."

Fernando, still clutching the jug, said nothing. Joaquín scrambled over and sat near his friend. For several minutes, they sat in silence.

Then the man who'd returned the cap asked quietly, "So . . . where you guys headed?"

Fernando remained mute.

"California," Joaquín said, with a wan smile.

"Long way. You got family there?" He took a dark kerchief from his pocket and wiped his neck.

"My brother," Joaquín replied. "He works on the coast." The thought of a coast breeze made the desert seem hotter.

"Me, I'm headed to Denver. I'm Raúl. And Eduardo here," the man said as he gestured to the Salvadoran crouched on his haunches, "he's goin' to LA."

Eduardo's skin was deeply creased from the sun. He looked up when he heard his name, but he did not smile.

"How do you get there—to Denver?" Joaquín asked, having only a vague notion of where Denver was.

"Bus. Probably one to wherever you're headed, too. That's why it's worth it to go with these guys. Once we're out of the desert, somebody'll pick us up along the road and drop us at the station. Worth it."

Raúl pulled a cloth from his backpack, put it on his lap, and untied the ends. Several pale tortillas lay in a neat stack. He held out the stack to Joaquín, who noticed delicate stitching on the corners of the cloth, the careful handiwork of a feminine hand.

"*¿Quieres un poco?*" Want some? Raúl said.

"No thanks," Joaquín replied. "We got our own." He pulled a can of beans from his pack and tugged at the ring on top.

Fernando still sat holding tight to the jug. Joaquín offered him the open can, but he just stared at it.

The coyote crouched apart from the others, gripping an open can and watching the group warily. He sat like a turkey vulture while he ate. When he was done, he tossed the can in the dirt and wiped his mouth with his sleeve. His eyes continued to scan the group. When he reached the woman and child, he fixed on them. The girl had taken off her shoe and was brushing the sand from her bare foot. The coyote's eyes fixed on the foot as she pushed her fingers between her toes. He made a slight sucking noise with his lips.

Suddenly, his head jerked up and he scanned the horizon. "Stay down," he said quietly.

He raised up a bit and shaded his eyes with his hand. They all could hear it now—the wasplike sound of a small motor at full force. Without saying a word, he motioned for the others to move. They stuffed their cans and plastic bags into their backpacks and scrambled to their feet—all except Fernando, who remained still, clutching his jug.

Joaquín bent down slowly and pulled him up. "Come on, *hermano.* Let's go." He helped Fernando to his feet. "You okay?"

Fernando nodded.

Joaquín gently pried the half-full jug from Fernando's grasp and helped him slip his backpack over his shoulders.

Quickly they scuttled through the wash, keeping their heads down. They could hear the sound coming nearer. When it got so close that they could hear pebbles spinning under tires, they froze against the wall of the wash, barely breathing. Joaquín could not look up. Some primitive consciousness took over his brain and convinced him that if he didn't see the danger, it would not find him. No one breathed.

Finally, the pitch of the motor changed, and its buzz faded. Joaquín could feel the tension between his shoulders ease.

When the silence of the desert returned, they began again, following the coyote north. The sun beat down ferociously on their heads and sweat burned their eyes. After another hour, they came upon a patch of mesquite that offered meager shade among the scrub that dotted the desert.

"Rest here," the coyote said. "Sleep if you can. From now on, we travel by night, sleep by day."

Exhaustion gripped Joaquín. He settled in the shade, wiped his face with his sleeve, and stretched out on the warm earth, his backpack behind his head. Fernando did the same, letting out a sound that was something between a sigh and a groan.

Nearby, the three *compañeros* jockeyed for what little shade they could find. After they settled, one of them dug deep into his backpack and pulled out an onion. With a pocketknife, he began to slice it, laying each ring carefully on the ground around him. A pungent odor filled the air.

Fernando raised his head. "What the hell?"

The *compañero* glanced up. "Onion. Keeps the rattlers away," he said.

"Rattlers?" Fernando sat up fast, checking the perimeter around his body and snatching his hand away from a nearby acacia root.

"Yeah. Want some?"

Fernando took a slice of onion, separated it into rings, tore the rings into tiny pieces, and surrounded himself with them. Then he hunkered down into the earth and curled up into a ball, pulling his arms and legs tight into his body. He looked miserable, but Joaquín was too tired to care. Finally, he closed his eyes, said a quiet prayer to the Señora de Guadalupe, and fell into a dreamless sleep.

He woke to the thud of a body hitting the desert floor. At first, he had no idea what was happening. It looked as though some multi-armed beast lay flailing in the dirt above the wash, near the pile of boulders several meters away. But he quickly he realized the arms were Fernando's—and they were pummeling the coyote, who was crouched on his haunches, shielding his head and neck.

Joaquín scrambled to his feet and raced toward the two men. He grabbed Fernando by his collar, wrenching him away. The coyote squatted motionless for a moment. Then he rose up, turned, and grinned at them, his hands open, as if to show no harm done. Fernando, his eyes wild with fury, kept kicking at the coyote. Joaquín jumped between the two and drove Fernando backwards, pinning his arms to his body. He could feel Fernando's chest heave from exertion.

"What's the matter with you?" Joaquín hissed, turning him away. "You want to get us left out here?"

That's when he saw the young mother in the shadow of the boulders, half-lying, half-sitting on the ground, her jeans unbuttoned and pulled down over her hips. She was looking at him, wild-eyed.

The coyote dusted off the desert from his fatigues. With measured nonchalance, he sauntered back toward the encampment.

"Cochino marrano!" Fernando growled, his whole body shaking.

The woman was on her feet now, her jeans buttoned up, her shirt tucked in. She stood in the shadow of the largest rock, her face stony. Joaquín glanced back at the encampment where her daughter lay sleeping. By the time he turned back, the young mother had brushed past them and headed back to the encampment without saying a word.

Joaquín put a hand on Fernando's forearm. He felt the rage coursing through his friend's body. "Get a grip," he whispered.

"Not happening," Fernando spat. "Not on my watch."

BY MIDMORNING OF THE second day in the desert, Joaquín's lips had begun to crack, and the skin on the backs of his hands burned as if he were holding them in a clay oven. The jug of water remaining in his backpack had become perilously light.

As he trudged along behind Fernando, eyes cast downward to avoid the blazing sun, he began to notice the flotsam from the other human beings who'd crossed this same dry stretch of land. He tried to remember what he saw, in part to distract himself from his own fatigue, and in part to test whether his brain still functioned in the intense heat. There was a bottle of nail polish, a set of rosary beads, a map of Tucson, nail clippers, a child's sneaker, a deck of cards, a small English-Spanish dictionary, an eyelash curler, a baby food jar, and a business card with the name of a furniture store in Tucson. This last bothered him most because it was someone's ticket out, and it was weightless—so why had it been left behind?

At noon, they stopped in the shade of several scrawny acacia.

Once again, the coyote sat separate from the group. He pulled a stick of beef jerky from his backpack and gnawed on it slowly.

"When I swallow, my throat sticks to itself," Fernando rasped as he squatted on the desert floor. His voice was thin, reedy.

"Where's your water?" Joaquín asked.

Fernando picked up one of his jugs and turned it over. Nothing came out.

"Here." Joaquín passed him his jug. "I still have some."

Sweat beaded under Fernando's eyes. He wiped it away.

"Thanks, man." He unscrewed the cap and took a sip, rolling the liquid around in his mouth before he swallowed. Then he passed the jug back to Joaquín and encircled his knees with his arms. "Where the hell are those water stations we were supposed to see?" he mumbled.

They sat together in silence for several minutes, their backs to the sun. Finally, Joaquín said, "What happened back there?"

"Where?"

"You know where," Joaquín said, annoyed.

Fernando looked away.

"You could have got us killed," Joaquín said. "You know that, right? What if he had decided to leave us—"

Fernando turned on him. "You said that," he hissed. "You already said that. Back there."

Joaquín recoiled. He stared, perplexed, as Fernando bunched up his body tight and started rocking ever so slightly, his breath ragged. This was so unlike Fernando, always quick with a joke, ready to make light of any situation. Now he looked shaken, drained. Joaquín knew he should shut up, knew he should leave his buddy alone. But he could not. He felt so vulnerable, out here with a bunch of strangers and a *comadreja* who'd just as soon see them dead, except for the money that would be exacted when they were delivered alive to their destination.

Joaquín waited until Fernando stopped rocking. Then he said quietly, "Look. You gotta get a grip, man."

Fernando flashed him a look, and Joaquín could see tears in his eyes. He realized then how little he knew about Fernando. His buddy had been quick to recount *how* he'd crossed into Mexico—the semi, La Bestia—but he'd never spoken about *why* he crossed. Joaquín waited quietly, watching Fernando compose himself. Finally, he said, "Tell me."

Fernando looked at him as if assessing how much he could say. After several moments, he turned his gaze to his own feet. "I had a sister," he said with a sigh. "Did you know that?"

Joaquín shook his head.

"Well, I did. She was older than me. I shared a plot of land with her and her *marido*." He touched his fingers to his temples. "It wasn't a big plot—just a little patch tucked back at the end of a dirt road. He and I grew poppies there. It was a good cash crop, and we did okay."

He paused and picked a pebble out of the sole of his boot. He looked as if he was unpacking memories stored deep inside his skull.

"But then my sister, she got pregnant. And they decided they wanted out. She didn't want any more to do with that kind of thing, with the baby coming and all." He raised his head and looked off into the distance. "I told them I didn't think it was a good idea, getting out. We argued. I told them we had a good thing and not to rock the boat. We argued some more. Then I told them I'd buy them out, but I didn't have the money. They knew that. So, one afternoon when I'd gone to town, he just went out and ripped up all the poppies. And planted *cala-baza*. I couldn't believe it." He looked away and spat in the dirt. *"Pinche pendejo."*

Joaquín sensed the story was not over. Fernando was edging toward something terrible, moving toward it slowly, deliberately. After several moments, Fernando began again.

"Before two days went by, they knew."

"They?"

"The mafia."

Joaquín looked down at his boots.

"And of course, they couldn't let that happen. Couldn't let that cash crop go." His lips tightened into a thin line. "Plus they wanted to make a statement. Because we weren't the only ones growing for them. We were just—just a small plot, a very small part of their operation." He stared at his fingernails, as if he were conjuring up images. "So they laid a trap. Not for him. *For her.* They picked her up. Took her to the dump. Kept her in some shack for six hours. God knows what happened to her there." His lip curled up in disgust. "And then . . . then they gave her back."

Joaquín became acutely aware of the silence of the desert around them.

"She was . . . damaged. Not right. She wouldn't say. Just sat with her arms around her belly and rocked. She was afraid. Afraid of them. And afraid of him, too, of what *he* would do. I don't know. But he was so out of his mind with rage that he"—and here, Fernando actually snickered—"he decided to turn them in. Ha! You don't go to the authorities in my country and complain about the *mafiosos.* You *never* do that. Because the *policía are mafiosos!*"

He rested his head on his knees again. His jaw was working furiously. "So," he whispered through gritted teeth, "they came for her again. Midday. To her house. While he was in the field."

He looked like he was going to vomit.

"I don't know . . . I only know . . ." His body began to shake. "I only know . . . when we found her, she was on the bed. They'd pulled her skirt over her head." he rasped. "Put a gun up inside her. And pulled the trigger."

Joaquín felt a jolt in his innards, a sharp stab that made him recoil into himself. It took him several moments to regain his balance. Finally, he put his hand on Fernando's back and left it there until the back stopped shaking. Then he said, "And him?"

"He went one way. I went the other. Neither one of us stayed to bury her."

Fernando turned away, curled in on himself, and lay on his side in the sandy dirt.

21

Speechless

Hilde hated going home after school.

When she dropped her books on the kitchen table, she could feel the empty house. Most often, her mom would be out in the milk house—brow furrowed, fingers pressed against temples—poring over a pile of pamphlets on cheesemaking as whey dripped from bags on hooks. If Hilde poked her head in, her mom would wave her away gruffly, reminding her of some forgotten chore that would keep her busy until dusk.

But it was worse when Mr. Booher was there. He'd be leaning up against a wall in the milk house holding forth on the fine points of ranching or milking or cheesemaking while her mother sat on a low stool arranging flower petals in the bottom of the cheese molds. On these days, Hilde could stand in the milk house door for a full five minutes and not be noticed.

And so she concocted a story about making the soccer team and having to practice after school—a story that would keep her mother happy, because her mother always said popular kids were made on the playing fields. Hilde's lies—about 4H, about soccer—allowed her to do as she pleased in the hours after school. Most days she hung out in town. She would buy a candy bar from the vending machine at the gas station, wander through the cluttered aisles of the thrift store, and then park herself on the bench across from the deli and keep an eye on her brother.

Her brother. She could see him through the plate glass window—his squared-off shoulders working as he wiped down the tables. He moved with animal grace, honed from years of wrestling. She longed to talk to him. But she never entered the deli anymore. It was too painful. He had unhooked from their private heartline, and she was adrift.

ONE TUESDAY AFTERNOON IN mid-November as she sat on a bench outside the thrift store sipping a soda, she noticed Toby trotting up the street. Nan appeared behind him, tethered to him with a long leash. She was dressed for the outdoors, in a drab green jacket and heavy hiking boots. As they got to the corner, Toby stopped and sat. Nan came up beside him, touched his head, and together they crossed the street.

Hilde jumped up and followed them. She was within an arm's length of Nan before she spoke. "You taking Toby for a walk?" she said breathlessly, matching her stride to Nan's quick pace. She knew it was an inane question, but she could think of nothing else to say.

When Nan saw her, she pulled on the leash. "Hold up, Toby. We got a friend here!" she said.

Toby swiveled his head around at the sound of his name.

"Can I walk with you?" Hilde asked.

"Sure. We're headed to the marsh. It's Toby's birthday, and this is what we do on his birthday. Well, truthfully, this is what we do a lot of days. But Toby'd be honored to have you along."

They walked together on the gravel path at the edge of the road, Toby reading the clumps of grass along the way. After a quarter mile, they turned off the road and crossed the footbridge into the marsh. High cattails and pampas lined the path.

As they approached the water's edge, Nan called Toby and unhooked his leash. "He loves this part," she said.

The marsh was full of birds. Tuxedo-suited birds on pink stilt-legs; football-shaped birds with white beaks; cinnamon-colored ducks; elegant stork-like birds with needle-sharp bills. The only birds Hilde could name were the mallards, which swam circles around each other in the pools hidden by the grasses.

Nan perched on a large rock near the edge of the marsh. Her round face softened. "Ahh," she sighed. "Toby and I do love this place."

Toby found a fallen tree branch at the edge of the marsh and tried to wrestle it from the mud.

"How old is he—Toby?" asked Hilde, after settling herself on a nearby rock.

"As of today, nine."

"And you've had him since he was a puppy?"

"Since he was about one. We found him on the edge of the Coast Road. We were coming back from Half Moon Bay. He'd been hit, and he was lying in the sand, trying to get up."

"How horrible," Hilde said, imagining the scene.

"But Pima—bless her heart—cannot *not* stop for animals. So we turned the car around, picked him up, and took him back up the road to a vet we know. His leg was broken, and he was in a lot of pain, but there were no internal injuries. So we had his leg set and took him home to recuperate." She paused to watch Toby sniff the sand along the edge of the marsh. "We weren't looking for a dog. But he wormed his way into our hearts. And the rest is history."

"That's terrible, that he got hit."

"Mm. Somebody probably dumped him at the beach. He came over the rise and onto the highway. He was lucky he wasn't killed."

"What kind of dog is he?"

"He's a mutt. Best kind."

"Does he ever go after birds?"

"Nah. He's too much of a pacifist. The birds seem to know that."

Toby trotted back to where they were sitting. When Nan put her hand out, he touched it with his nose, as if he were checking in with her. She took his head in her hands and massaged his ears. Then she leaned over and looked directly into his amber eyes.

"If you're very lucky," she murmured, more to Toby than to Hilde, "a great dog may grace your life." She kissed Toby on the forehead.

Toby shook off Nan's kiss and loped off toward the grasses near the marsh. As he did, Hilde felt a spike of pain near her heart. Jupe had been a great dog. Yes, and she had been lucky, very lucky, to have had him for most of her life. When she remembered, her eyes stung. She swiped angrily at the wetness on her cheek.

Nan looked surprised. "What?"

"Sorry," she said.

"Don't be sorry for your feelings. They're good for you. They're also good for the universe. Be sorry when you have no feelings," she said. "What were you thinking?"

"Oh, just about my dog. Jupe."

"Tell me."

She hesitated. She didn't know this pastor in hiking boots that well. But she was drawn to her, sensed she could trust her.

"Oh, you know. My dad hated the way he shed. I was supposed to keep the hair out of the house. But"—she could hear her father's voice in her head—"I didn't do such a good job."

"No?"

"I brushed him. A lot. And I swept up a lot. It was just—Dad would always find hair somewhere. He was good at that."

"And where's Jupe now?"

"Dead." The word jumped out of Hilde's mouth unbidden, surprising her. It sounded so cold, so flat, so unmatched to the feelings pent up inside her. She paused and picked at the grass until she regained her composure. Then she said quietly, "Just before we left."

"Ah."

Silence settled over them, and Nan seemed in no hurry to speak. Her face remained placid, untroubled, as if it were the most natural thing in the world to allow grief in—to give it light, to befriend it.

The tightness around Hilde's heart began to loosen. "He stopped eating a few weeks before he died," she finally continued. "He got pretty skinny. But I just thought he was upset because there was so much going on. Packing and all."

"Were you with him when he died?"

Hilde nodded. "He didn't show up for supper," she began, "and so I went looking for him. I looked everywhere—the cellar, the barn, the garage. I finally found him curled up under the porch. He'd made a little spot for himself in the shade. And he was panting. I ran and got him some water from the pump, and brought it back, but he didn't seem to want it."

"Go on," Nan said.

"Ethan—my brother—came home from practice, and when he saw me, he dropped his books on the lawn and crawled under the porch to be with us. I remember how relieved I was. He knows animals, you know? He felt Jupe's belly, looked into his eyes, checked his gums. And then he said—I remember exactly what he said—he said, 'I don't think he has much time, Scout.' "

She looked at the ground and her eyes blurred. The only noise was the lapping water at the edge of the marsh.

"I knew he was right. Jupe was old. So we sat there—and I just kept stroking his ears. They were so soft."

Nan nodded.

"And then . . . after a little while . . . he just slipped away."

Nan said nothing. But there was still an open space for Hilde to speak, and she did.

"We stayed there, under the porch, for a long time," she said. "Talking. Ethan reminded me of all the funny things Jupe used to do. Like burrowing his forehead in his bed after he ate to clean his muzzle. We laughed about it." She brushed away several grass seeds that had landed on her pantleg. "Later we buried him in the orchard. We even had a little ceremony. Dad was working that night, but Mom came out and stood with us for a while." She glanced up at Nan. "Mom's not much into that kind of thing though. She grew up around farm animals, so she sees things different."

"Different?"

"Different. From me."

"How so?"

Somehow Hilde had worked her way around to the question that had haunted her since Jupe's death.

"Um—she doesn't believe that animals have souls."

"Ah," Nan said quietly.

"Neither does the minister at our church. I asked him, and he said no." Her words came out sharp, staccato. "He said animals have 'no souls and no afterlife.' That's exactly what he said. I'll never forget." Then she turned and looked at Nan. "Do you believe that?"

Nan met her gaze. "That's a challenging question for any pastor."

"I'm not asking you—you know—as a pastor. I'm asking you as a person. What *you* think."

"Ah. Well, then, let me see if I can take a crack at answering"— she smiled a tiny smile—"as a *person*." She shifted on the rock, leaned forward, and gazed out over the marsh for a long time. Then she said quietly, "There's so much we don't know about the world, so much mystery. I've always believed it's important to hold that mystery alongside what we know, to make space for it."

Hilde nodded, though she had the feeling she was in over her head.

"And when we do that, when we make room for the mystery, sometimes, in my experience, we are graced by a deeper wisdom. We begin to sense the truth beyond what can be proven." She glanced at Hilde. "Have you ever had that experience?"

Hilde paused. "Um . . . maybe." She pushed her glasses up on her nose.

"I don't know anyone who can answer your question definitively. But for me personally, when I look into Toby's eyes—when he's calm and unafraid," she said, touching her chest lightly, her fingers outspread, "when I do that, I surely feel I'm looking at his soul."

Hilde could feel the muscles in her shoulders—the knots she had carried around for months from that awful day under the porch—loosen.

They sat together for several more minutes. Then Nan said, "How's the cheesemaking?"

Hilde stretched her back and sat up straighter. "Not so good. I don't think Mom quite has the knack. I don't know why. She really wants to make it work."

"And your dad—can he help?"

"He's not here."

When's he coming?"

"Soon." A thought as imperceptible as a shadow passed across her consciousness. She turned away from it. "But he doesn't know much about running a farm. He works at a college. We just rented out our fields around the house. I mean, Mom grew up on a farm. That's why she wants to do this so much. But Dad—"

"Your dad's gonna have a hard time working at a college around here. The nearest one is over the hill."

Hilde hadn't thought of that. She wondered whether her parents had. She changed the subject. "Mom hopes she can make it—the cheesemaking—into a real business."

Toby, exhausted now, stretched out on the cool dirt path and began chewing off the bark of a twig.

"Mm. Hope is a powerful thing. It gives people something to reach for."

"Yeah." Hilde didn't know where Nan was going with this.

Toby stood up and started coughing, spitting out pieces of bark on the ground. He retched hard and looked up at Nan, as if to say, *All good here.*

Nan glanced at him and then returned her gaze to the marsh grasses bending in the breeze. "What about you? What do *you* hope for?"

"Me?" Hilde puzzled over the question. It hadn't occurred to ask herself such a question. She'd spent so much time trying to keep the peace in her family, and to figure out what her mother wanted, that it hadn't occurred to her to want or hope for anything herself. Just asking herself the questions—*What do* I *want? What do* I *hope for?*—produced a tiny spasm in her stomach. There was something dangerous about such questions. "I don't know."

As they walked back to town along the road, with the sun low at their back and their own shadows lengthening before them, Hilde allowed herself the space to ask *What do* I *want*? She was only sure of what she didn't want. She didn't want to try so hard to make her family work.

22

Giving Up

L a Migra!" a voice hissed.

Joaquín bolted upright. For an instant, he didn't remember where he was—but grit pelting his face brought him to his senses.

Everyone was scattering in different directions. A white van was barreling toward them across the desert floor, kicking up clouds of sand and dust.

"¡Aquí!" Over here! Fernando called hoarsely over his shoulder.

Joaquín grabbed his pack and took off after him.

The two of them ran like they had from the bar the night they'd first met, feet pounding, boots kicking up pebbles.

Joaquín didn't look back. He didn't want to see how close they were. He didn't care what happened to the others. He just wanted to be gone. His heart raced, and his head pounded. Beads of sweat trickled into his eyes. He blinked to clear his vision, but it only made the stinging worse. He stumbled, and his calf brushed the spines of a cholla, which caused a painful zing in his leg. Still he ran, keeping Fernando's back in his eyesight.

Then it was Fernando who stumbled. He fell forward, hitting the ground hard, and scrambled up again. The terrain was rockier here, and the shadows longer. Fernando disappeared into a deep wash.

Joaquín dove down beside him, breathing heavily. Several minutes passed. When his breath was even again, Joaquín asked quietly, "You okay?"

"Yeah," Fernando croaked. He put his hand to his throat and coughed dryly.

They lay there for several minutes more, listening. Joaquín's calf throbbed. He twisted toward the pain and pulled a sharp barb from the fleshy part of his leg. Another zing raced through his body, making his hair stand on end. He closed his eyes.

When he opened them again, Fernando was lying flat on his stomach, peeking over the edge of the wash. "They got 'em," he said.

"Who?"

"Migra."

"All of them?"

"The boys. The onion guy. And his two buddies. But that goddam coyote. Where the hell is he?" He ducked his head and lay immobile. "Shit."

"What?"

"Looked this way."

"Did they see you?"

"Dunno." He flattened his cheek against the wall of the wash.

Joaquín slithered up the wash. Through a patch of scrub that lined its edge, he could see a man approaching, mirrored aviator glasses glinting in the sun. A yellow shield on the breast of his drab green shirt, a gun, a nightstick, a walkie-talkie. Border Patrol. As he sauntered forward, Joaquín could hear his boots crush the desert floor. He stopped just short of the wash, shielded his eyes, and looked out over the barren land beyond. Joaquín held his breath. Fernando, still on his stomach, rested his forehead on his hands and closed his eyes.

After a long moment, the man turned. He walked along the wash for a few yards, then headed back toward the van.

Joaquín exhaled quietly through pursed lips. They waited, motionless, until they heard the van start up and move toward the road.

"Gracias a Dios," Fernando whispered. "Let's get outta here. Which way is north?"

Joaquín oriented himself to the low sun. "That way," he replied.

They gathered their backpacks and started through the wash.

They had not gone more than a hundred meters when Fernando pitched forward again, landing hard on his forearms.

"Shit!" He flipped over and pulled one boot up close to his thigh. Joaquín crouched beside him and peered at the boot. The sole had pulled away from the toe and was bent back at a crazy angle. Sticky strings of glue stretched from the sole to the body of the boot. "Motherfuckers. They told me these were Timberlands."

Joaquín's mind started to race. You could live for days without food. You could blister in the sun. But you needed your boots to keep going.

Fernando kept pushing the sole back into place, and it kept curling outward, obstinately.

"You can't walk with that boot like that."

"Hermano, you're such a worrier," Fernando replied. "I got this." He pulled a tattered gray hoodie and a knife from his backpack. He fished for the drawstring at the neck of the hoodie, cut the end with one quick gesture, and pulled it out of its channel. Then he pushed the sole of the boot into place and tied the drawstring around the toe. "There. See?"

He grinned, but Joaquín saw a flicker of fear cross his face.

At just that moment, several small pebbles from the edge of the wash above them rolled lazily down the dry earth, landing just short of Fernando's foot. They froze.

Joaquín looked up through the scrub. *"Jesucristo,"* he whispered.

Peering down from the top of the wash was the face of a child. It was the girl who had crossed with them. She stood there, dumb. Then another face appeared over the edge. The young mother.

"Get down here," Joaquín hissed. The girl scrambled into the wash on her butt. The young mother followed.

"They didn't see you?"

"We hid," the young mother said in a small voice. "We ran, and then we hid." She was breathing heavily. "We didn't know what to do. We were lost." She looked at the jug poking out of Joaquín's backpack. "You have water?"

Joaquín pulled the jug from his backpack. It was frighteningly light. He twisted off the cap and offered it to her.

She took it and passed it to her daughter who took a small sip. Then she did the same, holding the liquid in her mouth for a long moment before swallowing. It seemed to calm her, that little sip.

"When we spotted you, we followed, and I prayed we'd catch up. But you were going so fast, we lost you. Two times we lost you. I told Aricela we had to keep going. She was so tired, but she did it." She stroked her daughter's hair.

"So you're Aricela," Joaquín said to the child. She offered a shy smile.

"And I'm Isobel," her mother said.

WHEN IT WAS FULLY dark, they started again. The air, which had been so searingly hot during the day, turned cold, penetrating their bodies and stiffened their joints. They moved clumsily in a line across the desert floor, one after the other, Fernando first, his gait hampered by his boot, then the girl and her mother, and Joaquín at the rear, scanning the vast expanse of land every few minutes. Sometimes they could hear vehicles—motorbikes, vans—on a road to the east. How far east, they weren't sure.

They were all exhausted. Joaquín could tell from the way they moved. His calf throbbed and his tongue stuck to the roof of his mouth.

When he swallowed, he felt his throat close—and for an agonizing instant he wasn't sure it would open again. The feeling made him claustrophobic, despite the vast expanse of desert around him.

For hours, they pressed forward, silent in the desert.

As the sun rose, they found themselves among rocky outcroppings with boulders as big as a man and acacia that produced enough foliage to hide them for a few hours. They needed rest and nourishment. There wasn't much water left, but they still carried canned fruit and beans, and Joaquín knew there'd be liquid in those cans.

"Hold up," he called to Fernando. "We gotta rest."

The little party stopped and looked around. Isobel slung her backpack to the ground, put her hand to her neck and groaned.

"*Gracias a Dios,*" she said. Looking toward the expanse of desert beyond Joaquín, she added, "Is it safe?"

Joaquín knew they were on a human-made trail, crude as it was, and it was probably not wise to rest nearby. He glanced around. The nearest boulders were about fifteen meters away. "Check over there," he said to Fernando. "See if there's a place we can sleep for a few hours."

Isobel sank down in the spotty shade of a mesquite. "Oh, my head," she said, rubbing her temples.

Aricela knelt next to her mother and pawed through her backpack. She pulled out a small fruit cup.

"Here, Mama," she said.

"No, you take it, baby," Isobel said, her voice weak with fatigue. She pushed it away.

Aricela sat back. Joaquín thought he saw a shadow of fear cross her face.

"Here," he said, pulling a can from his backpack and offering it to Isobel. "You take this one. Aricela can have that one."

Isobel did not move. She looked like she was going to cry.

"Take it, Mama," Aricela said. When her mother still did not move,

Aricela took the can from Joaquín, pulled open the pop-top, and gave it to her mother. Isobel took it with trembling hands. Aricela opened the other can, and as if they had sat down at a feast, they consumed the sweet syrup together, being careful to avoid the rough metal edges of the cans. Then they dug the fruit out with their fingers. When they were finished, Aricela sank down and rested her head on her mother's thigh.

Joaquín stood and glanced toward the outcropping. Fernando was standing next to a large boulder, staring back at him. He did not move. Puzzled, Joaquín put his hand to the brim of his cap, shaded his eyes, and looked harder at his friend's face, but Fernando continued to stand like a statue. Finally, in a gesture that was hardly noticeable, Fernando turned one hand outward toward the boulder.

Joaquín knew something was wrong.

"You stay here," he said. "I'm going to help Fernando."

Fernando watched as he approached. When Joaquín stepped into the shadow of the boulder, Fernando moved aside. "Not here," he said quietly.

The first thing Joaquín noticed were the sneakers, weather beaten and clearly unfit for such an arduous trek. They were splayed outward in opposite directions. The legs were twisted at obscene angles, pants still covering them. The T-shirt, once red, was tattered and coated with desert dust. Beneath it, the rib cage was still covered with desiccated skin. And the arms were nothing more than bleached bones, flung upward in what looked like a gesture of surprise, or perhaps great joy. One of the hands had been gnawed off, leaving a splintered stump.

"*Dios mío,*" Joaquín whispered.

"I almost tripped over him," Fernando said, staring at the corpse. "The shadows—I didn't see him."

Joaquín moved around to the skull. It had been picked clean, leaving only the eye sockets and hair. But the parts that Joaquín would never be able to forget—in their perfection—were the teeth—a full set, fully exposed and white as porcelain. "This guy was young," he said quietly.

"There's a ballcap over there. And a jug. Dry."

"No backpack?"

"No."

Joaquín squatted down. Gingerly, he slipped his fingers into the corpse's pants pockets and turned them inside out. Nothing.

Fernando picked up the cap and slipped his finger along the sweatband. He glanced up and shrugged.

"Shoes?" Joaquín asked.

"There's only one. Over there."

Joaquín stepped between two rocks and picked up the tattered sneaker. He pulled up the insole. Nothing. "You want this?" he said, holding out the sneaker.

Fernando shook his head. "Wrong foot."

"You sure? It's better than what you got."

Fernando stood there, looking forlorn. Finally, he took the sneaker. He sat on a rock and swapped it out for the boot tied together with laces. When he stood, he looked like he had two left feet.

"Fit?" Joaquín asked.

Fernando shrugged again.

"I wish we had some way to mark this place," Joaquín said, scanning the landscape. But the sameness of the desert was the only thing remarkable. He turned back to Fernando. "Leave the cap. It might help whoever picks him up."

Fernando tucked the cap gently under the torso.

As they returned to the trail, Joaquín said, "No mention of this."

But in fact, both Isobel and Aricela were fast asleep under the mesquite. Fernando collapsed at the base of a nearby acacia, and Joaquín gave up the idea of finding a safer place and lay down himself, exhausted in both body and spirit.

HE AWOKE TO FRIGID air. It was dusk, and Fernando was sitting up, a water jug on his knee. His eyes looked sunken.

"You okay?"

"Yeah," Fernando replied. "Dizzy."

"You have water left?"

Fernando turned his jug upside down. Two drops fell onto his pant leg.

"Okay, we gotta move. Wake Isobel. Let's get going."

"I'm awake," Isobel said, pushing herself up to a seated position. She touched her daughter's hair lightly. "*Hija,* wake up."

They moved through the night along the trail strewn with detritus from those who had made it this far, and somehow that gave Joaquín comfort. When the moon was high, they came up out of the wash and found themselves staring at a cattle trough, filled to the brim with water. So pristine did the water look, shimmering in the pale light, that Joaquín wondered whether the devil himself had placed it there. When Fernando saw it, he walked to the trough slowly, as if in a trance, and drew his finger over the surface, rippling it.

"Let's go," Joaquín said, coming up fast behind his friend.

"No, wait," Fernando said. He seemed mesmerized. He knelt, drew the empty plastic jug from his backpack, and submerged it in the water.

Isobel pulled Aricela closer and stared at Fernando.

"Hey, *hermano,*" Joaquín said, putting a hand on Fernando's shoulder and shaking it. "You don't want that."

Fernando kept his hand in the water, waiting for the jug to fill.

"You *know* that water will kill you." Joaquín's tone was insistent now.

Fernando continued to ignore him.

Joaquín grabbed Fernando's arm and tugged. The half-filled jug came loose from Fernando's grip and bobbed in the water.

Fernando whirled around and yanked his arm away.

"Leave me alone!" His face was contorted.

"Fernando—"

"Don't touch me!"

"But think what you're doing. Think! That water is unclean. If you drink it—"

"I won't drink it! I won't! I just wanna . . . touch it."

"You want to *touch* it?"

"Yeah. Take a little with me. In my backpack. I just want to . . . hear it slosh when I walk."

Joaquín was dumbfounded. He looked squarely into Fernando's face—and could see no light in his eyes. Nothing but a flat, dumb, spiritless look. It frightened him. He paused for a long moment, considering. Then he reached into the trough and retrieved the floating jug.

"Okay, man. Okay. Let's do this. Let's put in some water. Just a little. That way you'll be able to hear it, and it won't be too heavy." He filled the jug with just enough water to cover the bottom. "Give me the top." Joaquín stuffed the jug back into Fernando's backpack and helped him on with it. "You're still leading. Go. That way," he said, and he turned Fernando by the shoulders until he was facing north again.

Fernando complied without comment.

JUST BEFORE DAWN, A small yellow flag appeared on the horizon. It was waving in the breeze, a tattered cloth at the end of a thin metal pole arcing high against a pearl-gray sky.

Joaquín's heart jumped. He remembered. There *was* water in the desert, put there by volunteers, church people, Americans.

"There," he called to the others. "Water. Go that way."

They quickened their pace, but the enormous effort made them breathless. Isobel had begun to limp, and Fernando's mismatched shoes kept causing him to stumble. Nonetheless, they could see the drum, nestled on its side in a metal cradle like a keg of beer. *Fifty-five gallons of pure, sweet water.* And someone had even taken the time to write on it:

¡Buena suerte, compañeros!

Fernando let out a whoop when he got to the drum.

"Is it full?" Joaquín called, as he approached.

"*Sí, sí, sí,*" Fernando exclaimed, banging on the metal.

Joaquín knew there were people who emptied these drums with a few well-placed bullet holes. They were Americans too. But this one was full, heavy.

Fernando dropped his backpack and rooted through its contents. He pulled out a plastic jug, unscrewed the top, placed it under the spigot, and turned the flange. Clear liquid poured into the jug.

"Water, water," Aricela cried, dancing toward the drum.

Isobel fell to her knees and buried her face in her daughter's T-shirt. "*Santa María, Madre de Dios.*"

Suddenly, they all fell silent.

Then Fernando said, "What's that smell?"

Aricela looked at her mother, who was sniffing the air, a quizzical expression on her face.

Joaquín put his nose close to the jug. He sniffed once. Then again. His upper lip curled. "Gasoline," he said quietly. "Somebody put gasoline in the water."

Isobel let go of her daughter and sank onto the desert floor. Aricela stood ramrod straight next to the blue drum, color moving up her neck and into her pale face, turning it beet red. She began to cry, without tears. And then she retched.

Too enfeebled to continue, they lay in what shade they could find near the water drum. As the sun rose, it parted the gray clouds and began its work of bleaching the bones of the creatures that had died in the night. Exhaustion overcame the mother and her daughter.

When Joaquín was sure that Isobel and Aricela were asleep, he said to Fernando, "Walk with me. We need to talk."

He pulled Fernando to his feet and led him a few meters beyond the others. A breeze had kicked up, and the fresh morning air gave Joaquín courage.

"We can't go on much longer. We need help," he began, watching Fernando's expression carefully. "For all we know, we could be going in circles. Isobel is limping, and your shoes . . ."

Fernando looked at him, his eyes dull.

"We need to find a road," Joaquín said. "We need to get help."

Fernando's eyes flicked to the ground.

Joaquín ducked his head and tried to look Fernando in the eye, but Fernando would not meet his gaze. "You heard me, right?" Joaquín continued. "It's not what we want, but it's better than wandering out here until we drop."

Fernando squatted down, picked up a stick, and began to jab it into the sand.

Joaquín crouched next to him. "Without water, we could last— what? Maybe another day? Two?"

Fernando looked up. "No," he growled.

"But—"

"No, no, no, no, no! You hear me? No!" Fernando said ferociously.

The vehemence of the words stunned Joaquín. His mind raced.

"You go!" Fernando spat. "Take them with you. I don't care."

"Look, they'll pick us up. We can get some water, rest. A shower maybe. And some food. And after that, we'll figure out what to do. We'll call Gabe in California. He'll help." He kept watching for a flicker of rationality in Fernando's face. "And if they send us back, we'll try again. We'll *keep* trying."

"If I give up," Fernando whispered, the veins at his temples pulsing, "you know what'll happen? I'll be packed on a plane and sent back to that *hellhole country*—before the sun sets!" His eyes were ablaze now. "And then you know what'll happen then? Do you? They don't forget!

They *will* come for me. They *will* hunt me down. And they will butcher me like a hog."

"No, no," Joaquín said, gripping Fernando's forearm. "This is America. Tell them your story. Explain it. They'll understand."

Fernando looked up, incredulous. "Americans? They have *no* idea. They think everything in my country is just like America. They say, go to the police. Get protection there. Ha! They have *no idea* what it's like to live with no place to hide. To live where the police lie down with the politicians, and where both lick the boots of their narco bosses! Americans? They'll never understand why I can't go back. *Never.*"

They sat together, exhausted, for several more minutes while the sun rose over the saguaro.

"Okay," Joaquín said finally. "We'll go. You keep on."

"Okay," Fernando said hoarsely.

Once Isobel woke, Joaquín told her the plan.

She looked relieved, though when she glanced at Fernando, there was deep sorrow in her eyes. She staggered to her feet and approached Fernando who was squatting on the ground. *"Gracias,"* she said quietly, leaning over and touching his hand lightly. "For everything."

Fernando opened his hand and held hers lightly for a moment. But he did not look up.

Then Joaquín helped Aricela with her backpack, and the three scrambled up the gentle slope of the wash. Once they reached the top, Joaquín turned back toward his friend.

Fernando, still squatting on the ground, was watching them go. When Joaquín turned, an odd smile spread across Fernando's face. After a beat, he scooped up a handful of dry earth and held it up. "I made it," he said, letting the dirt sift through his fist. "To America."

Joaquín gave him a thumbs-up. Then he turned and followed the other two eastward.

THEY WALKED TOWARD THE sun, cursing it for blinding their eyes and welcoming it for warming their skin. After an hour, they came to a dirt road that looked newly worn and settled in the shade of a mesquite tree. Joaquín pulled out his map of the southern half of America—the one he'd brought from Mexico City—and the matchbook he'd squirreled away in the pocket of his backpack. He tore the map into small pieces, added some tumbleweed, and lit the pile on fire. Smoke drifted up in a lazy, gray plume. He sat down in the dust next to Isobel to wait.

23
Thanksgiving

It wasn't yet five o'clock and the day was already darkening. Hilde felt as though the world were closing in, like a shadow headache that never lifts. She leaned against the paddock fence, craving sunlight on her skin, and watched as Gabe refilled the water troughs. The goats were already headed for the barn.

"Hilde," Janine called from the house.

Hilde shivered and pulled her jacket tighter around her ribcage.

"Hilde, I need you. Now, please."

Her mother had been buzzing around the house all day, like an angry bee in a jar, setting up for what was to be Thanksgiving dinner. Mr. Booher was coming. And for that reason, her mother was at once eager and anxious. She was also angry that Ethan had to work at the deli for most of the day. She would surely sparkle when Mr. Booher arrived, but now—scrubbing the stains out of the kitchen counter, finishing the sweet potatoes, rooting around for a roasting pan for the small turkey breast she'd bought in Half Moon Bay—she would be in a mood. Which was why Hilde had been hanging out in the pasture, pretending to tend the goats.

Hilde stepped through the back door into the kitchen.

"Set the table, please," her mother said. "And take off your boots. You're tracking muck everywhere. I can smell it."

Hilde loosened the laces, stepped out of her boots, and set them outside on the stoop. Padding around the kitchen in her socks, she pulled open sticky drawers, counted out mismatched silverware, and arranged everything carefully on the kitchen table.

"Mom," she said, tentatively, as she gathered glasses from the cupboard, "I was thinking. Gabe's been working out there all day, and I don't think he has anywhere to go tonight. Maybe . . . maybe we could invite him in for dinner."

Janine turned to her daughter, meat fork poised in one hand. "Really? You think that's a good idea?"

"Well, I mean—"

Janine turned away. "You know, Hilde, sometimes you surprise me. You seem to have no idea how the world works." She opened the oven door and peered inside. "We're about to sit down to a beautiful dinner—a family dinner with Mr. Booher as our special guest, and you want the farmhand, direct from the pasture, to sit himself down at our dinner table. And he doesn't speak English."

A flash of anger shot through Hilde, derailing her train of thought. "He does speak English. He speaks it just fine."

"Okay, who speaks *some* English. But what does he have to say? What can he possibly have to say?"

Hilde turned away. This was not going the way she'd hoped, but it was going the way she expected. "I don't know, Mom. A lot, probably," she mumbled.

"What did you say?"

She turned back to her mother, feeling the energy pulsing through her veins. "I don't know, Mom. He probably has a lot to say," she said precisely. "You don't know, because you don't know him." She jammed her hands into her pockets and walked out of the kitchen.

Shaking her head, Janine turned back to the counter. She speared the raw turkey breast with the meat fork, positioned it in the roasting pan, and slid the pan into the oven. Then she wiped her hands clean.

"Darlin', this is one heck of a feast," Ned Booher said, reaching over Hilde's plate and spearing another slice of turkey. "I admire a woman who can cook like you do, I really do."

Janine passed a serving dish to him. "Thank you, Ned. More stuffing?"

"Oh, no. I couldn't." He patted his fancy belt buckle, an American eagle with rhinestone eyes. "Well, maybe. Hell, yeah. Pass it over."

The front screen squeaked, and Ethan came through the door. He glanced around the room.

"Ethan!" Janine beamed. "Finally! Glad you're home, honey. Come, sit down. We saved some dinner for you."

Ethan looked surprised at his mother's welcome, and a little suspicious. He crossed the room and sat down in the empty chair opposite Hilde.

"Here, hon, have some turkey. Hilde, pass the cranberry."

"You gotta try these sweet potatoes, son. They're great," Ned Booher said genially, pushing the dish toward Ethan.

At the word *son*, Ethan stiffened.

"So how was work?" Janine asked, laying her hand gently on his forearm.

"Fine." He withdrew his arm.

"Were there lots of people there today? I can't believe the place was open at all," she continued.

"Yeah, lots," Ethan said. He looked around the table. "Pass the biscuits, Hilde."

"That Carmine Cardullo," Booher said. "He'll do anything for a buck. And on holidays, those tourists come in droves—to enjoy a little sea breeze and some olallieberry pie. He's always gonna be open on the holidays. Trust me on that."

"Right," Ethan said, studying his plate.

"He's one wily coyote. You'll learn a lot from him, if what you want to do is to go into the restaurant business. Is that what you want, son?"

Ethan's upper lip curled just a bit. "I'd appreciate it if you wouldn't call me *son*."

"Oh, no offense, no offense. I'm just making conversation."

Ethan piled some sweet potatoes on his plate.

Booher continued. "Just want you to know that he's not the most upstanding character, if you're bettin' on learning the restaurant business from him."

Ethan looked up.

"Has he shown you his lockbox?" Booher said, bidding for Ethan's attention.

Ethan just stared at Booher silently.

"No," Janine said, shooting a warning look in Ethan's direction. "Tell us, Ned."

"Honey," Booher said, turning to her, "I just want your boy to know that skimmin' off the top ain't right. And that's Cardullo."

Janine turned and looked at Ethan.

"You watch," Booher continued. "Any cash payment he gets, instead of running it through his register, he just pops it into the lockbox."

"I don't get it," Janine said, perplexed.

"If he doesn't run it through the register, it doesn't show up on the books. And if it doesn't show up on the books, he doesn't have to pay taxes on it."

Janine nodded slowly.

"But that's not all," Booher continued. He waited for someone to take the bait.

"What?" Ethan said, finally.

"It's what he does with that money that tells you all about him," Ned continued. He speared a chunk of turkey on his fork and raised it into the air, examining it with relish as he stretched out the silence.

"What?" Ethan said again, thoroughly annoyed now.

"He stashes it away until he's got a good chunk o' change. And then he funnels it to them bikers. For the privilege of being part of their operation."

"What bikers?" Janine asked.

"You've seen those guys—the ones who come in on their Harleys and spend the afternoon tankin' up at the bar across from the deli, right?"

Hilde remembered the noise they made as they roared into town, flags on their jackets, insignia on their motorcycles.

"Those guys, they got nothing to do with their time but ride up and down the California coast, lookin' for a fight. I see what they're trying to do. But I got too much work on my ranch to pay them much attention."

"What are they trying to do?" Janine asked.

"Oh, you know. They figure out where them libtards are and make sure another point of view is in the air. They show up as unpaid security for certain bigwigs in the Central Valley. And sometimes they go all the way down to San Ysidro and spend the weekend crackin' heads at the border. They just do what needs to be done to flush out the woke and keep them off guard. You gotta understand this state is in a kind of civil war, and they're the muscle that keeps the other side from takin' over entirely."

There was an awkward silence. Ethan's fork scraped against his plate.

"And Cardullo," Booher continued, "he's a low-level peon in their organization. They gave him a leather jacket a couple years ago, and now he thinks he's an important cog in the wheel. He gives 'em free breakfasts and he gases up their hogs with the money he skims off the business. Fewer taxes for the business, more protection for the state. That's the way he sees it."

After several silent moments, Booher turned to Ethan. Hilde could see from the look on Booher's face that he was going to make another run at befriending her brother. He was that transparent.

"You know, son, workin' at the deli ain't bad," he said, wiping his mouth on a crumpled paper napkin. "But there's lots of things for a young man like you to do around these parts. Lots to do. Maybe you should take more advantage of where you are."

Ethan looked up.

"For instance, that's one big ocean out there," he said, pointing at the window with his fork. "And the deep-sea fishing can be pretty spectacular if you know where to go."

Ethan frowned.

"Hell, I'm heading out over Christmas with a couple of buddies. Maybe you should come with us. I can teach you just about everything you need to know about deep-sea fishing. Rockfish, lingcod, sheepshead—they're all out there for the takin'. And you can help us with the boat."

"No, thanks." Ethan dropped his eyes to his plate and shoveled turkey into his mouth.

Booher paused.

"Ned, that's so *nice* of you," Janine chimed in. "I know Ethan would love to go out with you sometime. He'll just have to figure out how to clear his schedule. I know he'd love to learn all you know about fishing."

Ethan leaned back in his chair, chewing slowly, and fixed his mother in his gaze.

Booher dislodged a piece of turkey from his teeth with his fingernail, watching Ethan. "Suit yourself, then."

There was a knock at the back door. Janine rose and opened it a crack. Hilde could see Gabe's face.

"Finished, *señora*. I penned the doe separate and gave her extra water. You might want to look in on her later."

"Thank you, Gabriel. Ethan'll do that after dinner."

"Sí, señora."

She closed the door, locking it behind her.

"How's that workin' for ya?" Mr. Booher said. "Havin' him here?"

"Oh, he's great." Janine replied, glancing at Ethan. "Works hard. Takes responsibility. Seems to know a lot about goats."

"Well, that's good—because, you know, you may be takin' a chance lettin' him work here."

"Chance?" Janine looked perplexed.

Both Ethan and Hilde looked up.

"Did you ask to see his papers?"

"Papers?

"Papers. Probably ain't got none. Most of them don't around here. You gotta be careful because if you get caught hiring 'em, you can be looking at a hefty fine. A lot of growers, they hire 'em because they work cheap. But me, I won't do it. I don't want 'em on my property, working with my cattle. No ma'am." He shifted in his chair.

Ethan glanced at Hilde.

Booher continued, "They show up at my ranch looking for work, or a handout, or even somethin' that isn't theirs in my sheds. I finally had to put up a fence around my property to keep 'em out. It's an electric fence. Won't do 'em permanent damage, that fence, but it'll surely make their eyeballs roll back in their heads." He broke off a piece of his dinner roll and sopped up the gravy on his plate. "To me, it's simple," he said. "You come to the USA, you *come in legal*. Then maybe, just maybe, I'll hire you."

Janine sat for a moment, considering what he'd said. She was clearly torn. "You may be right," she said finally, "but I did need help around here. I just couldn't do it all on my own." She gave Ethan a sideways glance. "Hilde, help me clear, please. Ned, I have pecan pie. Hope you like pecan pie."

Hilde got up and helped her mother clear the table.

"What's his name?" Booher said, leaning back in his chair and watching Janine clear his plate.

"Who?" Janine replied, scraping a plate into the garbage.

"That hand you hired. What's his name?"

Janine looked as though she could not remember.

"Gabe," Hilde said quietly.

"Yes," Janine said, nodding. "Gabe."

"Okay, then. But pay him in cash."

"I do."

"Because you don't want a paper trail."

Ethan stared at Booher, his face knit with disgust.

Another knock at the door. Janine crossed the kitchen and opened the door.

"*Señora,* two of the goats, they're missing. Probably across the creek. Okay if I take the truck to look for them?"

Janine turned to Ethan. "I hope there's gas in the truck, Ethan."

Ethan looked at her defiantly. "Yeah, Ma, there's gas in the truck."

"I'll go," Hilde cut in. "I want to help look." She knew that was only half the story. What she wanted was to get out of that kitchen, out of the house, anywhere but where her mother and Ethan were. She jumped up, scraping her chair across the floor, and headed for the back door.

Gabe held the screen door as she slipped past him and made a bee-line for the truck.

They were silent, bouncing over the rutted road in the darkening daylight. Hilde felt relief to be in the cab. She glanced over at Gabe, who was staring straight ahead, a little smile on his face.

"What?" she said.

He shrugged. His eyes remained glued to the road.

"You have something to say. I can tell," she continued.

He shook his head and shrugged again.

"Yeah, you do. What is it?"

There was a long pause. Gabe turned off the paved road onto a rutted dirt path that led to the bridge. "Your mama," he said, "she cares a lot about the farm."

Hilde snorted and turned away. "She cares, yeah." She looked out the window and let the grasses blur before her eyes.

"And the goats. And making it work. She cares." Gabe let the silence hang in the air. Finally, he said, "You don't want the farm to work?"

She looked down at her fingernails. They were short, dirty, and the cuticles were peeling. "I do," she said quietly. "At least about the goats. And the llama. I really like her."

Gabe nodded and produced that little smile again. "You have a good heart for animals. They know when they're being well cared for."

"Sometimes they feel more like family to me than my own," she muttered.

He let her comment hang in the air.

"My mom," she said finally, "she doesn't really like me. I guess you've noticed, right?"

"Why do you say that?"

"Oh, she loves me and all . . ." she hesitated. "But she doesn't really *like* me. I mean, she doesn't *like* who I am. She wants me to be a different kind of person." And after a pause, "Someone like her."

"Why would it be so bad to be like her?"

"I dunno. It just would." She didn't want to think about it.

"She's doing hard work," he said, after a pause. "And it's not easy doing what she's trying to do alone. Where is your papa?"

"He's back in Wisconsin selling our house. He's coming soon."

"You and your brother then, you're her only family." He paused. "And your brother—why isn't he helping more?"

"Ethan?" She took a deep breath. "He doesn't want to be any part of this. He's gonna leave. He's headed for Texas. Just as soon as he can save enough money." She could feel a pit opening beneath her ribcage.

They both retreated into silence as the truck bumped down the unpaved road.

Finally, she said, "You're waiting for your brother to come, right?"

"*Sí,*" he said. Then, "But he's been quiet."

"Are you worried?"

"No. I know him. He'll make it. He's smart." He seemed to say it more as a hope than as a conviction.

"When do you think he'll get here?"

"I don't know."

She looked at him. "Are you close? With him?"

He glanced at her and nodded. "He is my family."

As he turned into the pasture behind the creek, the truck bounced crazily, its shocks shot. The headlights swept across the high grass.

"There they are," he said.

In the darkening light, Hilde could see the two kids grazing on a mulberry bush.

"They're small," Gabe said. "We can take them in the cab."

They were easy to catch, as young as they were. Hilde carried one to the cab of the truck, and Gabe slung the other over his shoulders, catching its forehooves with one hand, its hind hooves with the other. Once settled in the cab, the two kids sat like fawns, one on Hilde's lap and one on the seat next to Gabe, their bony legs tucked neatly underneath their chestnut bodies.

The truck coughed and died several times before Gabe was able to get it moving. Finally, it came to life, its headlights illuminating the dirt road. After bumping along for several more moments, they turned onto the pavement and headed home.

"Jesus! What was that?"

When he heard the crash, Ethan jumped up from the table and headed for the front door. Janine and Booher, slower to respond, followed.

Outside, they saw the truck angled into the ditch next to the front gate, dust and smoke enveloping it. A midsize Pontiac was stopped in the middle of the road, perpendicular to oncoming traffic, its right front bumper crumpled like paper. Ethan ran to the truck, Janine to the Pontiac.

"Are you okay?" Janine said, poking her head into the passenger window of the Pontiac. She vaguely recognized the driver. He was the grandfather of the kid who sorted the mail at the post office. She had seen him there sometimes, tucked in a corner doing crosswords as his grandson worked. "What happened?"

"I dunno," the old man said. "They turned in front of me, and then . . . they just stopped."

"They stopped?" Her voice rose.

"Yeah," the man said, rubbing his shoulder where the seatbelt cut across his chest. Janine stood upright and turned. She looked at the truck for a long moment. Then, she walked slowly over to it.

"They're okay, Mom," Ethan said as she approached. "Hilde's just got a cut above her eye is all."

Janine didn't look inside the cab. Rather, she walked directly to Ethan and stood in front of him with nothing but a few inches between her face and his. "You said," she began icily. "You said you were going to *fix* the truck. You said you were going to *figure out why* it was stalling out."

"I did, but—"

"You said,"—she was shaking now—"you understood the danger of having a truck that stalls out. You even gave *me* the rationale"—and here she mimicked her son's voice—"'I've got to fix that before it stalls when somebody's turning left.'"

"Yeah, I did, but—"

By this point, Hilde had gotten out of the truck. She stood with a kid in her arms, blood trickling slowly down her forehead from her hairline, diverted by her eyebrow onto her cheek.

Gabe came around and took the kid from her. "Okay?" he said quietly.

She nodded. He started toward the barn, one animal under each arm.

"You're such an idiot!" Janine barked at her son. "You are the most irresponsible fucking idiot I know!"

It was a rage that Hilde had never seen before in her mom.

"Mom, it's okay. I'm okay—" Hilde broke in, though she was unsure whether her mother had actually seen her head wound. "Look." She plastered her bangs up against the top of her head so her mother could see the wound.

Neither Janine nor Ethan looked.

"Yes, mother," Ethan growled. "I *am* a fucking idiot. But I am *your* fucking idiot. You made me what I am, Mother. You *made me*."

She swung at him, and the palm of her hand hit his jaw with a resounding smack. He froze, and his eyes turned milky, as though he'd gone somewhere else, inside himself. For a long moment, only the grasses around them moved, swishing in the cold night air. He straightened to his full height, parted his lips, and tested his jaw, moving it back and forth with his hand. And then he looked at his mother again, but this time his eyes fixed on her as though he were seeing her for the first time. He turned and looked at Hilde, and something in his eyes—some mixture of pain and rage—made her own eyes well up. By the time she could see again, he had spun on his heels and gone.

Booher stood at the edge of the road, watching.

24

Truth Told

Alone and in the dark, Ethan strode along the road. He did not know where he was going. He just knew he needed to get away from his mother, away from her crazy pipe dream. *This is her idea. All her idea. I did not sign up for this.*

He'd been heading in the direction of town, but when he came to the bridge, he stopped. He could feel his heart pounding in his chest. He needed some silence, some peace, and the stillness of the riverbank and the movement of the water called to him. He found a path and began to walk along the bank. He sat down on a stump and waited for his anger to dissipate. He needed to pull himself together.

What *was* his responsibility here? Was he being a jackass not working for his mother? Was it his place to save her? From herself? He needed to break away. To figure out who he was and what he wanted. Maybe he would make mistakes. But it was his life. His decisions. And he was so close to that moment when he could step out, take the reins, a moment that seemed so full of promise, and *sweetness even.* Was it his job to stay back and save his mother? And what about Booher?

That was *flirting* at the dinner table. What about that? Should he tell his father?

He fished the phone from his pocket and dialed home. He didn't quite know what he was going to say, but he wanted him here. He needed him here.

"Hello?" The voice was groggy.

"Dad?"

No answer.

"Did I wake you?"

"Ethan?"

"Yeah, me."

"No, uh, you didn't wake me. Why are you calling? Is something wrong?"

Ethan paused. There was something off about his father's response. Why was he speaking in a low voice? It was late, sure—but not that late.

"Nothing wrong," Ethan said, carefully now. "I was just calling to see how your Thanksgiving went. Being alone and all."

"What?"

"Calling to see what you did for Thanksgiving, Dad. Did you go anywhere? Just wanted to check in and—"

"Ethan." His father had come to full attention now, but he was still whispering. "You're calling me now? For that?"

"Yeah, I just wanted to see—"

That's when he heard it—a female voice, sleepily: "Who is it?"

In that moment, Ethan's world shifted. He felt as though he were in a funhouse, with the floor beneath him heaving wildly. By the time he caught his balance, everything had become crystal clear. *He's not coming. He never planned to come. All those sanctimonious lectures about family and responsibility, all those Sundays sitting in church—and he's back in Kenosha screwing some woman, probably plucked from his staff at the college.*

Another moment passed, and the world lurched again. *Mom knows. Of course she does! That's why she's so focused on this damned pipedream. She cannot stand the truth, that he's done. And I've become a lightning rod for her rage. I brought those girls around and she lost her mind. It was this.*

Ethan felt the familiar fury—a fury ignited by years of fielding all the disappointment pitched at him by his father. But now, he understood. And instead of fury, he felt a deep sense of relief. *I'm not the cause of all this misery.* He could feel the ties to his family loosening. He had no need for his father's approval. He realized that while he was *of* his father, he was not *like* his father. And that thought brought breath back into his body.

"Not important, Dad. Just wanted to touch base." He took a deep breath, and the night air filled his lungs. "I'm sorry, Dad."

"That's okay. I wasn't asleep."

"No. I'm not sorry about that," Ethan said calmly.

He could hear his father's breathing.

"I'm not even sorry about finding out you're not coming."

Silence.

"What I *am* sorry about"—and here his voice began to break—"is that it took me this long to figure out I'm not actually a fuckup."

He hit the disconnect button and heaved the phone into the river.

25

The Dog Kennel

The Border Patrol arrived in a white SUV with its telltale green stripe. A man with thick forearms and a crewcut got out, followed by a young woman with slicked-back hair pulled tight into a bun. Both were dressed in olive drab, their black belts heavy with equipment. Tasers, batons, pistols—that much Joaquín could see.

The male agent stood apart—legs wide, arms crossed—as the female swung a small backpack from her shoulder and dug into it. She knelt and held out three bottles. *"¿Agua?"* she said.

Isobel took a bottle. A long sigh made its way from her chest as she twisted off the cap and gave it to Aricela. She accepted another for herself.

"Anybody hurt? *¿Alguien herido?"* the agent asked in Spanish, passing the third bottle to Joaquín. "Blisters? *¿Ampollas?"*

Isobel unhooked her daughter's arms from around her waist. She pulled off one boot and gingerly removed the heavy sock beneath it. As she turned the sole of her foot upward, Joaquín saw a blister the size of a silver dollar.

"Okay," the female agent said. "Let's get you to the station."

THE STATION WAS LARGER than the one Joaquín and Fernando had passed through a week before, but the agents behind the desk wore the same blue latex gloves.

Do they think we have rat mites? Joaquín mused.

After being processed and fingerprinted, they were ushered through a locked door into a cold, dank hall lined with chain-link. The place looked like a dog kennel, except for the low toilets that sat in the center of each cage.

"Familias aquí," the guard said as he unlocked one of the enclosures, which held twenty or so exhausted travelers, many of them women. Joaquín was initially surprised by the agent's assumption that they were a family unit, but he followed Isobel into the space without comment. The guard handed him three standard-issue mylar blankets before locking them in.

"Gracias," Isobel whispered to Joaquín. "I can't do this alone."

They settled into a corner of the cell and surveyed the other depleted captives, some of whom were already wrapped in mylar against the blast of the air-conditioning.

Within the hour, a female agent appeared with a first-aid kit and tended to Isobel's blister. Later, a phalanx of guards delivered bags of turkey sandwiches in plastic containers.

It didn't matter to Joaquín what the food was; he was famished, and he ate with relish. Once he had finished, a bone-weariness came over him, and within a few minutes, he was lying on the cement floor in a deep, dreamless sleep.

When he opened his eyes, it was the middle of the night. One bare lightbulb hung overhead, casting long shadows among the sleeping bodies. He turned over and found himself facing Isobel, who was fully awake and looking at him.

"Can't sleep?" he whispered.

"No."

"Are you cold?"

"No."

"You can have my blanket if you want."

She gave him a wan smile and shook her head.

"We almost made it, huh?" he whispered.

"Mm."

"Are you sorry? About giving up?"

"No," she said. "It's strange, but I feel . . . safe here."

"Safe?"

"There are rules here, laws. Yeah. Safe. I never want to go back."

Joaquín realized he knew nothing about Isobel. The trek through the desert and the worries about Fernando had absorbed all his energy, and he had never thought of asking her about herself.

"Where did you come from?"

"Juarez."

"Never been."

"It's a factory town. About a half day from Agua Prieta." She paused. "I had a good job there at an American factory."

"Doing what?"

"Making shoes," she said in a low voice. "You know. Athletic shoes."

"Why'd you leave?"

Her eyes glazed over.

"Tell me."

She looked away.

"Sorry. You don't have to tell me."

"It's a . . . complicated story."

"I don't need to know."

"It's okay," she said finally. "I'll tell you."

Joaquín waited, saying nothing.

"My husband," she began in a low voice, "he was foreman at the factory where I worked. That's how we met. He was big and funny, and he kept all the workers in line, you know?" She pulled her blanket tighter around her. "All the girls, they thought he was handsome." She looked away and her face softened a bit. "I was seventeen. I did too."

A cloud passed over her countenance. She said nothing for a long moment. Then she continued.

"The summer I turned eighteen, one of my cousins got married. The wedding was over an hour away, but I was determined to go. I took a bus to their town. It was my first time taking a bus that far, and by myself. After the ceremony, there was a big party. Of course, I went. There were a lot of people—I didn't know many of them—and a lot of celebrating. Drinking. Dancing. You know." She glanced at Joaquín. "The party went on a long time. I can't say what happened, but . . ."

Joaquín frowned.

"But I woke up in the bushes. I couldn't remember anything. Not how I got there. Not how I got the scratches, the bruises. And the blood . . ." She was whispering so softly now that Joaquín could hardly make out her words. "That's when I became pregnant." She looked over at the sleeping girl. "With Aricela," she whispered.

Joaquín scootched toward her. He could barely make out what she was saying.

She pinched her lips together as though she didn't want to say more. Then she let out a little gasp and continued.

"When I found out, I told my best friend, and she wanted me to . . ." A pained look crossed her face. "She said she knew where to go, and she'd help, but I—I just couldn't. Do it." She fell silent.

"I get it," Joaquín said.

She took a deep breath. "So instead, I came up with a plan. I decided the next time the foreman, the next time he tried to flirt with me—at the factory, you know—I'd flirt back. After that, things happened pretty fast."

"You told him?" Joaquín asked. He was treading on thin ice, he knew.

"No," she said. She stole a glance at his face. "We married quickly. I didn't tell him."

"Okay."

"But from the beginning, I think he suspected. The baby didn't look anything like him. His mother kept saying she didn't look like anyone in the family." She glanced at Aricela again. "I don't know. He let it go for years. But then one night he got into an argument at the bar with somebody he worked with. And that guy had been at the wedding. Somehow, he knew. He blurted it out in front of everybody."

Joaquín grimaced.

"So when my husband came home, he asked me—for the first time ever—he asked me outright. I was in the kitchen cutting up chicken for the next day. I was tired, and I was mad at him for staying out late and using up all our money on drink. He asked me. So I told him. The truth."

Joaquín's brow furrowed. "What did he do?"

"He got—he got *so* angry."

Aricela rolled over on the concrete floor. Isobel was silent for several minutes, watching her daughter, making sure she didn't wake. Then she continued.

"His eyes," she continued, "I'll never forget. His eyes, they were so full of fury. He grabbed a cleaver, and he brought the blade down hard—right next to my hand. He was aiming for my fingers, but he missed. He tried to pull the cleaver out of the wood. I remember just standing there staring at him while he tried to wrestle it free. And then . . . and then, Aricela was there. She was standing in the doorway in her nightgown."

Joaquín didn't breathe.

"I just grabbed her and ran."

Aricela stirred again. Isobel reached her hand out and touched her daughter's hair lightly, then turned back to Joaquín.

"I ran to my friend's house and we hid. She gave me money. And we got on a bus. In Agua Prieta, we slept on the streets. We waited for my friend to send more money—and when she did, I found a coyote. That coyote. You know the rest."

"Yeah," Joaquín said quietly. "But you're here now."

"And I'm happy. Even here. Because Aricela is safe. That's all that matters." She rested her head on her outstretched arm, and Joaquín could see that her exhaustion was finally giving way to sleep.

EARLY THE NEXT MORNING, two agents in khaki uniforms—a large man with a pocked face, and a portly matron with a mean, tight-lipped smile—pushed their way through the cage door. People poked their heads out from their mylar cocoons. The man drew his nightstick and smacked it several times on the metal door frame.

"Listen up, people," he said in English. His small eyes swept back and forth across the floor. "We need your cooperation." He pointed to the corner of the cage nearest the door. "Kids under eighteen—over here, please. *Niños aquí.*"

Several adults in the cage immediately sat up. No one moved.

"Rápido, por favor," the agent said in a commanding tone, his nightstick continuing to tap menacingly against the metal.

A teenage boy stood up. He looked to be about fifteen, slightly built. He stood amid the adults on the floor, nervously wiping his hands on his pants.

"Now!" the man with the nightstick bellowed. He slammed the nightstick against the bars. The boy startled and then moved quickly toward the corner of the cage.

Another boy, not yet thirteen, rose to his feet. He looked like a scared rabbit.

Aricela turned and looked at her mom. After a long pause, Isobel gave an almost imperceptible nod, and Aricela slowly got to her feet.

She picked her way across the bodies lying on the floor, following the boys to the corner of the cage. Joaquín noticed that one of her boots had come untied. She stumbled a bit as she stepped on the dirty lace.

"¿A dónde los llevan?" Where are you taking them? a woman called from the back of the cage. She had been seated next to the fifteen-year-old. Her voice was loud and high-pitched.

The female agent raised her hand. *"Los verán más tarde.* You'll see them later. They can't stay here. It's the law."

Joaquín saw the look of fear ricochet between Aricela and Isobel. Then Isobel's face went blank. She nodded again.

"¿Mamá?" Aricela called, her voice high and reedy.

"Ve con ellos, nena." Go with them, baby girl, Isobel replied, her tone lilting and reassuring.

"¿Mamá?" she called again, softer now. She stood there staring at her mother until the female agent turned her slender body toward the door. Aricela's eyes shone in the early morning light as she made her way through the cage door, never taking her eyes off her mother.

When she had disappeared into the dark hallway, Joaquín turned back to Isobel. She was staring at the cement floor, her mouth wide open, mute, tears pouring from her face onto the concrete floor.

IN THE MIDAFTERNOON, THEY came for the adults.

"Vámonos," said the agent in charge.

"¿Dónde están nuestros hijos?" Where are our children? said the woman with the high-pitched voice.

The agent ignored her. *"Rápido,"* he said as he poked and prodded people to their feet.

Joaquín saw the woman with the high-pitched voice stand, her legs wobbly, panic in her face. She seemed scarcely able to believe what was happening. *"No,"* she said. Then louder, *"¡No!"*

The agent banged on the metal door frame, and two more men

in khaki appeared. They surrounded the woman, grabbed her by the forearms, and muscled her out the door. As she passed, Joaquín saw her try to catch Isobel's eye, but Isobel's eyes were closed, and her lips were moving silently.

Then they were herded out of the building and into the hot sun. Joaquín stood looking at the back of Isobel's head as she waited to board the bus. She was still praying.

26

Cardullo

By Sunday late afternoon, the tourists had started home. The deli looked as though it had been hit by a swarm of locusts. Mr. Cardullo was totaling up the proceeds in the back room, and Ethan was sweeping up the napkins and sandwich crusts from beneath the counter stools. A young couple lingered over their burgers at a table by the front window, holding hands and talking low, oblivious to their surroundings. The man was slowly feeding fries to the woman as they talked, dipping each one in ketchup and poking it at her mouth playfully. She was giggling. When they finally got up to leave, the man dropped a bill on the table, his eyes still locked on his companion. She moved to the door with easy grace, leading him out into the fading light.

Ethan watched as they left. The man hadn't asked for a check. He'd just left a crisp fifty-dollar bill—maybe to impress the girl, maybe just to keep the party moving to wherever it was headed. Ethan had been stashing cash in a coffee can at home for months now, and he was still short of what he needed for a bus ticket to Texas and a first-month's deposit on a room to rent. *What would it be like,* he mused, *to have that kind of money to drop on a table?*

After glancing around the empty deli, he moved to the table, dishrag in hand. He stacked the dishes and silverware and wiped a few crumbs off the table. He was about to scoop up the bill when he sensed Cardullo watching him. Leaving the bill on the table, he picked up a coffee cup and stacked it on top of the dishes. He turned and headed for the kitchen.

As he was loading the dishwasher, he saw Cardullo move to the table and pick up the bill. He took it to the register, smoothed it out on the shelf above the cash drawer, and with a practiced hand, retrieved a gray metal lockbox from beneath the counter. Deftly, he tipped up the heavy pickle jar that sat on the counter next to the cash drawer and retrieved a key. He opened the box and dropped in the fifty-dollar bill. Then he wiped his hands on a dishtowel and helped himself to an apple fritter.

As he loaded the dishes into the dishwasher, Ethan began to consider what he'd seen. For all his blather, Booher was right about one thing. Cardullo was skimming. Skimming what he could off the top and probably funneling it to those jackasses who rode into town on hogs, a kind of Coast Road militia. Disgust bubbled up inside of him.

And then he began to consider his own situation.

27

Detention

They rode into the heart of the United States of America on a dilapidated white school bus, its windows covered in dark film. Shackled at the wrists and ankles—an insult to their depleted bodies— they stared out the darkened windows at earth scraped bare by wind and sun. By the time they reached their destination, many had nodded off in exhaustion.

The bus wheezed off the highway and onto a flat road that led in one direction only—to an enormous complex of buildings, a city in the middle of nowhere. The bus rumbled up to the main gate, which was flanked by flags and marked with an imposing sign. Because he could not read English, Joaquín had no idea what it said. But the place looked like a prison, its cinder blocks painted drab gray, its windows nothing more than narrow vertical slits in thick concrete. The entire place was surrounded by chain-link topped with razor wire and klieg lights. Passing through the gate, the bus ambled down a yellow line painted on the pavement to a building marked by a single metal door.

"Men out here, women stay," the driver barked.

Joaquín glanced at Isobel who was sitting across the aisle, holding the clear plastic bag that Border Patrol had returned to her just after they'd shackled her. He could see Aricela's pink sweatshirt in the bag. Isobel looked straight ahead, her body rigid, her knuckles white from clutching the bag.

After gathering up his own plastic bag, he leaned over and whispered in her ear. "We'll find her."

She turned away. "Don't," she whispered almost imperceptibly.

"But—"

"Let her go," she said.

"What?" He was dumbfounded by her response.

"Let her go!" she hissed, louder now. "I don't want her deported. She's better off here."

Joaquín pulled away as if he'd been burned. He stared at Isobel, not sure he'd heard her right. Would she leave Aricela with strangers? Here in America?

"You. Out. Let's go!" The driver pointed at Joaquín.

"Isobel, I—"

"Shut up!" she spat. "Leave me alone. I know what I'm doing."

"Okay," he said quietly. *Vaya con Dios.* He touched Isobel lightly on the shoulder and shuffled off the bus with the other men.

They stood for several moments on the hot pavement, blinking in the sunlight. When the bus started to roll by, he glimpsed Isobel's face in the window. She was looking at him now, and he saw in her expression a mixture of pain, regret and gratitude.

With a command shouted in English, a guard herded the weary men through the chain-link passageway into a squat building. They were buzzed through two thick doors and hustled into a holding room lined with low benches. The guard entered last, engaging a heavy door lock that echoed throughout the room. In front of them, a registrar looked up from his computer. He nodded, and the guard began to remove the detainees' shackles, one by one, hanging them on pegs on the wall—a still life of metal; a perverse, frozen waterfall. Once the din of metal subsided, the registrar started calling names. Each detainee was positioned for a mug shot, handed a folded set of scrubs topped with orange flip-flops, and led away.

Once he had been processed, Joaquín was ushered to a small cell, its heavy door sitting open. A table and chair, a metal sink, a toilet, and two bunks—with only the top one neatly made. Clearly, someone was living there, but the cell was empty.

Joaquín unrolled the thin mattress coiled on the bottom bunk, lay down, and fell asleep, his forearm across his eyes.

When he woke, he saw he was not alone. Sitting on the chair, leaning forward and looking at him, was a barrel of a man in blue scrubs, his elbows resting on his knees and his hands clasped loosely in front of him. His pale face was grooved, and the stubble that covered his chin was flecked with gray. His eyes were inquisitive, and not unkind.

"You better wake up if you want to eat," he said. "Speak English?"

Joaquín took a deep breath.

"*No.*"

"*Esta bien. Hablo español...*"

"*¿Hablas ambos?*" You speak both? Joaquín asked. This man easily could have passed for a red-blooded American football coach.

"*Sí.*" The man responded. "*Nací en Veracruz.* I was born in Veracruz. I know I don't look it."

Joaquín sat up and swung his legs to the cement floor. He felt stiff, and he smelled. His mouth tasted like cotton and his head throbbed. He rubbed his temples with his forefingers. "*Mi cabeza...*"

"You're dehydrated. When my last cellmate arrived, he had a headache so bad it made him vomit. If you're gonna vomit, do it over there, okay?" He nodded toward the forlorn toilet in the corner of the cell.

"I'm okay," Joaquín said. "Just need some water."

"C'mon. It's time for chow anyhow. I'll show you the way."

When they walked into the hall, a wave of nausea hit Joaquín and made his knees buckle. "I gotta sit," he said, moving to an empty metal table surrounded by backless stools. Both the table and the stools were welded to the floor. He wrestled his body onto a stool.

"Stay here. I'll get you a tray. Oh, and my name's Turtle."

"Turtle?"

"Yeah, well, my real name's Diego. But I got the name Turtle 'cause I'm a trucker. My wife made it up. She always said I was hard on the outside, soft on the inside." He smiled weakly. "My kids still think it's hilarious."

Joaquín watched as Turtle crossed the long hall and fell in line behind a group of men shuffling toward a window where trays were appearing one by one from a slot in the wall. They moved past a guard who did not look at them.

Turtle reappeared with two trays, one in each hand. Gingerly, he set one down in front of Joaquín, doing his best not to spill the jumbo-size water cup he'd procured.

Joaquín picked up the cup and sipped. He'd been unsure whether he could keep anything down, but the water was cool and sweet. He relaxed and discovered that he was mightily hungry, too. He pulled the tray closer and inspected the food: brown meat in a pool of gravy, spongy white roll, gray peas, and a pile of unnaturally orange macaroni. It was not what he was used to, but it was enough.

"That there," Turtle said, pointing his plastic fork to a cup of unnaturally red Jell-o at the edge of Joaquín's tray, "that's my favorite. If you don't want it, I'll take it."

Joaquín set the cup of Jell-o on Turtle's tray.

"Thanks. Eat up. We got twenty minutes—and the line just took up ten."

Turtle was a talker, and he talked as he ate. "Where you from?" he asked, sopping the gravy up with his roll. Mealtime was clearly the high point of his day.

"Mexico City."

"I don't remember much of Mexico." He shrugged. "Parents brought me here when I was five. Settled in Florida—Sweetwater, just west of Miami. And I've been there for thirty-four years. Got two kids in Sweetwater. Born there." He paused, looking away.

"How'd you end up here?"

"Picked up in Yuma," Turtle said. "It was my own damn fault. Had a big load going to San Diego. Almost made it too. But just before I hit the California line, I ran a yellow, and the cops pulled me over." He paused and stabbed at the macaroni with his fork. "I thought I was just gonna get a ticket. But before they're done writing me up, here comes ICE. That's what they do in Arizona—call ICE as soon as you get pulled over."

Joaquín listened carefully.

"'Course I got no docs. Nothing to show them. So they throw me in the *hielera* where I spend five days—they're not supposed to do that, you know, keep you more than seventy-two hours—and then they bring me here. And now? They're trying to deport me. Me! What am I gonna do in Mexico? I don't know anybody in Mexico. Nobody! My job, my kids, my life—they're all here."

He put down his fork and began picking at his paper napkin, tearing it into small pieces, worrying each piece between his thumb and forefinger. He continued.

"My kids, they're in high school. My wife passed last year, so it's just the three of us now. I usually call 'em every night when I'm on the road, but I couldn't in the cooler—and for five days, they didn't know where I was. My daughter was crazy worried. And I was crazy too. When I finally called them—from here—I told them not to tell *anybody* where I was. Just that I had a long haul, and I was gonna be home soon. They're good kids. They can take care of themselves. But I worry. I worry some-body's gonna find out where I am and yank 'em away from me." Turtle looked down at the shredded napkin, then up at Joaquín. "Sorry, man. Didn't mean to go on like that."

Joaquín nodded. "How long have you been here?"

Turtle mused. "A little longer than two months."

"Jeez. And they've been alone all that time—your kids?"

"Yeah. But what can I do? I'm waiting for my hearing, like every-body else."

Joaquín shuddered at the thought. *They keep you here two months without . . . ?*

When the buzzer sounded, Turtle dumped both trays, and Joaquín followed Turtle into the common area. It was a large, open room with chairs and tables bolted to the floor. Men milled about, some playing dominos, others chatting, some writing letters.

"Not much to do around here," Turtle said. He gestured to several men clustered around a TV mounted high on the wall, each wearing a set of heavy headphones. "You can watch TV, but you gotta pay to listen, and then you gotta watch whatever they put on that day."

They walked a few paces into the room. A man with a shaved head and enormous ears was hunkered down in the corner, together with two other men squatting nearby. As Turtle approached, the shaved head looked up.

"Hey, *Chicano*, you owe me two packs of ramen. Pay up or play." He held out a pair of dice in Turtle's direction.

Turtle swatted the man's head and squatted down. *"No te debo nada,* Chapo. I owe you nothing," he said, taking the dice from the man's hand. "And if I did, I'd never pay you in ramen. Cheetos, maybe. Never ramen."

The man with the shaved head reminded Joaquín of a prize bull—his body thickly rippled with muscle and fat. He eyed Joaquín suspiciously. "Who's the *pendejo*?" he said.

"My new cellie. Just arrived," Turtle said.

The bald man looked up at Joaquín. "You play?"

Joaquín shook his head.

"Whatever. We'll teach you," Chapo said, shrugging. A wooden toothpick appeared at the edge of his mouth. "What's your name?"

"Joaquín."

"Welcome to the Marriott, Joaquín," Chapo said, gesturing up at the double tiers of cells surrounding the common area. "They given you the tour yet? Showers that way, hole that way. That's about all you need to know." Chapo threw the dice against the wall.

Turtle shrugged. "It's not all bad. The basketball court you can use an hour a day. Chapel and visiting room are that way. And library through that door."

"Yah. In case you want to fight your case," Chapo added, a smirk on his face. "How many times you crossed?" He shook the dice hard and threw them again.

"Uh, twice—"

"Twice. Well, that's a felony, bro," Chapo said. "A fe-lo-ny. That means they gonna haul your ass into court. Give you a nice long sentence. And keep you here until you done your time. *Then* they gonna deport you."

Joaquín's eyes widened. He felt as though he were falling into a pit.

Chapo turned to Turtle. "How stupid is this guy?"

Turtle must have noticed Joaquín's despondency because he added, "You can fight it. Go for asylum." He paused.

"How do I do that?"

"You just prove they're gonna kill you if you go back."

"Prove they're gonna kill me?" Joaquín said dully.

"Yeah. Get documents. Something to show you've been marked," Turtle said helpfully.

Joaquín could feel himself becoming dizzy from the absurdity of it all.

"Or maybe you got some other kind of proof," Chapo said.

"Like what?"

"See that *wab* over there?" Chapo gestured in the direction of a skinny teenager pacing the perimeter of the common area. His skin was deep brown with reddish undertones—the color of rawhide. His face was bisected by a flat nose that pointed toward his chin like an arrowhead. Shiny black hair swept across his forehead and hid his eyes. As he walked, he talked to himself, one hand cupped over the other, as if he were praying. "He's goin' for asylum. He's from El Salvador. From what I hear, his mama had a pupusa stand in some shithole town, and a *mafioso* decided to shake her down. Protection money. She paid, big mistake, because he came back over and over. Finally, she had no more money. That's when he grabbed her son off the street—that *wab*—and lopped off his thumb. She found him outside the store with a note pinned to his jacket. *Pago recibido.*"

"Jesucristo," Joaquín said under his breath. He glanced at the boy—who, he realized now, was hiding one hand with the other as he paced.

"She sewed him up and sent him packing. He crossed the river at McAllen and headed straight for *la migra.*" Chapo snickered. "Hands up!" He held up nine fingers.

"By the time he got here," Turtle said, "his hand was black. Lucky he didn't lose more than a thumb. A church group heard about him. Found him a lawyer, and the guy's been working on his case for over a year."

Joaquín's eyes widened.

"Asylum takes time, *pendejo,*" Chapo said.

Joaquín scanned the thick walls. He could feel the claustrophobia setting in. "So, this place . . . is a prison," he said softly.

Chapo moved the toothpick from one side of his mouth to the other with his tongue. "No, *pendejo.* This is not a prison. In a prison, you know when you're getting out."

Part

III

❧

Another Way Home

28

A Way Out

By the third week, Joaquín had begun to recognize the groups. Mexicans, Salvadorans, Hondurans, Guatemalans—the *cholos*, with their elaborate tattoos and hand signals; the *compañeros*, whose leathered skin testified to long hours in the fields; and the *pochos*, living in America but drifting between two cultures. They were the ones who knew how far it was from San Diego to San Jose, from Miami Beach to Disney World. This mix of men, all trying to figure out how to make a life in the United States, or keep it—hopeful, cynical, perplexed, scared, angry, lonely.

It was late in the third week when he first noticed the small, sinewy man sitting on the floor of the common room, legs pulled up in front of him, elbows resting on his knees, head held in his hands. His eyes studied the floor.

"Indígena," Turtle said, spreading dominos on the table. "He doesn't speak Spanish."

"How do you know?" Joaquín asked, helping him turn the dominos face down.

"I asked him for his Jell-O. He just looked at me. I thought he was gonna cry," Turtle said as he shuffled the dominos with the palms of both hands.

Joaquín studied the man for a long moment. He looked spent, as if all the life had been sucked out of him. "Why don't we ask him if he wants to play?"

"Him?" Turtle scoffed. "Nah."

"He might like it," Joaquín said.

"He doesn't exactly look like a barrel of laughs," Turtle said. "Besides, we don't even know if he knows how to play."

To Joaquín, the man's pain was almost palpable. It reminded him of the human husks who inhabited the garbage dump of Ciudad Neza, scrounging for food or drugs among the debris the rest of the world had chucked. When he was a boy walking with his mother past the dump, she would remind him of their humanity. "Don't be afraid of them," she would say. "And if they speak to you, answer them with respect. They are lost, but they are not irredeemable."

"If he doesn't know how to play, we can show him," Joaquín said.

He stood up and picked his way through the bodies over to the *indígena* on the floor. When his feet came into view, the *indígena* looked up. His eyes were sunken and dull, drawn down at the outer edges, and his stubble was raw and unkempt.

"*¿Quieres jugar?*" Wanna play? Joaquín said. He held out his palm and showed the man a domino.

The man didn't look at the domino. His gaze fell to the floor again.

Joaquín squatted in front of him, trying to position his face within the sightline of the man. "*¿Sabes jugar al dominós?*" Do you know how to play dominoes?

The *indígena* looked up again, and it was then that Joaquín noticed the blankness in his eyes. It was as if he were dead. Or didn't care whether he was dead or alive.

"Dominos?" Joaquín said again.

The man's face registered nothing. But when Joaquín did not move, the man finally reached into his shirt pocket and pulled out a small blue card. He offered it to Joaquín.

Joaquín looked at the dog-eared card. He had no idea what it meant. He held up a finger. *"Momento,"* he said, and he walked the card back to Turtle, who had engaged another man in dominoes and was playing his hand with gusto.

"You have any idea what this is?" he said, slipping onto a stool next to Turtle and laying the card next to his dominos.

Turtle took his time playing a domino, poking the corner so that it lined up perfectly with the one next to it on the table. When he was finished, he picked up the card and flipped it over in his hand.

"No wonder nobody talks to him." He handed the card back to Joaquín. "He's *Q'eqchi.* They give these cards to any *wab* who doesn't speak Spanish or English. Supposed to make it easier for the guards to speak to them in their native language. But hasn't been a guard knows *Q'eqchi* in this place in the last fifty years."

"He's—?"

"Mayan. Probably from Izabal. Petén, maybe. Keeps to himself, is all I know."

"How long has he been here, d'ya think?"

"Dunno. Longer than me."

Joaquín fingered the card. Finally, he stood up and picked his way back through the hubbub of the common area. He wanted to return it to the *indígena.* But the man was gone.

The buzz rippled quickly through the common area the next morning. On rounds, a guard had gone up to the *indígena's* cell—the last one on the third tier—and found him in the corner, his eyes lifeless, his skin dusky, his mouth wide open in a silent scream. The guard hadn't known what he was looking at. But when he inserted his finger into the gaping mouth, he felt something soft. Something dark. He reached deeper and hooked his fingernail into the softness. He couldn't get it. He rolled the man onto his back, put one hand under his neck and opened his gullet. He dug his thumb and forefinger deep into the man's throat, stretching the jaw as wide as he could, and pinched the dry softness between his fingertips. Then he tugged. He lost it. He dug deeper and tugged again. Finally, he snagged it and pulled it out—a heavy black sock. It was then that he noticed the man's bare foot.

29
Court

Cardenas, Ayala, Lorta," the guard barked. "Perez and Garcia. Front and center."

Joaquín didn't like this guard. His head was shaped like a torpedo, with hair shaved short except at the top where it stood up like a bristle brush. He had a moustache that ran down both sides of his mouth, and small deep-set eyes. What's more, he was clearly *pocho*, so Americanized that he probably couldn't speak Spanish. So why was he here anyway, on the wrong side?

They were hustled into the processing room. Two other guards watched as they entered.

"Cuffs on."

The detainees looked at each other as they held out their hands, wrists touching. The guards cuffed them, then secured the cuffs to a leather belt around each man's waist.

"What's going on?" Joaquín asked Perez.

"Court," the guard said, looking over his list.

"Why us?" Perez asked.

"It's just your day, buster," the guard replied indifferently. He shackled Joaquín's ankles and attached each cuff to a heavy metal chain running between his feet.

They rode in a white bus without markings for a half hour, silent except for the occasional sound of metal chinking against metal.

Joaquín wished he understood how the system worked. He felt like a tumbleweed in a dust storm, unable to alter its course, at the mercy of powerful and capricious winds blowing across the desert. His only connection to the outside world had been a crackling phone call to his brother on the second day he arrived, and he was afraid if that lifeline snapped, he could be lost in the wasteland of detention forever.

He knew they were approaching a town when the road smoothed and widened into four, then six lanes. Buildings appeared—fast-food restaurants, gas stations, tire shops, grocery stores. Finally, they turned a corner and slowed. The courthouse was everything the detention center wasn't—tall and stately, with marble walls and tinted glass windows, its entryway covered by an arched portico. They passed by the front entrance and pulled up in the alley behind the building.

"Out. Here," the guard said, his hand on his holster.

THEY WERE LED INTO the building, up some stairs, and into a waiting room, shackles clanking against the marble floor. Within a few minutes, a bailiff appeared and ushered them from the waiting room into the courtroom. As they entered, a second bailiff slipped a headset over each detainee's ears. The first six rows in the room were already filled, so they shuffled to seats in the back. Several lawyers sat at wooden tables at the front of the room, casually chatting with each other, their expensive suits in stark contrast to the tired clothing of the detainees. Beyond the men in suits, perched on a platform impossibly far from everyone in the courtroom, was a carved mahogany desk and heavy leather chair, flanked by two United States flags.

"All rise," the bailiff called out.

The judge entered from an invisible door to the left of the platform and lumbered up the steps to the bench. He was a walrus of a man, his jowls heavy, his eyes puffy, his body shrouded in black robes. He settled himself in the leather chair, took off his glasses, and rubbed them with a small cloth.

"Be seated," the bailiff said.

Chains clattered as the detainees took their seats.

The judge arranged some papers on the desk, taking his time as if no one else were in the courtroom. Finally, he nodded at one of the attorneys.

With an unmistakable gesture, the attorney signaled to the front row of detainees, who stood up in unison and filed to the railing.

"Good afternoon, ladies and gentlemen," the judge began, perusing the courtroom. A court reporter and an interpreter sat to the side of the bench. A handful of observers watched from the gallery at the back of the room.

Joaquín's earphones leaped into life. *"Buenas tardes, damas y caballeros,"* a female voice said in his ear.

"Addressing myself to the defendants, you have each been charged with the misdemeanor offense of improper entry of an alien, which carries a sentence of five thousand dollars and six months. You have also been charged with the felony offense of illegal reentry after removal. This carries a sentence of two years in federal prison and can extend up to twenty years if you have a criminal record. Do you understand the charges?"

It took a few moments for the translation to reach the ears of the detainees at the railing, but once it did, they nodded in unison.

Joaquín snapped to attention. *This court can throw people in prison for years?* He glanced down his row to see if any of the others had caught that detail, but he didn't know these men well, and no one glanced back.

The judge singled out the first detainee at the balustrade, fixing his eyes on him. "Mr. Flores-Gomez, I understand you are not a US citizen, and that you entered the US through the southern Arizona border without inspection at a US port of entry. And that after being removed, you reentered the US through the same border this past June. How do you plead to this felony charge of illegal entry: guilty or not guilty?"

The lawyer behind him whispered something in the man's ear.

After a moment of silence, the man replied in English. "Guilty."

"Mr. Flores, we need your answer in Spanish, please," the judge said.

"Culpable," he said.

"Thank you, Mr. Flores. Given your cooperation in this matter, you are sentenced to one year, followed by removal. You will receive credit for time served."

A pit opened in Joaquín's stomach. Could they do this to him?

The judge went down the line of bedraggled detainees one by one. Each detainee was addressed by name, and each person replied *"Culpable."*

"Why are they all pleading guilty?" Joaquín whispered to the man sitting next to him. "They must have reasons for being here."

"That judge—he don't want to know," the man replied quietly.

Joaquín's heart beat against his chest. He felt dizzy and weak. The room closed in on him as the past months flashed through his brain— two chancy crossings, a perilous trek through the desert, the corpse behind the boulder, Fernando's craziness at the cattle trough, Isobel's panic in the holding pen, her small daughter disappearing into the dark corridor. *Has it all been for nothing?*

There was a ruckus at the front of the room.

"Counsel," the judge growled. His thick eyebrows closed in over his nose. "You've been admonished before. This man appears to understand neither English nor Spanish."

"Yes, your honor." Flustered, the attorney glanced at the interpreter, who looked back at him and shrugged. He flipped through some papers on a clipboard. Then he pulled the man away from the railing and led him over to the bailiff, who ushered him out the door.

"Where're they taking him?" Joaquín whispered.

"They can't try him 'cause he don't understand the language," the man replied.

"So he's going back to detention?"

"Maybe. Or they'll find somebody to interpret—a relative, maybe. If they do that, they'll send him home with the relative, give him a court date, and hope he'll learn a little English before he shows up again."

"They do that?"

"They don't care. They don't want to deal with him."

The judge continued to address each detainee in turn. Once he'd finished, the row shuffled toward the bailiff, and the next row stood and filed to the railing.

"Addressing myself to the defendants. . ." the judge began again in a monotone.

Joaquín felt raw desperation driving its way upward from his gut. He took several deep breaths and tried to calm himself. He looked around the court, at the back of the row in front of him. Two rows remained before his would be called.

And then it came to him.

He pulled against the metal that shackled his cuffs to the chain around his waist and inched his index finger into his front pant pocket. It was still there—the paper the *indígena* had given him. He fished at it desperately, sitting up straighter and straighter until the man next to him looked at him quizzically. Finally, it loosened, and he slipped it from his pocket. It was bent and torn at the edge, but it hung on his index finger like a tiny flag. He looked up.

The bailiff was staring at him suspiciously. He turned in his seat and glanced down at the paper and up at the bailiff again. The bailiff sauntered over, stood behind him, reached over his shoulder and picked the paper off his finger, spreading it out in the palm of his hand: *I speak Q'eqchí.*

The bailiff glanced at Joaquín, frowned, and looked down at the paper again. Joaquín realized the man next to him was watching the drama play out from the corner of his eye. In the moment when the bailiff looked away, Joaquín flashed his seatmate a look begging for silence. The man turned his gaze to the judge at the front of the room, his eyes glazed.

The bailiff poked Joaquín on the shoulder and moved away. At the door, he turned and beckoned.

Joaquín rose, making as little noise as possible, and followed the bailiff out the door. He wanted to turn and take one last glance to the man who sat next to him, a glance of gratitude, but he didn't dare.

AFTER SOME PAPERWORK, WHICH Joaquín and the foreigner signed even though neither could read English, they were divested of their shackles, loaded into a van, and driven to a small, seedy Greyhound bus station twenty minutes from the courthouse. By the time they pulled up, the late afternoon light was fast fading. The driver stopped at the entrance, hopped out, and opened the sliding door of the van.

"*Vámonos,*" he said with little inflection in his voice.

As they climbed out, the driver rifled through a satchel in the front seat. He pulled out two envelopes and handed one to each of them. Then he hoisted himself into the driver's seat, slammed the door, and pulled away.

Joaquín looked down at the envelope. The top flap had been tucked into the back. He pulled at it. Inside were official-looking papers, printed in English, together with a laminated card and a black marker.

Joaquín was stunned at how fast it had all happened. When the bailiffs realized they'd hauled into the courtroom two un-prosecutable grunts with the detainees of the day, they were annoyed. And so they'd processed the paperwork for these two insignificant fish without fanfare. They just wanted them out of sight, out of mind, out of town.

As Joaquín and the foreigner stood on the curb next to the bus station, envelopes in hand, wondering what to do, a skinny young *gringo* with paper-white skin, scraggly beard, and long hair eyed them, then approached. He wore a torn red T-shirt and baggy shorts. A tattered clipboard was tucked beneath one arm.

"*¿Buscan ayuda?*" Need help? he said in perfect Spanish. His eyes were a piercing crystal blue.

Joaquín looked at him suspiciously. Across his T-shirt were the words *No Más Muertes*.

The skinny young *gringo* saw him staring at the shirt. "No More Deaths," he said, pulling the shirt taut from the hem. "You heard of us?"

Joaquín nodded tentatively. These were the people who put water in the desert.

The young man turned to the foreigner. "*¿Habla español?*"

The man remained silent.

The young man perused the foreigner and then said something in a language Joaquín had never heard.

The foreigner looked up in surprise. Then he responded in kind.

"You speak his language?" Joaquín asked.

"He's Mam. I could tell. I spent a summer in Huehuetenango. Don't speak it well, but I can get by."

Joaquín shook his head and cracked a small smile.

"Court doesn't explain much," the young man said, pointing to the papers in Joaquín's hand.

Joaquín drew in a deep breath and nodded.

They sat in turquoise plastic chairs, and the young man pulled out the papers from Joaquín's envelope and spread them on his lap.

"This bus voucher, this'll get you a ticket over there," he said, nodding at a counter window where a ticket agent with a green visor sat tapping on a computer keyboard. "Wherever you need to go. And this," he continued, holding up a green paper, "is a court order. Says you need to check in with the court once you get to wherever you're going. Says you need to give 'em an address. The deadline's here." He pointed to a date on the paper.

Then he turned and looked at Joaquín directly. "You're Mexican, right?"

"Yeah."

He paused. Joaquín could tell he was pondering something. "Look," he said finally. "I'm gonna tell you something straight. *He* should report to the court," he said, gesturing toward the Mam. "He might have an asylum case, if he can back up his stories."

"Yeah, I'm gonna go for asylum too. It was bad—"

"But you," he interrupted, "they're never gonna give you asylum. They don't give asylum to Mexicans. Ever. So, between you and me, I'd think twice about doing what this paper says. You don't want to get sucked back into the system."

Joaquín listened, motionless.

"'Course, I never told you that, right?"

Joaquín nodded.

"And this"—he held up a laminated card—"this says, *I don't speak English. Can you help me get to —.* You fill in the blank and carry it with you. Show it when you need to. The farther away you get from here, the more likely you'll find people who'll help. Where are you headed, anyway?"

"Pescadero." Just saying the word made Joaquín's heart leap. He was near, now.

"Where's that?"

"California. Near San Francisco. On the coast."

The young man took the card and wrote the town's name on the card, adding *San Francisco* in parentheses. He exchanged a few words with the Mam, took his card and wrote *New Jersey* on it. "Look," he said, "you can get a bus going west this evening. But this guy's gonna have to wait until morning." He exchanged a few more words with the Mam, and they both rose. "He can stay at our shelter tonight. Let me help you get that ticket before we go. And, oh yeah, you need money for food." He handed Joaquín a twenty-dollar bill.

"*Gracias,*" Joaquín said softly. He'd never held a US bill before. It was beautiful.

The skinny young man and the foreigner drove off in a faded VW bus. Joaquín stood in the bus station, ticket in hand, wondering how to make time pass faster. It would be an hour before the bus appeared, and the anticipation he felt for seeing his brother was almost unendurable.

Suddenly, he realized how hungry he was. Across the street, at the other end of an enormous parking lot, he spotted a Walmart. The store was decked in Christmas lights, which cut through the dusk and made the place glow like a jewel. Inflatable snowmen and life-size reindeer lit from within flanked the entrance. He headed for those lights, making a mental note to remember this exquisite moment—his first, unimpeded steps in the United States—and to share it with Gabe.

As he reached the entrance, the doors slid open and the aroma of ground beef and onions hit him, causing his body to tremble. A MacDonalds, tucked just inside. *Eating American food, bought with American money, in an American store—what could be better?*

Twenty minutes later, he was leaning against a lamppost in the darkened parking lot, unwrapping a juicy burger. He took a big bite. The taste in his mouth, and the satisfaction of the moment, brought tears to his eyes.

He was almost finished when he noticed a battered delivery truck turn in to the far end of the parking lot. It lumbered toward him, and as it passed, it slowed and a shadowy figure in the front passenger seat leaned forward and looked out the driver-side window. The vehicle headed around the side of the building and disappeared into the shadows.

In a few moments, from the darkness came a small flood of people hoisting backpacks onto their shoulders and looking around warily. In a flash, Joaquín knew what he was seeing: it was a drop of human cargo in the Walmart parking lot. And what a place for a drop—bathrooms, food, clothing, money-wiring services, and it stayed open late. He remembered, when he forked over the cash for passage back at the border, that was where they said they'd be doing the drop—at a Walmart in Tucson. He stood under the light, sandwich poised in one hand, feeling empathy for these travelers. And then, his throat began to tighten. Was *this* the Walmart *he* was supposed—?

"Amiiigo." A raspy voice came from the darkness. "We have been looking for you."

Joaquín jumped, the remains of the burger falling to the asphalt. The face was so close he could smell the breath. And below the right eye, that tat—two teardrops.

The man grabbed Joaquín's wrist and tightened down on it like a steel vice.

"We couldn't find you," he growled. "We thought you were dead. But no! Here you are!" He began to torque Joaquín's wrist, causing Joaquín to wince in pain. "And I never forget a face. Especially one that owes me money."

Anger shot through Joaquín. *This scum, this cerote, who vanished into the washes like a snake when la migra showed up, is gonna shake me down for payment? Now?*

"Fuck you," Joaquín growled.

"Hey, what's your problem? You made it here, *hermano*," the coyote said, shrugging dramatically. "Better late than never, right?" He scanned the bushes behind Joaquín. "Where's your friend?"

"None of your fucking business." Joaquín wrenched his wrist from the man's grasp.

"Oh, but it is my business. He owes me, too. You both need to pay. ¿Lo entiendes?"

Joaquín's rage made him speechless. And so, he spat into the coyote's face.

At that moment, two police cars rounded the corner and sped into the parking lot, lights sweeping the dark, sirens blaring. The coyote grabbed Joaquín's throat with one hand, tightened around it mercilessly, and push him into the shadowy bushes at the edge of the parking lot. A bowie knife appeared in the coyote's other hand. Time slowed.

"You owe me, *canalla*. You owe me three thousand dollars. For you and your buddy," he said. The knife point traced its way slowly over Joaquín's jawbone, past the corner of his mouth, lodging delicately in one of his nostrils. "I'll be here tomorrow night. To collect. And please don't make it any harder than it needs to be. We all have eyes on you." He flicked his wrist, and Joaquín felt a searing pain in the fleshy part of his left nostril. "That's so we remember what you look like."

He gave Joaquín a final shove and disappeared into the darkness.

Joaquín lay writhing in the bushes for several seconds, unable to catch his breath, his windpipe crushed, his nostril on fire. After a mighty gasp, his throat opened, and night air filled his lungs. For several minutes more, he lay cradled by the bushes, wracked with coughing. When the fit finally subsided, he staggered to his feet, cupping his nose in his hands. Warm blood dripped through his fingers. He looked around, but the delivery truck had vanished, and the police cars had disappeared. The parking lot was silent, save for some Christmas music wafting from the interior of the Walmart. A mother and her young son emerged from the store and headed to their car, the child skimming along on a shopping cart filled with goodies.

Joaquín stood for several moments on unsteady legs. When he could walk again, he headed toward the bus depot, craning his neck forward so the blood from his nose dripped in front of him rather than on his shirt. He passed through a gas station where he grabbed a handful of paper towels from the dispenser near the pumps and held them to his nose. He could feel the warmth as he bled through the towels. He entered the bus depot from the rear and saw a bus idling in the parking bay. He hesitated for a moment.

The ticket agent with the green visor glanced up from his computer. When he saw the bloody paper towel, he stopped what he was doing, leaned back, and looked carefully at Joaquín's face.

"*Qué te pasó en la nariz?*" What happened to your nose? he said in perfect Spanish, though he looked like a *gringo*.

"*¿Es ese el bus a San Francisco?*" Is that the bus to San Francisco? Joaquín replied, ignoring the question. He wanted nothing more than to get on that bus.

"*Sí,* but—is that your final destination?"

Joaquín wavered. He felt faint.

"Let's make sure you get to where you need to go." He held out his hand.

Joaquín produced the ticket he'd purchased an hour earlier. His nose was throbbing badly.

"Pescadero, huh? Where's that, exactly?

"On the coast. West of San Francisco," Joaquín managed to say.

The agent handed him back the ticket. "That's your bus then," he said indifferently.

Joaquín retrieved the ticket, crossed the waiting room as quickly as his wobbly legs would carry him, and boarded the bus. He took a seat in the last row, scrunching low to keep his face in shadow.

The agent watched as the bus pulled away from the platform. Then he turned and picked up his cell phone.

30

Posada

To Hilde, Christmas had always been magical. She would spend hours making gifts—hand-knit scarves, clay-fired dishes, bourbon-soaked fruitcakes—wrapping the packages carefully and trimming them with yards of ribbon fashioned into rosettes or curls or puffs. She would squirrel them away in the back of her closet until the big day. The pleasure of Christmas, for her, was mostly in the anticipation of family opening the gifts she'd gathered or made for them.

But this year, things felt different. There had been little discussion of the upcoming holiday throughout the early weeks of December, and her own anticipation was flagging. She had a hard time imagining Christmas morning without her father, and her mother seemed so distracted that Hilde wondered whether she was even tracking the date.

Finally, two days before the holiday, her mother arrived home with a tree in the back of the pickup. She hauled it into the house and set it up in the corner of the front room. It was a small, scrawny pine, held up by two flat pieces of wood nailed crosswise to the trunk, but still, it filled the front room with the unmistakable sharp scent of the holiday.

"How are we going to decorate it?" Hilde asked, examining a bald spot among the branches. She reached between the prickly branches, found the trunk, and twisted it until the spot faced the wall.

"I'm putting you in charge, honey," her mother said, pulling a twenty-dollar bill from her wallet. "Here. Take this and see what you can find in town for ornaments tomorrow."

On Christmas Eve day, Hilde took the money to the thrift store and found a small collection of ornaments in the shape of Peanuts cartoon characters. She bought them, together with a string of multicolored tree lights. When she got home late in the afternoon, she found her mother dressing for dinner. She had laid out several bags of pre-popped popcorn and cranberries, along with some heavy twine and a thick needle.

"Ethan's working late, and Mr. Booher wants me to join him for dinner tonight," she called from the bedroom. She emerged in flowy pants, a scoop-neck top, and earrings that looked like tree ornaments. "His brother's in town—here for the fishing trip, and I just couldn't say no." She grabbed her purse and jacket. "You don't mind, do you, sweetie? You're so good at this kind of thing. I know whatever you'll do will be stunning." She swept out the door, leaving behind the scent of Evening in Paris.

Hilde spent a half hour stringing the cranberries and popcorn and hanging ornaments on the tree. To fill the room, she turned on the radio and cranked up the Christmas music. But it didn't help. *Everything is fractured. Everyone is lost,* she kept thinking. She could feel darkness seep into her soul, weighing her down so heavy it scared her. The simple task of trimming the tree seemed both too difficult and too pointless to finish. Finally, she put on her parka, poured herself a bowl of cereal, and ate supper on the front porch.

Dense gray clouds were rolling in from the west. For a good fifteen minutes, she watched as wind caught the dead leaves on the street and whipped them into loopy arcs. As the gusts increased, treetops began to dip and bend. She drew her parka around her as she felt the first heavy drops of rain hit her face.

She was sitting in the dark, her cereal bowl empty on her lap, when a procession of people rounded the corner of the elementary school and began moving slowly up the road. There must have been twenty or thirty of them—many with flashlights, a few with candles. They stopped at the first house they came to, surrounded the tiny porch, and began to sing, a single guitar accompanying them. Soon a light from the interior spilled through the doorway, and a couple emerged. The woman offered something in a large basket. They crowded around the basket, then turned and continued up the street.

Hilde watched as they came closer. She recognized the guitarist as one of the farmworkers from La Sala. Alejandro was his name, and when he played, his guitar sounded like poetry.

In front of him, leading the procession were a girl and boy, obviously dressed as Biblical figures. The girl was in a blue robe, too young to be pregnant but with a bulging belly nonetheless. The boy moved alongside her with the help of a shepherd's staff. Several younger children, angels with cardboard wings and tinfoil halos, surrounded them. As they approached, Hilde heard their voices. They sang first in Spanish, then in English.

> *En el nombre del cielo*
> *os pido posada*
> *pues no puede andar*
> *mi esposa amada.*

> *In the name of heaven*
> *Can you give us lodging?*
> *My sweet wife is so weary*
> *After hours of walking.*

They stopped at the home across the street from Hilde's and continued to sing, flashlights illuminating their faces. Again, they were met by a couple, the woman offering treats. Hilde didn't know what it all meant, but it was surely more appealing than sitting on the front room alone staring at the street. She set down her bowl, flipped up her hood, and melted into the procession as it headed up the street.

By the time the little parade reached the white church where the road bent and led into town, the rain was heavy and relentless. Everyone was soaked, their clothes sticking to their bodies, their candles snuffed out. Alejandro had stopped playing and was stuffing his guitar into his rubber poncho. Only the flashlights lit the way. Yet the revelers seemed unfazed.

Nan stood at the door of the church, handing out paper towels.

"Come in, everybody. Woo! Is it wet!"

The revelers wiped their faces and hands with the paper towels, dropped the dead candles in the trash, and moved into the sanctuary, dripping rainwater everywhere. Despite the cold, people were energized, and the room was filled with chatter.

Nan's face broke wide when she saw Hilde step through the church's old wooden doors. "Girl, you are clearly drowned. Come in and warm up. And take a seat in front. I want you to see everything."

Stealing up the side aisle, Hilde took a spot in the corner near an old upright piano. She watched as people found their places, reaching over one another to shake a hand or bump a shoulder. The children from the parade assembled at the front and gazed out shyly at the congregation, the little ones dressed as angels fidgeting in the front row.

When the sanctuary was almost full, a man with bottle-bottom glasses rose from his pew and moved toward the piano. His fingers fumbled on the keyboard, found their place, and rested there. As he did, a young mother sitting in the first row passed her toddler to another woman, rose, and stood beside the sodden angels, who had become part of a live tableau of the nativity scene. In a voice as clear as water, she began to sing without accompaniment. The room went silent.

O come, O come, Emmanuel
And ransom captive Israel,
That mourns in lonely exile here . . .

The dark and delicate carol filled the room as the pianist began to lay quiet chords beneath the young mother's voice. When the last chord dissolved into the humid air, nothing could be heard but rain pounding the roof. Then the room exploded in raucous applause and foot stomping.

This was nothing like church in Wisconsin. No parade of well-dressed parishioners nodding at one another as they took their seats in the pews. No tuneless hymns, no droning sermons, no mumbling prayers. The pleasure and downright joy Hilde saw on the faces of the people in *these* pews—a motley group of very wet worshippers—seeped into her soul like water into dry soil. It was as though she had stepped into a new world, an expansive space where people showed up in dripping rain gear, muddy boots, goofy Christmas ski hats—and it didn't matter. She breathed deeper than she'd breathed in months.

No one stayed long after the service. Instead, they gathered their coats and scarves, pulled their hats low on their heads, flicked on their flashlights, and headed out again into the driving rain, singing as they paraded through the town.

Hilde let herself be buoyed along the route, not knowing where the group was headed. As they passed the deli, she caught a glimpse of Ethan wiping down a table near the window. The sight of him scrubbing the laminated tabletop—on this night of all nights—caused a familiar rush of pain that ambushed her in the middle of a carol. She pressed the heels of her hands to her eyes. Everyone's face was wet with rain, and so she let her tears flow, remembering what Nan had said: *Let your heart break. Let it crack open. And trust that over time it will heal. Because when it does, you will find yourself a different person.*

The parade passed beneath the town's one stoplight. When the revelers reached the white clapboard porch of the community center with its windows glowing in the dark, they pushed the costumed Mary and Joseph to the front of the procession and began to sing that special song again. This time the doors flung open, and the crowd inside cheered and invited them in. They scrambled up the steps, chortling and greeting one another as they shed their wet coats and muddy shoes in the hall's cloakroom.

Hilde followed, blending in as best she could. She wriggled out of her coat and boots and shook the water from her hair. When she stepped into the big room, she saw that it was festooned with colored lights and tissue-paper flags. Tables near the kitchen were piled with serving platters of food, and a showy seven-pointed pinata swung from a ceiling rafter. The aroma of chili and cinnamon permeated the air.

"Los tamales están calientes." The tamales are hot, one woman called from the kitchen area. "Get over here, everyone!"

Hilde dried her face on her sleeve and shuffled forward together with the others.

31
Arrival

Twenty minutes after the last reveler headed home, ten minutes after the janitor put out the last trash bag and locked the doors of the community center, a bus pulled into town. It paused at the intersection of the two main roads. A single figure stepped into the muddy street, his boots splashing rainwater onto his pants. He stood under the stoplight as the bus barreled away, his nose swaddled in a makeshift bandage patched from a paper towel.

32

Christmas

The dull dawn seeped through Hilde's bedroom window on Christmas morning. She opened her eyes and lay still for several minutes, listening to the rustling of the animals in the barn. They would need to be tended to, and Gabe wasn't coming today. She swung her feet over the edge of the bed, pulled on jeans and a sweatshirt, and headed for the back door. There was no stirring from the other bedrooms. The house was dead.

It was good to be in the barn, to feel the goats' eagerness as they sniffed for their feed. When she finished the chores, she stood for a moment looking back at the house. Still no sounds. She stowed the rake, closed the gate, and tiptoed back inside. On a scrap of paper from the kitchen drawer, she wrote, *Gone for a walk. Back soon.* She left it on the table.

She walked through the morning fog, her hands jammed in her pockets. At first it felt fine to be alone with the rhythm of her steps. But she did feel a niggling guilt, leaving that note. *What kind of girl takes a walk on Christmas morning. Should I be home, trying to make like things are fine? Like we're a family? I'm tired of jollying up everyone else.*

She wasn't sure where she was going, but she soon found herself in front of Nan's cottage. Since it was not yet eight, she was surprised to see lights ablaze inside. She stood for several moments, then approached and stepped onto the porch. The boards creaked under her weight. She was about to knock when Nan opened the door.

"I thought I heard somebody out here," Nan said, filling up the doorway. She wore oversized flannel pajamas, and she was holding a glass of orange juice. "Look at you! You're already up and dressed. Have you had breakfast?"

Pima peered around the kitchen corner, spatula in hand. "Oh, hallelujah. Company! Nan made way too much batter," she said, holding up a glass measuring cup of butter-colored liquid. The smell of bacon, mixed with syrup and orange juice, and spiced with the piquant scent from the spruce tree by the fireplace, was exactly what Hilde needed, though she couldn't have said so when she set out from home. She bent down, took off her muddy boots, and padded into the room. Toby, who was stretched out on the couch, lifted his head and flopped his tail when he saw her.

Nan asked no questions, and Hilde offered no explanation for why she had shown up on Christmas morning like a stray. It felt like some kind of grace—this gracious, no-questions-asked hospitality—and it made Hilde wonder how Nan had learned what she knew. Had *she* been raised in a family where she felt miscast, mismatched? Had *she* found it necessary to choose between having a life and having a family? And if so, did she regret her choices?

After breakfast, Hilde watched as Nan and Pima opened the few sparse presents scattered under the tree. Nan gave Pima a pair of waders made of olive-green rubber. Pima gave Nan a new ladle for her water bucket. The rest of the presents went to Toby, who eyed each indifferently—a bottle of dog shampoo, a retractable leash—until Pima dug out his "big" present, a bunch of rawhide chews packed in a tin decorated with reindeer. For that, he roused himself and ambled over for a chew.

He had just settled down when they heard a knock at the door.

A man in his twenties, compact and wiry, stood on the porch, grinning broadly. He was holding a stack of neatly folded blankets.

"Jorge. *¡Hola!* Come in." Nan said.

Hilde recognized the man. He'd been coming to La Sala for the past few weeks, mostly looking for work. Nan had fed him, given him a bike and some blankets, and had introduced him to the others, always ending with "and if you know of any work..."

"*Gracias, señora,* but I cannot come in today." His eyes sparkled. "I got a job at the mushroom farm. And today I have overtime."

"Good news!"

"I came to say *¡Feliz Navidad!*" He said the words with gusto. "And to return your blankets. Today I move into a trailer on the ranch. No more camping under the bridge."

"*Gracias a Dios,*" Pima said, wiping her hands on a dishtowel as she came to the door. "That bridge is tough in winter."

He set the blankets on a chair.

"You sure you don't need them? We have plenty," Nan said.

"No, *señora.* They give us sleeping bags."

There was a scraping sound on the porch. Jorge glanced toward the noise and nodded.

"Last night," he began, beckoning in the direction of the noise. A face appeared behind Jorge's shoulder, a makeshift bandage on his nose. "Last night, this guy showed up at the bridge." He stepped aside and muscled the man until he stood in front of Nan. "He's looking for his brother. I told him maybe you could help."

It didn't take Nan long to figure out who he was. She spoke to him in rapid Spanish, and while Hilde could understand none of it, she could see his rising excitement as Nan responded. "*Sí, sí. Lo conozco. Sí, sé donde vive.*"

"Okay, then. Let's go," Nan said in English, turning to Pima. Pima started to gather up coats and car keys. Nan turned to Hilde. "Do you know who this is?" She pulled the stranger gently into the room. "This is Gabe's brother. Joaquín.

Hilde stared into Joaquín's face. Despite the makeshift bandage, she could see the resemblance. He was smaller and thinner than Gabe, but he had Gabe's dark eyes and that shiny hair that fell over one eye.

Nan touched Joaquín's forearm. "And we're gonna take him up to find Gabe. Want to come?"

They piled into Pima's Chevy, a low, wide-bodied boat of a car whose original brown finish had been eaten away by the salt air. Pima and Nan sat in front, Hilde and Joaquín in back. Nan had thrown on a coat, and as they headed up the road, Hilde noticed Nan's pajamas sticking above the collar.

Halfway up the hill, Hilde glanced furtively at Joaquín. He was looking through the front window, anticipation in his face. *This is the guy,* Hilde thought, *this is the guy Gabe worked so hard to help. This is the guy Gabe wired money to whenever he got paid. And now—finally—he's here. How far has he come? Where has he been?* She glanced at him again. He was looking out the window now, his right leg bouncing nervously.

At the top of the hill, they turned off the pavement and traveled for several minutes over a farm road, nothing more than two mud-packed ruts separated by a strip of high grass. The car twisted through fields and around battered outbuildings, jostling everyone so much that Hilde had to brace herself against the roof. Finally, the road dead-ended in a semicircle of asphalt and matted vegetation. A lone trailer sat at the far end of the asphalt. Water and salt stains ran down its corrugated sides. One of the windows had been broken out, and a piece of cardboard was taped over it. Pima cut the motor and they all got out.

It was quiet on the hill. The only sign of life were two turkey vultures soaring lazily against a blue sky.

Nan approached the trailer. The wooden steps that led from the ground to its door were flanked by a banister that wobbled fiercely when she grabbed it.

"Hilde, give me a hand here," Nan said. "Hold this thing steady and let me see if anyone's home."

Hilde braced her body against the railing and watched Nan climb the steps.

She knocked on the door. *"¡Hola!"* she called. "Anybody home?"

No answer.

After a few seconds, she twisted the door handle. It was unlocked. She pushed the door open, and Hilde could see into the trailer. There were several sleeping bags on the floor, a lantern, a small stove, and the bottom half of a watercooler in the corner. From the ceiling dangled an extension cord with at least half a dozen plugs attached. It looked dangerous.

"Nope," Nan said, turning back toward Hilde. Her eyes flicked over Hilde's shoulder, and she began a slow grin. "Ah. There he is."

They turned, and Hilde saw Gabe trudging back to the trailer, eyes downcast, an enormous jug of water perched on his shoulder.

Joaquín, who was standing by the stairs, let out a whoop and began running toward his brother. The sound made Gabe look up. He stopped, his mouth agape. It was clear he was trying to see who it was running toward him. Suddenly, he slung the water jug to the ground and began to run.

They met in the middle. Gabe threw his arms around his brother, grinning madly and pounding him on the back. Gabe grabbed his brother's shoulders, pushed him back and looked at him, as if to make sure he saw what he saw. Then he wrapped an arm around Joaquín's neck and wrestled with him, hollering and laughing.

Hilde watched them both, a half-smile pasted on her face. She was happy for Gabe, happy that his brother had made it. But inside she felt a hole open in her heart, a wound from which deep sorrow spread, touching her skin from the inside out. Their bond was so strong, so deep. And she was adrift and alone.

"I think our job is done here," Nan said, coming up behind her. "Let's let these guys catch up." The brothers walked toward them, arms over each other's shoulders, both beaming. "Gabe, bring this guy to town tomorrow. Let's introduce him around."

"*Sí, señora. Gracias!* Thank you! Thanks for bringing him home!"

"I only brought him up Bean Hollow Road. He brought himself the rest of the way. I'm sure he has plenty to tell you, so we'll leave you to it."

As the car headed back down the rutted road, Hilde saw Joaquín grab his brother, kick his foot out from beneath him, and wrestle him to the ground. They were both laughing and gasping for air.

"Where have you been?" Janine said, thoroughly annoyed. She was sitting at the kitchen table, gripping a mug between her hands. "It's past noon."

Hilde looked around the room. It was empty.

"Where's Ethan?"

"He's out looking for you."

"Sorry. Nobody was up. I went for a walk."

Her mother waited for a better explanation, her lips pursed.

"Really. I went for a walk." When she sensed her mother's suspicion, she added, "And when I went by the pastor's house, she saw me and invited me in. For breakfast."

Janine face turned from suspicion to disgust. "And you did what?"

"I said yes. To the pastor. I went in."

Janine's grip on the mug tightened. "The pastor," she said, her mouth turning down in disgust. "The one with the *girlfriend.*"

Hilde stiffened. There was a time when she would have shrunk from her mother's glare, but this time what she felt was a growing heat in her gut. "Actually, Mom, that's her wife. They're married."

Janine's hands flew up in the air. "Oh, and that's better?" She said, her eyes blazing. "Good God, Hilde. First, you invite the farmhand to dinner. Then you take up with a pair of—" She stopped herself. "Jeez! I don't know why I thought California was a good idea."

"A pair of what, Mom? A pair of what?" Hilde said, fixating on the words her mother did not say. She could feel the heat move up into her face.

"Honey—"

"*Dykes*, Mom? Is that what you're gonna say? Dykes?"

"Hilde—"

"They're *gay*, Mom. They're a *gay couple*. And so what?"

"I just don't want you to—"

"It's not catching. Mom! Why do you always think the worst of people?"

Janine stopped and stared at her daughter. Then she stood up, slamming the mug onto the table. "Jesus Christ, Hilde! Haven't I got enough on my plate? Haven't I?" Tears sprang into Janine's eyes. She grabbed the mug and turned toward the sink.

Hilde had never seen her mother cry. It both shocked and pained her. Her mother had always been the tough one, but now she looked haggard and beaten. What was this?

What she wanted to say was, *Mom, they take care of each other. They're a family. They're what family does.* But she couldn't. She didn't want to hurt her mother anymore. What she did say, very gently, was "Mom, really. I'm okay."

33
Dots

The rain began again on Christmas night. It blustered in from the coast in frigid sheets of water. It soaked the streets and swept through the town, bashing into the Coast Range and doubling back on itself. Every leaf, every rock, every tree on the hills above town gathered the wet from the wind and returned it so that it flowed back from the hillcrests and rocky outcroppings in rivulets, streams, cascades, waterfalls, and rivers, into the town and surrounding fields. The marshes filled, the fields flooded, and the rows of dark, rich earth disappeared in puddles that ran together into pools, the pools into ponds, the ponds into lakes.

By the time Hilde awoke on the following morning, she could see the creek across the road had risen so high and gained such fury that it dislodged branches the size of a grown man's leg. The power of the water caused the limbs to dance crazily as they careened down the banks to the ocean. Mesmerized by it all, Hilde dressed quickly and headed toward the bridge. She knew farmworkers lived beneath the bridge, and she worried that she might find someone in trouble. But when she reached the bridge, she saw no one. She sat down on the bank and watched as the branches cracked against the cement pilings, the foliage disappearing under the roiling waters.

How bad must it be that people prefer living under a bridge in winter to living where they were born, where they grew up?

She stood up. Perhaps those guys had gone to the church to get out of the rain. Turning away from the creek, she picked her way up the slope, flipped up the hood of her parka, and headed for the church.

A minute later, a large tree limb tumbling through the water caught at the mouth of the bridge and stuck.

She was drenched by the time she arrived, her boots squeaking as she mounted the steps to fellowship hall. Through the window, she could see Nan and Pima inside setting up tables. One of the cooks had shown up, too, and looked to be chopping onions. The rest of the room was empty.

"Oh, so glad you're here!" Nan exclaimed as Hilde pulled the door open. "We could use some help. Weather's getting worse. I expect we'll see quite a few folks today."

Hilde peeled off her heavy jacket and hung it on the hook next to the door. It began a steady drip onto the floor.

Nan was right. Over the next half hour, several familiar faces appeared at the door. They hung up their sodden jackets and lined up their boots near the potbelly stove to dry out. Standing in stockinged feet, they filled their plates with beans.

It was midmorning when Gabriel appeared with his brother. The mud that clung to their boots was so heavy that Hilde saw Joaquín stumble as he mounted the steps.

Nan's eyebrows shot up when she saw them. "How in the world did you get here?"

"We walked," Gabe said, stepping out of his boots and over the door sill. Water was trickling down his face, dropping from his nose to the floor.

"All that way? How long did it take?"

"Couple hours. It was not so bad—slippery on the way down." Gabe looked bedraggled, but he managed a smile. "My brother, he's worried—and he wants to know if you can help."

Nan turned to Joaquín. *"Podemos sentarnos y hablar.* Please come in. Let's get you something hot to drink. Hilde, get Gabe and his brother some hot coffee, will you?"

They sat at a table in the corner of the room, Gabe and Joaquín on one side, Nan on the other.

"Sit with us, Hilde. You don't mind, do you, Gabe?" Nan said.

"No, *señora*. She's family to me."

Hilde felt a rush of warmth inside her. Was she? She hoped so. She slid onto the bench beside Nan.

"Please," Nan said, turning her clear blue eyes on Joaquín.

Joaquín wrung his hands. He was silent for several moments, as if trying to figure out where to start. He looked at the ceiling, glanced at Nan, then looked down at his hands.

Gabe gave him a light bump with his shoulder. *"Puedes confiar en ella."* You can trust her.

It looked to Hilde as though Joaquín was gathering his courage. He glanced over at Hilde. *"No Inglés,"* he said sheepishly.

"Le explicaré." I'll explain it to her, Gabe said gently.

Joaquín took a deep breath and spoke in Spanish.

Nan listened carefully, nodding, her clear eyes never leaving his face.

Gabe leaned over to Hilde and murmured, "He says he tried twice to come over the border. On the second time, when he was crossing the desert, *la migra*—Border Patrol—found them, and his guide disappeared. Most of them were picked up. But he got away"—Gabe hesitated—"he and a few others."

Joaquín continued haltingly, and when he could not find the words, Nan would ask him a question in Spanish, bringing him back to his story. All Hilde could do was catch a few phrases and try to read the body language around the table.

After another bit of conversation in Spanish, Nan turned to Hilde. "I was just saying there are lookouts on the hills working with the coyotes—the guides—and they probably swooped in and picked up his coyote once Border Patrol showed up."

Hilde nodded.

Joaquín began again, and again Hilde found herself deciphering the conversation through the expressions on Nan and Gabe's faces. She caught a few fragments—the name Fernando, a mother and daughter, and water, or lack of it. *No suficiente agua.*

Then Joaquín stopped. He looked off into the distance and said quietly, *"Y esa noche se llevaron a Aricela."*

"Took her? Took her where?" Nan said. *"¿A dónde?"*

More back and forth, incomprehensible to Hilde.

Then Nan caught Gabe's gaze and held it. "I don't know what we can do to track them if we don't have their last names," she said in English.

There was a long pause. Gabe put his hand on Joaquín's forearm. *"Pero, ¿qué hay de Fernando?"*

Joaquín winced. *"Sí. Fernando."*

His tone now was wary, and his hands worried the coffee cup. He seemed unable to look at either Nan or Gabe. Finally, he raised his head, and when he spoke, his voice cracked. Hilde thought she saw his eyes glisten.

"Entiendo," Nan said, nodding. "That I may be able to help with. *Ven conmigo."*

She led them into a small office off the communal room. An old computer sat on a desk piled with papers. She reached around back of the computer, flipped a switch, and sat in the only chair in the office. Gabe and Joaquín stood behind her, and Hilde stood in the doorway.

After a few taps on the keyboard, the screen came to life. *Fronteras Compasivas.*

"This group," she said. "They keep maps." She clicked on the search bar. "Translate for your brother, will you, Gabe? I can't read English and speak Spanish at the same time. He crossed where?"

"Nogales. West, outside of Nogales," Gabe said after exchanging a few words with Joaquín.

"How many days did they walk?"

"Three and a half days. Until they split up," Gabe replied.

"And Border Patrol picked him up where?"

"Beside a road."

"I'm guessing it was somewhere along here," Nan said, tracing her finger along a line labeled Route 19 on the map.

She tapped the mouse again. A topographical map appeared, an odd landscape of greens and browns, overlain with almost-realistic shrubs and hills.

"This'll be the area," she said.

As Hilde watched, small red dots began appearing on the landscape, each with a black center. They looked like blood corpuscles from her science textbook. She took a step closer. More red dots, and still more—dozens of them, then hundreds—on the gray-green landscape.

"What are those?" Hilde asked, peering over Nan's shoulder.

No one answered. The air felt close in the little office.

Then Nan said quietly, "They're deaths, honey."

"Deaths?"

"Yes." Nan placed her hands in her lap.

Hilde steadied herself on the back of Nan's chair. Could this be? So many people—people like Joaquín, like Gabe—out there dying? In the desert? Did she want to see this?

Nan replaced her hand gingerly on the mouse and began to scroll down the page. Below the map, a list appeared, with headings—name, gender, age, cause of death, body condition.

Hilde's eyes skidded through the lines.

Maria Cristina Acevedo, female, age 24, heatstroke
Alejandro Mendes, age 19, skeletonization w/articulation/
*   ligamentous attachments*
Oscar Bustamante, age 38, hanging, skeletonization w/
*   mummification*
Unidentified female, age 20, blunt force trauma
Unidentified female, age 2, blunt force trauma
Alicia Castillo Rojas, female, age 14, hypothermia, decomposed
Daniel Acevedo, age 24, GSW to head

"GSW?" Gabe whispered, pointing to the last entry.

"Gunshot wound. A lot of vigilantes out there," Nan replied, her lips tight. Then she leaned over the keyboard, put her elbows on the desk, and pressed her fingers to her forehead. "There must be a better way," she mumbled. She turned to Joaquín. "*¿Cuál es el apellido de Fernando?*" What's Fernando's last name?

"Hernandez López."

She pecked at the keyboard, and a search box appeared. She typed in the name, hesitated, and clicked.

The map zoomed in to a patch of land with sagebrush on one side and a black field on the other, divided by a road. One red dot appeared near the road. Slowly, she let go of the mouse and let her hands fall into her lap.

Gabe reached around her, gently moved the cursor over the red dot, and clicked. A box appeared over the map.

Case Report ML 02-01454, Hernandez López, Fernando, male, age 19, heat stroke and dehydration. Fully fleshed.

Silence.

Nan raised her hand and traced a line on the computer screen with her finger. "That road," she said quietly. "It leads to a subdivision."

"He was close," Gabe breathed.

Hilde looked around at the others, bewildered. Nan was staring at the screen. Gabe had turned and was watching his brother intently.

Joaquín was standing stock still, his face a mask.

There was a commotion in the common room. Nan looked around from her office chair.

"Hilde?" Ethan's voice, breathless.

Hilde poked her head around the corner and saw her brother standing at the door. He had on heavy rubber boots. His face was pale, and she thought she saw him shaking.

"Need your help." His tone was ugly. Imperious.

"How did you know I was here?"

He shook his head as if to say *That question is too stupid to answer.* "Need you now." She heard the edge in his voice.

"What? Is it Mom?"

He looked flustered for a moment, then angry. "No. It's the creek. It's overflowing. It's flooding the road. And it's heading toward the barn. Now."

Gabe appeared behind her. When Ethan saw Gabe, his shoulders relaxed a bit. "The goats," Ethan said. "We need to get them to higher ground. Gabe, need your help, bro."

Gabe's eyes flicked to his brother. Joaquín continued to stare stone-faced at the computer.

"Not now," Gabe said quietly.

Ethan stiffened. His eyes narrowed, and his jaw set menacingly. Hilde could see he was struggling to control his anger. For a long moment, no one said anything.

Nan broke in. "Go, Hilde," she said. Then to Ethan: "Gabe will come when he can."

34

Flooded

By the time they got home, the road in front of the house had turned to a river. Muddy water from the creek was creeping up over the pavement, as if unable to remember the way to the ocean. It spread out and oozed to the other side of the road, crawling up driveways and lapping against porch steps.

"Goddamn him!" Ethan muttered as they waded through the muck to their porch railing. "He's the hired hand, for Chrissakes. Who does he think he is?"

Hilde dragged her boots through the water and up the steps of the porch, keeping her distance from her brother. She'd had enough of him. For now, anyway.

"Where's Mom?" she said sharply. Her tone of voice surprised even her.

"In the barn. Go help her. I'll bring the truck around."

Hilde found her mother on her knees amid a swarm of goats, her arms around two kids who were bucking and bleating, clearly terrified by the chaos around them. She looked exhausted and close to tears.

"I'll take 'em, Mom," Hilde said as she grabbed one of the kids and tucked it under her arm.

The other kid squirmed away and bolted from Janine's grip. Janine grabbed it by its leg and yanked the animal back.

"Take it easy, Mom," Hilde said more urgently. "Let me help." She wrapped her other arm around the animal's belly and picked him up. He had been struggling wildly, but her steady pressure around his middle calmed him.

Ethan backed the truck close to the barn, and Hilde and her mother loaded animals one by one. When the truck could take no more, they heaved themselves into the cab, and Ethan headed through the muck, onto the flooded road, and toward higher ground. Back and forth they trekked, the truck making a bigger wake each time it approached the barn, the rain falling in steady sheets, the creek spreading beyond its banks. Distracted by the panic of the bleating animals still trapped in the barn, they did not notice the water creeping into the milk house and surrounding the brown shipping cartons full of cheese, turning them soggy gray. They failed to see it steal up the porch steps, seep beneath the front door, run across the slanted floorboards of the parlor, and find its way out the back door.

By the time Ethan made the final trek and unloaded the llama—nostrils flaring, eyes bulging—into the back pasture, darkness was blanketing the landscape. They drove home in bone-weary silence, Hilde hemmed between her mother and Ethan. As they pulled up in front of the house, a cloud parted, and the moon lit up the property. It was then they saw the porch coated with heavy sludge.

"Oh, jeez," Hilde breathed like a silent prayer.

Her mother remained mute, her eyes fixed on the damage.

"Can't stay here," Ethan said flatly. "But the barn loft is still dry. C'mon. We'll sleep there and figure this out tomorrow."

JOAQUÍN SAT ON THE floor of Nan's office, covering his head with his forearms and rocking back and forth, trying not to see what he'd seen, trying not to know what he knew. He couldn't catch his breath. He couldn't stop the pounding in his head. He had left Fernando—his buddy—on the desert floor. He knew how frail he was, how dehydrated, how wrung out by the sun. He knew how off he was, off in the head. He should never have let Fernando stay.

That simple but terrible red dot, those words—*fully fleshed*—so battered Joaquín's mental defenses that he was flooded with guilt. And without those defenses, his brain began to deliver up the other dark failure lodged in his heart. Where was Isobel? And what had happened to Aricela? The image of Aricela turning desperate brown eyes toward her mother as they led her stiff, sticklike body through the cell door bloomed in his brain. And the memory of Isobel sitting on the bus, unmoving, her eyes dead, her knuckles white, overcame him. *What had happened to them? Where are they now?* Nothing had worked out. Nothing. He had failed everyone. At every turn. He rocked and rocked, feeling lightheaded, staving off nausea.

Finally, he heard Gabe's voice, and he tried to stand. He lurched to the side and banged into the wall. Gabe grabbed him under the arm, steadying him, and he stumbled into the community room and sat hard on a chair, gasping. Nan gave him a brown paper bag to breathe into and stood behind him for several minutes, gently rubbing his shoulders.

Finally, she said, "Pima and I—we gotta go sandbag the house."

"Go. I got him," Gabe said, still staring at his brother.

"Put him to bed on the sofa," she replied. "There's food in the fridge. We'll be back in the morning."

As Nan and Pima gathered their slickers, Gabe moved to the kitchenette, opened a can of refried beans, and dumped the contents into a pot to heat.

IT WAS EARLY MORNING when Ethan shoved open the door to the house. He entered first, followed by Hilde and their mother. The water had left a slurry of mud along the baseboards and produced a nasty wainscoting around the room. It had climbed up the wallpaper, discoloring it with fingers of moisture. It had seeped up the skirt of the upholstered chair. And it had produced a smell—musty, rank—that called from the walls and floorboards the odors of all the strangers who had ever lived in the house.

"Got us good," Ethan said, bending down to touch the damp mudline on the wall.

Hilde watched her mother survey the damage. Janine moved slowly around the room, looking. She ran her fingers over the windowsills, the backs of chairs. On the bookshelf, the books had ballooned up from the water that saturated their pages.

Hilde picked her way over to the stairs that led to the bedrooms. Sitting on a low step, she pulled off her boots and set them aside. In stockinged feet, she climbed the stairs and took a quick tour of the hall, peering into each bedroom. "Things are okay up here," she called to cheer her mother.

But Janine's face remained stony.

They spent the morning cleaning up. Ethan shoveled sludge while Hilde wiped down the walls with a bucket and rags. They made piles on the porch of foodstuffs and books and household goods that needed to be pitched, and they wiped down whatever they thought could be saved, though there was precious little of that. Janine, curiously disinterested, wandered out the back door and disappeared into the milk house. When Hilde went looking for her half an hour later, she found her sitting on the damp floor digging out mud from the cheese molds with two fingers.

"Come back to the house, Mom," Hilde said, quietly. "We can do this later."

Her mother stared up at her with vacant eyes.

Hilde helped her mother up. "Why don't you go lie down. We'll finish here."

Janine just stared at her.

"Okay, then," Hilde replied. "Let me clean off the rocker on the front porch, and you can sit there. Look, the sun's coming out."

After clearing a space in the muck and wiping down the rocker, Hilde lined it with a dry blanket from the bedroom.

Janine sat down and began to rock.

After noon, Gabe appeared at the back door. He knocked gently. Hilde saw her brother's eyes flick to the door and harden. When he did not move, Hilde went to the door and opened it.

Gabe stepped inside. *"Jesucristo,"* he whispered, surveying the damage. He ducked back outside and returned with a shovel. For the rest of the afternoon, he worked shoulder to shoulder with Ethan, digging out the muck, neither of them saying a word.

As dusk settled, Gabe said, "Those pesticides in the shed. They need to be put up or they'll contaminate the water. I'll do it."

Ethan only nodded.

When Gabe had disappeared into the barn, Ethan said, teeth clenched, "Goddamn him!"

Hilde, still on her knees, turned to her brother. She could feel the bile building inside her. "You know, Ethan. He did come," she said quietly. "He came today."

"Yeah. A day late," Ethan spat, turning away and picking up a shovel.

Hilde rose to her feet. "Ethan," she said, her heart starting to pound, "you don't know what was happening yesterday. You just—" she stammered, "you just waltzed in and said, 'Let's go.'"

"He's the help, Hilde," Ethan retorted, driving his shovel into a pile of muck behind the couch. "That's what he's *supposed* to do."

She could feel the heat rising into her cheeks. "He doesn't *belong* to us, Ethan. You act like he's some sort of beast of burden, or something."

Ethan waved her away. "Oh, Hilde. For God's sake, take it down a notch. You're so dramatic."

Hilde felt a blast of anger, as though her insides had been coated with gasoline and his words were the match. She threw down her rag.

"Don't, Ethan. Don't call me 'dramatic.' You, Mom, Dad—you do that. You all do that!" Her eyes narrowed. "And of course, what does that do? *It shuts me up.*" Her voice was shaky now. She had no idea where this rage was coming from, but for the first time she allowed it out, and it erupted from her like a bazooka-fired missile. "I shut up. And you just move on, like some water bug skimming over a pond. You just skim away." She waved her arm wildly across an imaginary pond. "You don't take in anything I said. You don't think about how *you* come off. So long as *I'm dramatic*, you're in the clear."

He stared at her, stunned.

She turned away. "What's happened to you, Ethan? You don't see what's around you. Or if you do, you don't care. You're always running out the door, peeling out the driveway, leaving me with Mom—and all her problems. It's like you're blind to everyone—to everything around you. Look at what you've become!"

Her fury hung in the air between them.

He slowed. "Me?"

"Yeah, you." She wasn't done. "Like yesterday. You had no idea what was going on. No idea! And you didn't even try to understand. You just bulldozed your way in, and . . . you treated him like *shit*!"

He stared at her, uncomprehending.

She stopped, trying to gather her wits. Then she said quietly, "It was his brother—"

"His brother?"

"Yeah. Gabe's been sending him money forever, trying to get him out of Mexico. And he *finally made it*."

"Okay . . ." he said tentatively.

"Joaquín is his name. The brother."

Ethan nodded.

"And there was someone else. Someone who crossed with him," she continued. "Gabe knew him too. And that guy—he *didn't* make it. There was a map, and all these dots, and one of them was him. Or his body. They'd just figured that out, and then you walked in."

She stepped back and let out a long breath. She could smell the sweat on her own body.

"They're just people, Ethan," she whispered, all the energy drained from her now.

At that moment, Gabe walked through the back door, shovel in hand, and Hilde's words evaporated into the air, replaced by an awkward silence.

Ethan stared at Hilde for several moments, his face reddening. Then, glancing at Gabe, he picked up his bucket and shovel and clomped through the front door. He passed his mother, still rocking in the rocker, and disappeared into the barn.

HILDE AND GABE SPENT the rest of the afternoon washing down the walls, while Ethan mucked out the barn and milk house. Every time she caught a glimpse of her brother through the screen door, she felt a pang of guilt about what she'd said, but at the same time, she was relieved she didn't have to deal with him. At dusk, he reappeared.

"Where's Mom?" he said curtly as he stowed his shovel on the back porch and stepped inside.

Hilde glanced out the front window. The rocker was empty, still.

"Don't know." She crossed the room, stepped out onto the muddy porch, and scanned the road. A vague sense of dread fell over her.

They could see footsteps leading off the porch and disappearing into the standing water on the road. "Where would she go?" Hilde murmured. "Everything's such a mess."

"Maybe she's up at Booher's place," Ethan said.

"He's gone fishing, remember?" Hilde said.

"Yeah," said Ethan, absently. Then, as if waking himself up, he gave his head a little shake. "I'm gonna take the truck and get us something to eat. I'll watch for her along the road. You stay here in case she shows up."

"Please," Gabe said out of the blue.

They both turned to look at him.

"I need to check on my brother."

"Where is he?" Ethan asked.

"At the church."

"You stay here," Ethan said. "I'll bring him back with the food."

35
Reckoning

Ethan parked the truck behind the taquería and stared out the windshield. Raw clouds scudded across the sky, whipping in from the sea beyond the dark cliffs as if not yet done with their devastation. The air was thick with the smell of mud, and the lights from the dash cast a dim glow in the worn-out cab of the pickup.

He couldn't get out. Too much was roiling in his brain.

What did she mean—that I'm blind to what's going on? I know what's going on: Mom's pipe dream—the farm, the goats, the cheese—all a joke. Mom doesn't know how to run a farm. She's just running away. She knew from the beginning Dad wasn't coming. She knew. What was she thinking? And when was she going to tell us?

He stared out the windshield at the black underbellies of the clouds.

And Dad, with all that moral compass crap. Character, he said, you gotta have character. All that—while he's bedding some bimbo. What a goddamn hypocrite.

His hands tightened around the steering wheel, and he tasted disgust in his mouth.

This family is so fucked up. I gotta get out of here.

He thought about Texas and all the freedom there. Freedom to do what he wanted, be what he wanted, find out who he really was. He'd already conjured up images of the seaside town on the Texas coast where he'd land, with its weathered buildings, its small fleet of oil rigs off the coast, its wide-open sky. He could imagine himself walking the streets, breathing the salt air. And now he almost had enough for that bus ticket. Did it make him such a bad person to want to get away from this fucked-up family?

But then, there was Hilde.

If he took off, what would happen to her? A pain took hold of him, starting in his stomach, working its way into his chest, and tightening his throat.

She doesn't know the whole of it. Maybe she should.

He had been blind about Hilde. In his mind, she was still a kid—nine, ten years old—with skinny stick-arms, turned-out feet, straw for hair, and stars in her eyes whenever he came into view. But that's not the person she was now. That's not the person who just cut him off at the knees for his behavior toward Gabe. No, not the same. It was as if his little sister had been body-snatched, and in her place was someone quite different. How had that happened? When had she changed?

I should tell her. She's old enough.

And then a cold thought came to him.

She's old enough to hear it, but she's not old enough to get away. It's not the same for her. She's stuck. Stuck here with Mom. And God knows, Mom isn't holding things together very well.

He'd been his sister's protector for so long that he had come to expect it would always be that way. And—surprise—he didn't want to give it up. Mom was always badgering Hilde about something—her hair, her posture, her clothes. It was true that Hilde wasn't going to be a homecoming princess—not like Mom—but she didn't deserve to be her mother's punching bag. He couldn't imagine Hilde hanging here alone without him.

But then again, Hilde had changed. In all that had happened this past year—the acrimony, the uprooting, the lies, the disillusion, the instability—she had made an astonishing transformation. That little kid that was so meek and fragile had developed a steeliness he had not noticed before.

And her allegiance had somehow shifted, too, without his notice. He—Ethan—was no longer the one she sought out. It was Gabe she was listening to now. Gabe she was seeking out. She had opened a space for Gabe, hung with him, watched him work—and somewhere along the line, she had learned his story. And she had developed a bond with him. A deep connection with him, and now some surprising compassion for his brother.

It's ironic, really, he thought. *Here we are, a family who was doing just fine on our little Wisconsin farm, now falling apart at the seams, with parents who can't stand each other, and me so fed up I'm about to chuck it all for Texas. And there they are, two brothers—who grew up in some godforsaken place in Mexico—walking miles through the desert, shaking off the feds, risking everything—to be a family again. How fucked up is that?*

He slumped over the steering wheel, his arms encircling it, his hands meeting at the top, his forehead resting there, and began to rethink all she had said.

IT WAS DARK WHEN he returned to the house. He climbed the porch steps with two bags of food in hand and Joaquín trailing behind.

Hilde had set several candles around the parlor, and a Coleman lantern was sitting on the table, casting massive shadows on the walls.

Gabe met Joaquín at the door and put an arm around his brother's shoulder.

"Taquería's busy," Ethan said, handing the bags to Hilde and bending down to take off his boots. "Only place that's still got power."

"No Mom?" Hilde said.

"No Mom." Seeing Hilde's face, he added, "Not yet."

"I'll go. I'll look for her," Gabe said.

Ethan glanced at Joaquín, who looked pale and weak. "After the food," Ethan said.

They sat around the table, lantern illuminating their faces, and ate ravenously, saying little.

At one point, Ethan turned to Joaquín. "You've been here how long?"

Joaquín only smiled and replied, *"Gracias por la comida."*

"He thanks you for the food," Gabe said.

"Ah. No problem," Ethan said. Then, to Gabe: "When did he cross?"

"Two months ago," Gabe replied.

"Two months? Where has he been?"

"Detention."

"Detention? Why?"

As Gabe recounted the bones of Joaquín's journey through his words, Hilde thought she saw Ethan's face soften. He was listening from some deep place within himself. His eyes fixed on Joaquín, then Gabe, then Joaquín again, in a way that reminded Hilde of the brother she'd remembered from home.

He was so focused that several times he forgot Joaquín didn't speak English and he would ask questions of Joaquín that Gabe had to translate. He was sucking in details as if he were a reporter. They talked, and Gabe translated, until the Coleman lantern abruptly went out.

They sat for a moment, surprised by the darkness.

Then Hilde said, "Shouldn't Mom be home by now?"

"I'll go," Gabe said again, scraping his chair across the still-damp floorboards. To his brother, he added, *"Ven conmigo."*

Joaquín rose.

"Hilde, you stay here," Ethan said. "Find some more oil and relight the lantern. Put it on the front porch. Mom'll want to know what's happening when she shows up. You can tell her we'll be back soon."

Hilde cleared away the paper dinner sacks as the three of them pile into the truck. Ethan backed out of the driveway and drove slowly through the standing water in the street, heading east.

She waited up until midnight. Finally, exhaustion overtook her, and she dragged herself upstairs, lay crosswise on her bed, and fell into a deep sleep.

SHE SURFACED AN HOUR later to the sound of voices in the kitchen, a thick fog still enveloping her. For a moment, she could not place where she was, nor why she still had her boots on. An unfinished dream—mud-slicked water, a missing llama, a plate of beans—pinned her down in the depths of her consciousness. Then she heard her mother's voice.

Her mother. That was it. It was her mother's voice. And then Ethan's. And Gabe's, a low response. They were home. All home. Safe.

Hilde closed her eyes again, and the weight from her exhausted body weighed her down. She craved more sleep. As she was drifting downward, she heard Ethan say, *See if you can light the stove. There's tea in the cabinet.* But that must have been the start of another dream because Ethan had never in his life made a cup of tea.

WHEN SHE AWOKE AGAIN, it was late morning. The light was streaming in the window. She twisted and sat up, her boots clomping on the floor. How could she have slept so long? It wasn't like her. What's more, she could smell coffee and hear murmurings from the kitchen. Apparently, everybody else was already up.

She stumbled from the bedroom to the stairs, her hair disheveled and her mouth cotton.

When she entered the kitchen, Ethan was sitting at the table, together with Gabe and Joaquín, all three clutching mugs. A propane stove was set up on the countertop, and a jar of instant coffee sat between them.

"Hey," Ethan said when she stepped into view, "I was just about to get you up. We're gonna go check on the goats. Maybe get some more sandbags. You should stay here."

They were all looking at her expectantly. Something seemed off about this scene, but Hilde could not put her finger on it. "Where's Mom?" she asked.

"She's asleep," Ethan said quickly, nodding as he spoke. "She's fine. But she needs some rest. You should stay. Be here when she wakes up."

"Okay," Hilde said, perplexed.

As Ethan brought the truck around and Gabe and Joaquín loaded feed into the back, Hilde peeked into her mother's bedroom. The lump under the covers was unmoving, an odd contrast to her mother's hair, which was strewn wildly across the pillow.

36

Coyote in Town

Joaquín helped Gabe and Ethan check the herd over the next hour, counting carefully. When they realized at least a half-dozen kids and four nannies were missing, they spent the better part of the day searching for the lost, finding only one small kid drowned in the creek bed at the edge of the pasture, its stick-legs bent wildly among the branches of a fallen log.

Gabe waded into the waters and disentangled the carcass, bracing his body against the swift-running current. He cradled the lolling head in his arms. "I'll bury her tonight," he said as he laid the lifeless body on a tarp in the truck bed.

"Okay. I'll help," Ethan added quietly.

For the rest of the afternoon, they hauled sandbags from the county's pickup station at the high school in case the rains returned.

Joaquín found the work to be a balm to his spirit. He laid his back into every chore—lifting hay bales onto the truck, packing sandbags against the barn walls until his muscles screamed. He wanted to

"

be exhausted. Because when he was exhausted, he couldn't think. And that's what he wanted: not to think.

At dusk, they returned to the house. Silence hung in the air as they entered, though Joaquín knew they'd left the girl and her mother there. The girl, Hilde, emerged from a back bedroom when she heard them come in. She came into the kitchen and rummaged through the cupboard, pulling out several cans of warm cola and set them on the table. They pulled up chairs and popped the tops.

Joaquín didn't know what to make of this family. Gabe had told him some. The girl and her brother were both hard workers, but they didn't know much about goats. What's more, there seemed to be tension between them—something he could not understand. In his world, a brother watched over his sister, protected her. And the mother? There was something broken here, something terribly wrong.

After a few minutes of rest and some conversation in English, Gabe turned to him and said in Spanish, *"No hay comida en la casa.* There's no food in the house. We're gonna go get some. You come, too." He and Ethan stood up, their chairs scraping the kitchen floor.

Joaquín rose and followed them to the door. As they left, he glanced back at Hilde, who was sitting at the table, her hands around a can of cola. He smiled, and she gave him a little wave.

The aroma of tortillas, peppers, and onion that filled the little taquería produced a deep longing in Joaquín. It brought back memories of his mother calling him to supper as he and his brother passed a soccer ball one to the other in the field next to the little *casita* where they grew up. Such vivid memories brought tears to his eyes. That powerful, magnetic draw toward his brother, his only family now, was what had propelled him from Mexico City through the desert. It had sustained him in the detention center. And it had finally gotten him to Pescadero. Following Gabe into this taqueria, with these smells—it was like finally coming home.

They ordered at the counter, and when the food came, they could not wait. They found a table by the window and dug into the bags, setting aside the larger one to bring back to the house.

Joaquín inhaled two tacos without saying a word, and then sat back and stared at the darkened restaurant across the street. *Maybe there's work there,* he thought. *Maybe I could work in the fields with Gabe during the day and wash dishes at night. Two jobs. Twice the pay. That would be good.* He could feel the food begin to nourish his spent body. He could feel himself coming back to life.

A figure moving along the sidewalk just outside the window flickered in front of him. He blinked. Did he see what he just saw? Or was he dreaming? The cowbell on the door of the taquería clanged, and a rush of cold air hit the back of his neck. He heard boots on the floor. And then the raspy voice, the one he would never forget.

"*Tacos. Dos.*"

He slouched in his chair and pulled his ballcap low over his brow.

Gabe noticed. "*¿Estás bien?*" You okay? he asked quietly from across the table.

Joaquín shot him a look.

Gabe glanced at the man at the counter. Ethan, sitting next to Gabe, looked up too. As the man groped for his wallet, they both glimpsed the leather-sheaved bowie knife partially hidden by his coat.

Gabe pushed the chips closer to Joaquín. "Eat," he said quietly in English.

Joaquín picked up a chip and put it in his mouth. He tried to chew, but the sound was so loud he stopped. The chip softened on his tongue.

Gabe lowered his eyes and took a bite of taco, but Ethan sat straight up, trying to work out what was happening as the man helped himself to salsa from the bar. With a chip in one hand and a plastic cup of salsa in the other, the man turned casually and surveyed the tables. Ethan met his gaze for a moment, and then looked away.

"Dos tacos," the cashier called.

The stranger turned, took a bag from the cashier, and headed out the door.

"Jesucristo," Joaquín whispered.

"¿Es él?" That's him? Gabe asked.

"Tengo que salir de aquí." I gotta get out of here, he wheezed. He scrambled for his jacket.

"Wait," Ethan said, putting a hand on Joaquín's forearm. "Let me see where he went." He got up from the table, strolled outside, and stood in front of the taquería, his hands riffling through his pockets as though he were searching for a smoke. He looked left. He looked right. He stepped into the street and peered down toward the bridge. Then he turned and nodded to Gabe, who had already thrown the table scraps in the trash and collected the bag for home.

"Vamos," Gabe said, loosening Joaquín's grip on the edge of the table.

They stepped into the night air. Joaquín could feel the chill over the darkened street.

"Get in the truck. I'll keep an eye out here," Ethan said.

Joaquín headed around the back of the building and toward the truck. Gabe followed.

As they rounded the corner, Joaquín saw a shadow move. Suddenly, an arm like a vice wrapped around his neck, and the point of a knife lodge delicately in the soft flesh beneath his jawbone.

No one moved.

"Hola, amigo," said the raspy voice. *"Te he estado buscando por todas partes.* I have been looking for you. We had a deal. You remember. Pay up at the Walmart. But you never showed. Now you've made me come all this way, just to collect my money."

His eyes flicked toward Gabe.

"Y éste debe ser tu hermano." And this must be your brother. He nestled the knife a little deeper. Joaquín flinched at the pain. "The one

who lives up the hill?"

How did he know?

"People are so helpful here," the man continued as if reading Joaquín's mind. "They tell you everything, if you are polite." He smirked. "They even told me I didn't need to trek up the hill to find you, because you were helping your brother at that little goat farm." He edged forward. "But when I got there, all I could see from the back window was a tender little *chica rubia*, all by herself, mopping out the mud. How old is she anyhow?" He puckered his lips and made an obscene kissing sound.

Joaquín could smell his breath.

"So, my friend, here we are. And I still need my money. But I'm a reasonable man." He growled into Joaquín's ear now. "I'll give you four hours. Bring the money to the bluff north of town. I'll be waiting for the bus out there, the last bus—so don't be late." He shrugged. "And we'll part company happily. But if you make me come after you again"—he began scraping the blade gently against Joaquín's neck—"you, your brother, maybe even *la chica*—somebody will end up paying. I'm sure of it."

Ethan, watching from the shadows, understood fully.

37

On the Bluff

Hilde could not fathom where they were. By the time the truck pulled into the driveway, it was close to nine o'clock and the sky was inky black.

Ethan entered alone. He had nothing in his hands, no food. Just a dirty canvas sack.

"Where were you?" she asked sharply.

He looked at her as though he didn't understand the question.

"Did you bring food?" she said, fully irritated now. "You've been gone so long. I'm starving."

"Oh. I forgot," he said as he headed to the back of the house.

"You forgot?"

He stopped, turned, and she could see the confusion on his face. It was as if he had been so deep in thought he hadn't even heard her. And then something else flashed across his face.

"Where's Mom?" he asked, his eyes suddenly alive and darting around the room.

"Bed. She came out a while ago. I gave her a soda, but she didn't drink it. She just sat there—"

Ethan let out a breath. "I'm really sorry. About the food," he said, and he disappeared into his bedroom, shutting the door behind him.

Hilde stood in the center of the kitchen, dumbfounded. What was going on? Where were Gabe and his brother? Why was Ethan acting like that? Her mother was in such bad shape, and he didn't seem to care. All of it suddenly made her feel untethered, lightheaded. She knew something was terribly wrong. She grabbed the edge of the chair and began gasping, her heart pounding, her palms sweating, her scalp burning as though a thousand tiny wasps were stinging from the inside. She closed her eyes and began rocking back and forth on her feet, hoping to reground herself.

After several moments, she found herself squatting on the floor, her arms cradling her head. She tried to breathe deeper, gather her wits, center herself. When she finally felt ready, she stood up and approached Ethan's door. She knocked. No answer. She opened the door a crack, peeked in, and saw Ethan perched on the edge of his bed surrounded by money. Lots of money. Ten-dollar bills. Twenty-dollar bills. Fifty-dollar bills. He was putting them in piles next to the empty canvas sack.

She pushed the door open. "What are you doing?"

He looked up. "Stay out, Hilde."

"Geez, Ethan, what is all this?"

He gathered up the bills and stuffed them into the sack. The cigar box where he had kept his tip money lay open on the bed.

"Ethan, where did you get that money? It's way more than your tips."

"I said stay out of it." He brushed past her, sack in hand, and headed out the front door.

"Wait," she called, following him into the night air. "What's happening? Are you leaving? For Texas? Tell me, please!" Her voice was high and shrill.

He stopped at the door to the truck. "No," he said, his eyes softening just a bit. "I'm not going to Texas. I'll be back. You stay."

She felt her spine stiffen. "No way. Wherever you're going, I'm going."

"Hilde, you can't go." He looked back at her. "I'm just going to meet Gabe and Joaquín, that's all. You stay here."

"What's all that money for? Please, tell me, Ethan. What's going on."

"Oh, for God's sake!" He turned on his heels and headed toward the truck.

She crossed to the truck, swung the passenger door open, and pulled herself into the seat before he could reach the driver's side.

"I'm not getting out of this truck," she said, clutching the wheel with one hand and the door with the other. Her knuckles turned white with the effort.

Ethan stood beside the truck, looking in at her through the driver-side window. Finally, he climbed in. "Okay, then. Okay." He batted her hand away from the wheel.

He backed up the truck up and headed for town. A dense fog rose from the ground, producing a blanket that blinded her when the truck's headlights hit it. He slowed only a little as they bore through it, causing her to brace herself with one hand on the dash and the other on the door. When they turned the corner and headed into town, she saw that most of the buildings stood damp and darkened, silhouettes against the night sky. But the deli was illuminated by the lights of several police cars. The sheriff was standing with a group of men in the doorway.

As Ethan's truck sped by, Mr. Cardullo stepped away from the group and stared into the dark street. For a spilt second, he locked eyes with Hilde as she peered through the passenger window.

In a flash, she knew. "You stole that money."

Ethan said nothing.

She could feel the truck accelerate. "You stole it. From the deli. Didn't you?"

He kept his eyes on the road, his jaw working.

She glared at him. She wanted him to know how much he was scaring her, but she could find no words.

His jaw tightened. "I didn't have enough," he growled.

"Enough for what?" she asked, incredulous.

"Enough for the payoff."

"Payoff?"

"Joaquín. To pay off the goddamn coyote, Hilde."

"What coyote?"

"The guy who brought him over the border. He's here—in town. And he wants his money. Tonight."

He was about to say something more when his demeanor changed. "Oh, shit," he said in a low voice. He adjusted the rearview mirror and stared at it for a long moment.

"What?"

"Hold on."

Just before they came to the Coast Road, he swerved and headed down the access road that led to the marsh. The truck bounced heavily, and Hilde's head hit the ceiling of the cab.

"For god's sake, Ethan!"

The truck came to a stop past heavy brush just high enough to shield the cab from view. He cut the motor. "Shut up, Hilde. Just for a minute, shut up!"

"No!" She was furious now and not about to take any of his guff. "What is wrong with you?"

He grabbed her wrist and looked hard at her. "Listen to me!"

She ripped her arm from his grasp. "What? You're gonna tell me *what* about stealing that money?"

He glared at her for a moment. Then he said, "That cut on Joaquín's nose! How do you think he got it?"

"What cut?"

"Joaquín's nose. Sliced open. You saw it. He couldn't pay the money they thought he owed. For the crossing. Jesus, Hilde, don't be so thick!"

Hilde was silent.

"And now he's here—the coyote. In Pescadero. He wants his money. And he'll slice open the face of any fool who gets in his way."

"I—"

"And did you know? He came by the house today."

"What?"

"Our house. He watched you through the window. He was looking for Joaquín. But he found you."

She sat for a moment, absorbing this information. She could feel her body pulling in on itself as though she were a hermit crab retreating into its shell.

"This money"—he touched the canvas sack between them—"this money is enough to send that shitbag back to where he came from."

"But . . ." she sat there, her mind bouncing like a ping-pong ball. Finally, she said, "But why pay? He left them in the desert. He didn't do what he said he would. Call the cops. Just call the cops."

"Call the cops?" He looked at her, incredulous. "And tell 'em *what*? That an illegal alien has been overcharged by his coyote after stealing over the border? There's no law here. We're not working inside the law here."

She paused. "Yeah, but he's such a lowlife—"

"Oh, worse than that," he interrupted. "He's probably running drugs for some cartel. I'm probably shooting the money into the veins of some moron in Indiana."

"But why would you steal that money? For *this*?"

His hands gripped the top of the steering wheel. He leaned forward and rested his forehead on them and took several deep breaths. Then he whispered, almost to himself, "I didn't have enough—on my own. Hilde, I'm not who you think I am. I never was. But dammit, I'm tryin' here."

Tears came to her eyes. She turned away.

They sat together for several moments. And as they did, she saw his grip on the wheel tighten again. That's when she knew he wasn't through. She could still read him.

"You know Dad's not coming, right?" he said. "Ever."

At that precise moment, she realized *she did know*. She'd resisted the idea, pushing it down in her mind, burying it in the unremarkable routine of her daily chores. Perhaps she'd known it from the day they left home, in the way he turned, not watching them go as the car lumbered down the gravel driveway. Mounting the steps to the porch like a man with a purpose, a purpose that didn't include them.

"Yeah," she said simply. It was a relief to say it out loud.

She could tell he was thinking furiously, as if he were trying to find a way out of a maze that had no exit.

"What else?" she said.

He rocked slightly forward and backward in in his seat, trying to find the words.

She fixed her eyes on him. "Tell me." *Say what you have to say. Maybe I already know this too.*

"When Mom went missing that night . . ."

"Yeah."

"We went to find her."

"Uh-huh."

He stopped.

She felt like she was prying the top off a can.

He began again. "When we went to find her, we were in the truck. We were driving along the road near the bridge, looking for her."

"Okay."

"And we got out and started to walk the creek. Gabe took the far side. And Joaquín and me, the near side."

"And?"

"And Gabe, he was the one who spotted Mom first. I didn't see her. I was too far away. She was in the water."

He turned and stared at her. His eyes were so piercing she looked away.

"In the water," she repeated.

"Yeah." He seemed to be waiting for her to comprehend. But she didn't.

"She fell in?"

"No."

"She didn't fall in?"

"No," he said again.

"Then what?"

"She *waded* in, Hilde." His mouth was tight, as if he were trying to stop himself from talking. "She waded in, and she had *rocks in her pockets.*"

A moment passed. Then a flash of white lightning hit Hilde's brain. Had he said what he'd said? Did he mean what he said? She gripped the seat with both hands. *He didn't mean it. This cannot be right. He's wrong.* The cab of the truck closed in on her. There was no air to breathe. She was hot. She was cold. She felt she might vomit. She kneaded the seat with her grip.

He waited for some time, saying nothing. Then he began again.

"Gabe pulled her out. She"—he paused, looking away—"she struggled." Then he inhaled slowly and deliberately, as if he'd been holding his breath. "But he got her out."

She struggled? Mom struggled? She didn't want to come out? She wanted that grimy water, that swirling current to suck her down? She wanted that more than she wanted us? Why? Why would she want that? What's wrong with us? An odd, animal sound escaped from her mouth.

Just then, a sheriff's car barreled past. Ethan snapped his head toward the noise and listened as the police car slowed at the Coast Road. Its siren whooped once, its lights flashed. It turned and headed south.

"Thank God," he said softly. He shifted into reverse and backed up the access road. The wheels spun in the mud, caught, and propelled them up the bumpy grade onto the main road. At the Coast Road, he turned north.

He drove for only a hundred yards before they reached the turnoff. Suddenly, they were bouncing along a poorly marked road leading to the bluff. The fog was thicker here, but still there were patches of starry sky. As they reached the edge of the parking lot, the fog cleared, and the headlights leapt out over the cliff. Reflections from a pale gibbous moon played in the water some forty feet below.

Ethan braked, doused the lights, and killed the engine. The sound of the ocean crashing against the shore filled the silence.

"Look," Ethan said. "I don't know what's right. I don't want you to think I'm—I just gotta do this. It's something I can do."

When she didn't respond, he put his hand over hers and pried it from the seat. "You're okay. You stay here."

He grabbed the canvas bag, opened the door, and slid out of the cab. He scanned the darkness behind the truck. Then he peered through the open window. "I didn't want you to come. But you're here. So please. Stay in the truck."

A scuffling sound from the edge of the bluff drew her out of her stupor. She peered out the window and into the fog. When she turned back, her brother was gone, heading toward the cliff, his silhouette disappearing into the darkness.

Suddenly, from behind the truck came the crunch of footsteps. Instinctively, she shrank down in the cab.

A figure passed by her window, heading for the bluff. A compact man with a broad back and a slight limp. She thought she saw him glance her way, but he did not stop.

"*Hola, amigo,*" he called in a raspy voice. "Finally, we do some business." The sound carried clearly through the fog.

Hilde saw Joaquín stand, canvas sack in his hands.

"And you brought me payment. *Bueno, bueno,*" the man said magnanimously, as if he were congratulating a teenage son. "I'm just sorry you made me come so far for it." His tone shifted abruptly, and he growled, "Now count it for me."

"Count it?"

"*Sí.* On your knees. Count it out. Let me see it."

Joaquín squatted. He turned the canvas sack upside down and dumped the contents onto the sandy earth.

"Slowly," the man growled.

Joaquín counted the bills, stacking them in piles and securing each with a rock. Wisps of fog settled around him and disappeared as he worked. "Three thousand," he said finally.

The man surveyed the pile of bills for a long moment.

"A little short, I think, *amigo.*"

"Short? That's it. That's what I owe."

Hilde, slouched down, peered over the dash. She understood only a little of the Spanish, but she could see Joaquín's upturned face in the moonlight. He looked terrified.

"*Sí.* That *was* what you owed. But you didn't pay on time. And so now"—he gestured to the piles on the ground—"it's not enough. You made me come here. You kept me waiting. Now you owe interest."

Joaquín's mouth fell open.

"You're surprised," the man observed. "But what did you think? You crossed in early November. It's end of December. That's two months. Let me think." He put his fingers to his temple in a mock calculation. "Another thousand will cover it."

"What?"

"Another thousand. You have it."

"No. I don't have it. I don't."

"Oh, so sorry." The coyote glanced over his shoulder at the truck.

Hilde shrank down in the seat, hoping he did not see her in the dark.

"Too bad, too bad," the man *tsked*, then he waited a beat. "Tell you what," he said. "I'm gonna forgive *all* that interest," he said, gesturing magnanimously with his hands. "And instead, I'm gonna take the truck."

Hilde heard the words, but her Spanish was too poor to make out the meaning.

"I gotta get back to business, *amigo*. And I just don't like buses. They're too slow. And they stink. That truck, it isn't worth a thousand. But I'm willing to take it. Can you believe your luck? We all win."

"But . . . it's not mine," Joaquín said in a small voice, still on his knees.

The man's head flicked from side to side as if he were looking for someone in the dark.

Hilde felt a presence on the other side of the truck.

"They coyote stepped forward and held out his hand. "The keys, *imbécil!*"

"But I—"

The man's right boot swung back and arced forward, finding the soft flesh beneath Joaquín's jaw. Joaquín's head snapped back, and his body fell into the dirt. He lay on the ground, stunned and woozy. The man walked to him, stood over him for a moment, and kicked him in the kidneys. Then he started rifling through Joaquín's pockets.

A silhouette appeared at the edge of the bluff.

"Yo! Shitface!" Ethan called in English.

The coyote paused a split second to assess this new threat.

"*¿Y quién es este?*" And who is this? the man said, standing. He reached beneath his jacket. Hilde saw a blade flash in the moonlight as he flicked his wrist, adjusting his grip. He crouched and moved toward the silhouette on the cliff.

Ethan coiled his body low into a wrestling stance and began to dance along the edge of the cliff. "C'mon, shitface!" he taunted. "Let's do this."

Time slowed to a crawl, and through the swirling mist Hilde saw the coyote slash the air, first at Ethan's chest and then in front of his face. Ethan bobbed and weaved at the edge of the cliff, dodging the blade each time like a matador dodging the horns of a bull.

"Too low," Ethan baited. "No good there either."

Finally, in frustration, the man dove at Ethan's midsection. The blade flashed again.

Hilde screamed.

Suddenly Gabe's body flew across her sightline, barreling toward the cliff, his head tucked like a boulder. Ethan darted aside, and Gabe struck the coyote low in the spine, transferring the full force of his fury into the man's body, flinging him out beyond the edge of the cliff. For an instant, the man remained suspended in the thin night air, his legs and arms flailing wildly, his eyes bulging. Then the ocean pulled him down, and he disappeared into the dark.

Hilde jumped from the truck and ran to her brother who was on his knees at the edge of the cliff, breathing heavily and peering into the inky water. She didn't want to look down. She just wanted to throw her arms around her brother and haul him away from the cliff. But when he turned to face her, she could read in his eyes all that had just happened.

"Go look after Joaquín," he said.

"Is he . . . dead?"

"Go look after Joaquín," he repeated.

She moved toward Joaquín who was curled up in the dirt nearby, squirming.

"You okay?" she said, kneeling and touching his rounded back.

Moaning softly, he rolled onto his side and pushed himself up. He touched his jaw gingerly, spit blood into his hand and fished a tooth from his palm. He looked up at her with doleful eyes.

Gabe was sitting some distance away, holding his right shoulder with his left hand. He looked stricken. She had seen so much empathy in him, in his work with the animals, that she'd assumed his gentleness was woven into the fabric of his being. But clearly, she was wrong. There was something else in him—something fierce and frightening—and even he seemed appalled by it.

Ethan moved toward Gabe, who looked up with a mixture of panic and pain on his face.

"Self-defense, buddy," Ethan said, kneeling next to him. "Self-defense."

For a moment, Gabe looked like he was trying to convince himself that what Ethan said was true. But then he buried his head in his arms. "*No. Muy malo.*"

The whoop of a siren sounded from the north, carried along by the fog. Ethan and Gabe both swiveled their heads toward the highway.

Hilde could see Ethan trying to calculate his next move. He turned back to Gabe.

"Look. You need to get out of here," he said, reaching for the bills that lay scattered on the ground. "Here," he said, his hands full of bills. "Take these and go."

"No," Gabe stammered. He sat on the ground, glassy-eyed.

"That man," Ethan said, his hand gesturing to the cliff, his eyes fixed on Gabe, "he left your brother for dead in the desert. And he damned near killed him here."

Gabe looked over at Joaquín, who was still bleeding from the mouth. Hilde saw tears in Gabe's eyes.

"Listen," Ethan said. "This—all this—it never happened. You weren't here." He glanced toward the road again. "But you gotta go, 'cause they're coming for me now."

"What?" Gabe's expression was glazed.

"I got this," Ethan said.

The wind started to whip up the bills. Joaquín dove for them, collecting what he could from the ground. When he winced, Hilde scrambled to help.

Gabe continued to stare at Ethan.

Ethan curled his fingers into a ball. "Go. Please. I got this. You. And Joaquín. You need to disappear. Just get out of town."

From the bluff, they could see the sheriff's car heading toward them, looking like a bubble machine with lights blazing. It slowed at each turnout, checking for unusual activity, then sped to the next outturn in the road.

Ethan grabbed the remaining bills and stuffed them into Gabe's hands. "But before you head out—figure out how to get Hilde home. Okay? Take her now."

"What?" Hilde's head snapped up. She didn't want to go with Gabe. She wanted to stay with her brother. "No way," she said, standing up.

Ethan, still on his knees, turned and looked up at her.

"Look, Scout—"

She felt a pang in her heart. He hadn't called her that in months.

"You can't be here," he continued. "Whatever happens, it won't make sense. You need to get home. And you need to get Mom some help. You got that? Get her help."

Hilde stared at him, her eyes stinging, wondering whether she had lost her brother at the same moment she had found him.

"Go home. Please," he said. "I can handle this."

He was desperate to have her go—she could read him. Reluctantly, she turned away.

Gabe helped his brother up, steadying him. He glanced once more at Ethan, then led the others out into the darkness.

Ethan watched as they picked their way over the beach grass toward the footpath that led to the Coast Road and back through town.

38

Arrest

Much of what happened between Ethan and the sheriff that night was picked up by the local radio station. Nan came over to the house as soon as she heard the news and sat with Hilde and her mother.

> *Eighteen-year-old Ethan Sabin of Pescadero was arrested Tuesday night after allegedly burglarizing the deli where he worked on Stage Road. Deli owner Carmine Cardullo called authorities around 10:30 p.m. after noticing a light in the window of his store. As he and the sheriff inventoried the crime scene, Cardullo saw the suspect drive by. The sheriff pursued the suspect and arrested him without incident on the bluff north of Pescadero State Beach.*

No other crime was mentioned.

NAN STAYED ALL AFTERNOON, helping Hilde clean up, while Janine rocked in the metal chair on the porch. Hilde was surprised at her mother's passive acceptance of Nan's presence in the house.

As the light ebbed, Nan sat Hilde down at the kitchen table and squared Hilde's face in her warm hands. "Talk to me," she said quietly.

Hilde looked across the table. She was so tightly wound she could hardly breathe. The silence of the kitchen, its dampness, and the sound of her mother rocking on the porch all worked on the pressure inside her head until she thought she would burst. Words riding on emotions began to force their way out of her mouth.

"I don't—" she stammered. "I can't. I don't know where to start."

"Middle will do."

In the quiet of the kitchen, with her mother safely outside, she finally let go, the words spilling out of her like a dam breaking. How exhausting it had been to live through the fierce battles between her mother and brother. How lonely it was losing her brother to his own anger. How burdensome the farm had become, producing nothing but weepy cheeses and dead goats. She was embarrassed by her mother's new relationship with another man and enraged by her father's unforgivable deception. And then her mom—her mom just gave up on them all. She chose grimy swirling waters instead of them. When she got to that part, she could barely speak, her teeth were chattering so.

"And now . . . without Ethan . . ."

Nan waited patiently.

"I don't know what to do. Mom, she needs help. I'm supposed to take care of her." She looked away, holding her breath and shaking her head, tears streaming down her face. "But I don't"—she gasped—"I don't know how."

As they sat across from one another in silence, Nan's steadiness, her hands resting atop one another on the kitchen table, began to work on Hilde, bringing her down from the horrible headspace she was in.

Finally, Nan spoke. "Your mom," she said, glancing at Janine through the front window, "let me talk to her. Okay?"

Hilde nodded, mute.

Nan scooted her chair back from the table and made her way outside to where Janine was sitting. Hilde watched through the window as Nan squatted beside Janine. Soon her hand was on Janine's forearm. She was looking up at Janine and nodding, listening. It seemed an eternity, the time Nan spent on the porch. Finally, she stood up and came back into the kitchen.

"We're going take her where she can get some help. We're going today," she said. "She's ready."

Air rushed out of Hilde's chest. She closed her eyes and rested her head on her forearms atop the table.

That afternoon, they drove Janine over the hill to the hospital where she was admitted for observation. She made no fuss when they brought a wheelchair to take her to her room—which surprised Hilde because she knew how obstinate her mother could be. But she obeyed the orderly when he asked her to sit, and as he wheeled her down the long, polished corridor and around the corner, she did not look back.

Passing through the glass doors of the emergency room into the darkened parking lot, Nan put her hand around Hilde's shoulder. "You stay with us tonight," she said. "We'll put you up on the sofa with Toby. He likes company."

Nan didn't say much as they drove back to Pescadero, and for that Hilde was grateful. She needed the quiet. It was enough to let her head rest on the cool window of the car and watch the crop rows whip by.

THE NEXT MORNING, SHE woke on Nan's couch, her face buried in Toby's fragrant fur. The dog stirred and lifted his head when Pima shuffled into the kitchen and put the kettle on to boil. Pima gathered three mugs from hooks below the cupboard, set them on the table, headed toward the back door. Toby roused himself and slipped off the couch.

"Good boy," Pima said quietly as she held the screen open for him. Then she let out a low sound. "Whoa—"

Hilde sat up.

Pima stepped out onto the stoop and peered into the light, shielding her eyes from the early morning sun.

Nan appeared from the bathroom, toothbrush in hand. "What?"

"Check out the creek," Pima said, holding the screen door open. "Looks like it's jumped its bank. It's flowing *around* the bridge, not under it. I've never seen anything like that before."

"Found a new way to get where it wants to go, I guess," Nan said, bemused.

39

Sentencing

Ethan was brought up on charges on a Tuesday in January, in a somber courtroom with no windows. The judge, a sour-faced man with rimless glasses perched atop a pointed nose, listened with interest as the case was laid out. Hilde hoped the judge might go light on Ethan, but the district attorney, who it turned out was Carmine Cardullo's brother-in-law, added looting to the charge of burglary since the crime took place during a natural disaster. They made an example of him, which neither Hilde nor Nan expected. And he was sentenced to eighteen months, plus restitution of the money he'd taken from the deli.

Hilde was crushed.

A week later, Hilde went to visit her brother at the jail where he was being held before his transfer. She knew it would be difficult to see him after that week. The place was a long bus ride away.

"They told me you could be out in six months," she said in a husky voice, sitting across from him at a small counter, plexiglass between them.

He met her gaze and his face softened. "Hope so," he said quietly. "But I wouldn't count on it."

"But you told them what they wanted to hear. I thought they'd see you were cooperating, and they might not send you away at all—"

"Guess not," he replied, looking down.

"Oh, Ethan," she said, feeling the tears begin to well up. "How could this happen?" She could not believe her brother was going to jail.

He raised his head and leaned in toward the plexiglass. His eyes were fixed on hers now.

"Look. You know what happened—you know all of it. Weigh it in your mind. If I had to do it over, I'd do it all the same way. I would."

"But—"

He placed the palm of his hand on the plexiglass. "I don't know, Scout. It just seems like to do the right thing, sometimes you gotta do the wrong thing."

She swiped at her eye angrily. Then she put her hand on the plexiglass in the shadow of his and let out a deep sigh. It felt as though she had let go of an entire lifetime.

40

Grave Wax

A week after the trial, a body was fished out of the rocks near Point Lobos, some eighty miles south of the Pescadero cliffs. The Monterey County coroner noted in his autopsy report that the greenish-black skin had blistered, and the tissue that clung to the skeletal remains turned to the soapy fatty acid he knew as grave wax. He affixed a special toe tag on the skeletal remains, one he used for unidentifiable bodies.

41
Misfits

So how do you feel about Mr. Booher bringing your mom home on Monday?" Nan asked.

It was early February, and they were walking Toby to the marsh to look for blue herons. Hilde held Toby's leash as he ranged in front of them.

"Okay, I guess," Hilde replied. "She's gonna stay up at his place for a while. He's got a full-time nurse to help out."

They passed the vegetable stand, which was closed for the winter season. As they found the path that led to the water, Toby veered hard to the right, pulling Hilde off balance. She stumbled down the steep grade behind him. When they reached the marsh, Toby began sniffing the grasses near the water. Several avocets took wing, but the larger birds—the herons—simply turned their heads and watched him warily.

Nan settled herself in her usual place, the rocky outcropping at the edge of the water, and gazed out over the marsh. Hilde sat beside her.

"And what about you?" Nan asked.

"He said since I was so good at raising goats, he'd teach me how to raise cattle. The kind you eat." She glanced at Nan and rolled her eyes.

Nan offered a slight smile.

Finally, Hilde said in a small voice, "But I don't want to live up there. With them."

The moment she said the words, she felt a familiar guilt seep through her gut. How could she not want to live with her mother, broken as she was? She felt responsibility for her mother's happiness return like a heavy wave, overwhelming her.

"So, what do you want?" Nan asked gently.

Now Hilde felt an undertow pulling her hard in the opposite direction. "I don't want—" she began, "I don't want to be with them right now. I know it's terrible to say, after all that's happened, but I can't breathe around her."

Nan looked at her impassively.

"I just want some space. Some air." Hilde looked away.

"I hear you," Nan said. "Sometimes people don't quite fit with their families. And when they don't, it can be hard to figure out who they really are. Because families are always pushing back. Wanting you to be what you're not." She paused, twirling the ring on the finger of her left hand. "If you can't negotiate being yourself with your own family, it's gets really tough, growing up."

They sat in silence for several minutes, both watching Toby explore the wet spots along the marshy edge.

Finally, Hilde said, "So do you think maybe I can stay with you for a while?"

Nan leaned over and bumped shoulders with her. "Let's see what we can do."

42
Another Way Home

By the time Hilde graduated from high school, Ethan had been out of jail for several months and was working on an oil rig in Texas.

In early June, she received a graduation present in the mail. When she opened the mailer, she found a small velvet-lined box holding a delicate enamel pendant—the silhouette of a young goat, his horns barely budding, in mid-jump. The accompanying note read:

Been in touch with Gabe and Joaquin. They've been picking grapes in Bakersfield, but I got them jobs on the rig. They're headed down here in the next couple of weeks. Pay's a lot better. Plus, half the guys on this rig are felons, turns out.

Have fun in Madison. But remember, all that book learning you'll be doing—it's not the same as life learning. Never forget.

—Ethan

Hilde drove herself back across country in late August, her admission letter to the University of Wisconsin tucked in the glove compartment of the peppy Kia Ned Booher bought for her as a graduation present. She took the same route the family had driven three years earlier. She even looked for the Denny's they'd stopped at outside of North Platte, but it was lost among the endless plains. The miles of highway she drove with the windows open, smelling the air—the feedlots, the grasses, the diesel—gave her time to think, time to take the measure of where she had been and where she was going.

Her mother and Ned Booher had come down from the ranch to say goodbye, Janine in that same yellow sundress she'd worn the first time she brought Ned to the house. He was as boisterous and overbearing as ever, but her mother looked happy to have his arm around her waist.

Nan and Pima, bleary-eyed from the raucous game of rummy that had kept the three of them up late the previous night, had helped pack her stuff into the car. Toby was the only one not in front of Nan's house when Hilde drove away. He was still curled up on the sofa bed Nan purchased when it became clear Hilde was staying for more than a couple of weeks. They had become her true family for two full years, so that now, crossing back across the plains on her way to a new destination, she felt like a polished stone, skipping across a pond, hardened by the water but still vulnerable to the air, sunlight, and the passage of time.

As she passed through Illinois, she considered whether she would stop and see her father. But he had a new family, a new home, a new baby even, and the wounds were still raw. She would wait another year or so; she would wait until she was ready.

But the old house, the farm—it drew her like a magnet. Despite everything, there was still some sweetness in those early days, moments she had kept safe behind the scrim of her memory, and it was those she wanted to recapture, to tuck away for the future. And so, as she crossed the Illinois line into Wisconsin on that humid summer evening, she turned onto Route 50 and started up the rolling hills.

She spotted the barn first, though she could hardly recognize it. The white siding had been painted red and given over to a Mail Pouch Tobacco ad. As she drove nearer, she saw that parts of the silo had caved in. And the driveway, which used to curve toward the house, had been paved with asphalt, and rerouted straight through the apple orchard, dead-ending at an enormous corrugated aluminum building whose sign marked the farm's new profit center: aquaculture.

She parked the car under the old linden tree and stood beneath it for a minute, surveying the grounds. The outbuildings, the gardens, the driveway all had been rejiggered, which made her feel dizzy and disoriented. But still, she knew the pitch of the land so well that she could reimagine the old places, superimposing them on the new. When she came upon the horseshoe pits, even though the stakes were gone and the indentations covered in grass, she could almost feel the rusty metal shoe in her hand. She wanted to pitch it, to hear it clang against the stake before settling into the sand. She realized that this was as near to time travel as she would ever get.

The house looked empty, its windows darkened, its shades drawn, but there was washing on the line, so somebody clearly lived there. As she passed the doors to the root cellar, she saw that the old wooden stairs to the back porch had been replaced by a cement stoop, and the dark hiding place that Jupe had favored was gone.

She walked down the long slope to the barn, sliding the door open and slipping into the dark interior. The ceiling—the floor of the loft— had broken through in several places, and jagged timbers hung above the stalls that once housed the animals. How beautiful and well-tended this barn had once been, with animals resting in those cool stalls. She tested the rickety stairs to the loft, careful not to disturb the wasp's nest that still clung to the window frame, and when the wood held, she mounted the steps and emerged onto what was left of the loft's floor-boards. The cavernous room was empty save for a few sweepings of hay that lay in the corners, remnants of past harvests. Tiny motes floated in the air, illuminated by shafts of light from broken shingles. It was here that she and Ethan had spent many hours piling up heavy bales to make forts and jumping into soft mounds of straw. Where were those days?

She eased out the barn door and made her way back toward the house, hoping no one would appear on the porch. She knew that around here, if they were home, they'd come out and greet her. Would she tell them who she was? What if they asked her in? Did she want to see how they'd updated the kitchen? Painted the living room? Replaced the fur-niture? Maybe not. Because if she did see, if she saw how the walls had been scraped clean of her family's photos, the carpets scrubbed free of their scent, it would weaken her own memories. And that was not why she was here. She was here to revive those old memories, to tuck them away for a little longer until she could fully sort them out.

And so, she hurried by the house and headed to the car. She knew the place was no longer hers. Her home was irredeemable, except in her own imagination. She might have felt bereft, having lost it, but she did not. She had those memories. And she had a home on the coast that she'd made for herself, one that suited her better. And that was enough.

She turned once more toward the alfalfa field and stood for a long moment in the driveway, breathing in the familiar night air. Then she slipped into her car and headed north.

Acknowledgments

This book would not have happened were it not for my serendipitous acquaintance with Wendy Taylor, former pastor of the Pescadero Community Church, who was looking for an editor for her nonfiction book about her experiences with undocumented laborers in Pescadero. The stories that she and her late co-author Margaret Cross captured in that book got under my skin and stayed there, and when Wendy invited me to join her on an educational trip to the Border at Juarez, I jumped at the chance. My own subsequent trips to the Arizona border, and the superb programs offered by the nonprofit Borderlinks, gave me the opportunity to hear the stories first-hand from migrants and from those helping them on their journeys. Those trips, which were organized through First Presbyterian Church of Palo Alto, were especially enriched by Javier Hernandez, First Pres Facilities Technician, and Maria Marroquin, Executive Director of the Day Worker Center in Mountain View, California, both of whom shared their own stories of coming across the southern Border to the United States.

Once the seed was planted, I enjoyed the support and encourage of many people in writing this story. I owe them all a debt of gratitude:

To my fellow writers Susan Wolfe, Richard Abramson, Marcia Kemp Sterling, Chandrama Anderson, Ron Ott, Scott Gordon, and the members of the Pacific Coast Writers Collective JoAnneh Nagler, Julia Erwin-Weiner, and Katrina Ryan, who critiqued portions of my manuscript with grace and grit.

To my teachers Lynn Stegner, Alice LaPlante, Rachel Herron, Lisa Cron and Jennie Nash, from whom I learned the craft of fiction. And to Bill Pflaum, who has served as writing and publishing mentor to me throughout my career, and who has gotten me out of a few jams.

To my first readers, who kept my nose to the grindstone: Meredith Wheeler, Gina Anderson, Twila Slesnick, Eleanor Laney, Julie Noblitt, Tib Hotson, Jackie Wheeler, Karen Walker, Judy Ocken and Rosemarie Menager. And especially to Annie Kolar, who spent numerous hours helping me sort out character motivation based on her own deep psychological wisdom.

To my team of publishing professionals who helped to polish the book: developmental editor Susan Dalsimer, copyeditor Kim Bookless, cover designer Swapan Das, interior designer Lorie DeWorken, cover consultant Ina Saltz, and sensitivity reader Yazmin Lopez Pease. Special thanks to book designer Diana Russell who finished the covers.

And finally, to the community of First Presbyterian Church of Palo Alto, especially Nan Swanson, Pat Kinney, Craig Wiesner, Derrick Kikuchi, Sally Nordlund and Rob Martin, who helped shape my thinking on progressive issues over two decades, and who changed the way I look at the world.

About the Author

Hollis Brady is the former director of the Stanford Publishing Course and other publishing ventures at Stanford University. Her longstanding activism in border issues has taken her to Nogales, Juarez, Agua Prieta, San Ysidro and Pescadero where she has collected stories from migrants and those supporting them in their journeys. She lives in Northern California, over the hill from Pescadero.